A Brush with
Betsy Flak

Cover design by Melody Simmons

ISBN (paperback): 978-0-9990419-4-9. ISBN (ebook): 978-0-9990419-3-2.

First Edition

Happy reading!

FREE DOWNLOAD

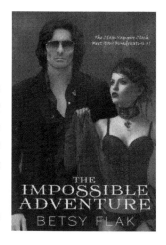

PROLOGUE

Rain slashed at the windows.

Staring into a computer screen, Duncan plotted the annihilation of his eternal enemies. His plan — the result of well over a decade of gathering intelligence, recruiting his army, and growing the necessary funds — would begin tonight. It needed to be ready. No, more than ready, it needed to be perfect. They would get but a single shot. Failure meant certain death.

Only after hours of double- and triple-checking was Duncan satisfied. His plan was as good as he could make it. The rest would be up to her.

As if summoned by that thought, a slender woman entered his office. Her raven waves tickled the laces of a gown dyed silver to match her eyes. Long years ago, those eyes — sea blue back then instead of silver — had pulled him to her. Kane was his creation, the one that made everything possible.

"Sire, I thought you may have need of me." The scent of lavender followed Kane like a handmaiden.

Shivers cascaded down Duncan's spine. His fangs wore twin grooves into his lower lip. Blood-stained fields dotted with corpses instead of wildflowers filled his mind. Their future called to him.

Duncan's office door clicked shut.

The sound shattered Duncan's daydream. He slid his gnarled hands over the cool marble of his desk. Unnecessary breaths slowed unnecessary heartbeats.

Beside the door the color of sun-bleached bone, Kane glanced at the windows behind Duncan.

The tingles radiating along Duncan's shoulders flared. Twisting in his chair, he faced three panels of floor-to-ceiling windows. Sure enough, the late afternoon sun peeked through clouds heavy with rain. The leaded glass protected Duncan from most of the sun's danger, but not all.

"Sire, you should be more careful." Her bare feet padding against the tile floor, Kane strode to the windows overlooking the courtyard below. She snapped the black-out curtains shut in one fluid movement.

For an instant, Duncan longed for the days when the sun had warmed his human body. "Thank you, my dear."

After a quick nod, Kane perched on one of the sleek chairs across from him.

Duncan folded his hands on his desk. "As you may suspect, the moment to begin has at last arrived. I'd like you to lead the charge, Kane."

Kane's chin dipped into another nod, confirming his implied request.

But another, more important question loomed before Duncan. "Are the others prepared to take your place?"

"Yes, Sire. Eight are available, two of which show promise."

Scarred fingers — the result of Duncan's early encounter with Adara — steepled in front of his narrow nose. He couldn't hope for another Kane, no matter how often he sent Adara on her fruitless searches. But eight of them should be enough to squash his troops' rebellious instincts. Even one on its own could maintain the spells Kane had created. It just wouldn't last long.

But eight could last an entire year. If not, Adara could find more. And there was always brute force, although that never worked for long. But Duncan could no longer spare Kane for something so trivial.

Kane angled forward in her chair, catching Duncan's ebony eye. "And I will be but hours away should you need me. If all should fail."

Duncan's lips twitched, threatening a rare smile. He had yet to disclose the pilot location, but his base sat in the mountainous middle of the country. Kane couldn't help but be correct. Not that he would have hours if her replacements failed. "I daresay you will have your hands busy enough, my dear Kane, even if everything goes as planned."

Rustles emerged from the stables a courtyard away.

Duncan's thick-lashed gaze flicked toward a computer monitor. By now, the sun would be nearly set. Soon the clatter of battle would reign.

"We have the eight replacements. We'll just have to hope that they—and any additions Adara finds—will be good enough. It's time to shift to our true purpose: destroying our eternal enemies. It's no secret that their waves of mindless soldiers have suppressed us for centuries. Even our historic numbers cannot compare to theirs. No, at this moment, it would be useless to fight them directly. First, we must demolish those waiting in the wings. Only then can we fight them in earnest. Only then can we bring an end to this unfortunate chapter in our history." Duncan leaned back in his chair, surveying the impact of his practiced speech.

Kane's face remained smooth as glass, but her torso tilted forward. Her hands lay clenched on her lap. Her toes

3

dug into the electric blue rug. Kane was excited, though she refused to show it.

"Now, I have plans for battling them directly, but as I mentioned, first we must attack their backups, which is where you come in, Kane. This part of the plan is straightforward: we attack their young. As you know, our enemies keep their children tight and safe within those villages of theirs. They cannot be our targets, not yet. Instead…" Duncan's obsidian eyes glittered as he stretched out the suspense. If only he could be the one…but no, he must remain here. He must focus on their long-term goals. "We'll attack their trainees — those sequestered away in their boarding schools, far away from the action. Far away from meaningful assistance."

Kane's coral lips pursed. "And how do you intend to do this, Sire?"

"Ah, *that*, my dear Kane, is for you to unearth. You, Fang, and three of our best fighters will go. The five of you are to act as an independent nest. Once you have a detailed proposal for your attack, you'll report back to me. Together, we'll finalize it into something suitable for testing. If the test is successful, we'll apply your plan to the entire country, maybe even the continent. Remember: whatever plan you create, we'll use it to destroy each and every training Cell hiding in those boarding schools. Now, where is our first target, you may wonder?" Without waiting for a response, Duncan twisted the secondary monitor toward Kane. He extended a talon toward a crimson circle drawn over a satellite image. In the center was a cluster of brick buildings. "This…Eversfield Preparatory Academy."

Kane assessed the map, probably noting the acres and acres of uninterrupted forest separating Eversfield from any notable cities where the Clan's regular Cells would hunt. Yes, Duncan had provided them with more than enough room for shelter — and for their other needs.

"I presume I do not need to ask this, but what is the objective, Sire?"

Duncan responded with a toothy grin a millimeter away from a snarl. "It's simple: to kill them all."

THE CLAN-VAMPIRE CLASH

Episode One: A Brush with Vampires

Lila's Sophomore Year, First Semester

August

CHAPTER 1

Charcoal clouds raced across a dark sky. The wind whipped tree branches and clawed at their leaves. Goosebumps crawled over Lila's arms. Of course she would flee one storm, only to enter another.

"Here you go, honey." Lila's dad deposited a purple polka-dotted suitcase and matching duffel next to her flats. His brown eyes scrunched with concern.

Lila turned away from him and toward a brick monstrosity. Two matching buildings peered around it as if all three stalked fresh prey. Jungle-green ivy climbed up the walls to press against rows of iron-framed windows. Bushes with thorns as long as Lila's pinky guarded the cobblestone path leading from her sidewalk to an archway. In the arch's center hung a bronze plaque engraved with "Eversfield Preparatory Academy."

A field mouse facing an adder, Lila wiped her clammy palms against her khakis. She demanded that her heartbeat slow, her breaths deepen, and her butterflies climb back into their cocoons. None listened.

Lila dug her fingers into the straps of her backpack like it was the source of her dwindling courage.

Stilettos clicked against the asphalt behind her.

Lila's insides clenched. Her spine stiffened. Her hands flew into the pockets of her ugly pants.

Her mother planted a hand with glossy nails on Lila's shoulder and squeezed. "Baby, it's not too late. We can just

9

pack you right back up in that car," her mother whined in an overripe tone.

It reminded Lila of all she'd learned about her mother in the past few months, none of it good. Lila's voice hardened, becoming low, cold steel. A force to be reckoned with. "No, I'm sure. This is the right thing for me." Lila almost added "for us," but guilt stopped her. Both her parents had taken an entire day off work to prepare her for Eversfield.

Her mother released her shoulder. "If that's what you want, baby. And you're sure you don't want to come home during the fall break in a couple months? We, er, one of us can pick you up."

Lila's frizzy braid lurched from side to side as she shook her head. They'd discussed that very point at least five times in the last twenty-four hours, ever since they'd found out about her last-second admittance to Eversfield. "No, I told you. I'll have too much studying to do."

Her mother turned her head to stare at the pine trees flanking the lonely road leading to Eversfield. A ruby nail brushed a tear away from the corner of her lined eye. A single, elegant tear…that was all for show.

Squashing her frown, Lila shifted to her dad and spread her arms wide. He—unlike her mother—yielded and smothered her in a bear hug. He lifted her off the ground and swung her side to side like she was five years old again. Lila buried her face in his neck, swallowing the tears. His salt and pepper goatee nibbled at her forehead. Lila was sad—no, devastated—to leave him. But sometimes you hurt the ones you loved to save yourself.

As he set Lila down, he murmured, "You sure you don't want *one* of us to come in with you?"

Lila drew a shaky breath. "No, it's okay. We just had breakfast with the headmaster and the sophomore grade leads. I want to do this on my own. I *need* to do this on my own."

Her dad didn't press the issue. For that, Lila was grateful. She wasn't sure she could have denied him twice.

"And besides, this isn't goodbye, right? We're doing dinner tonight?" Lila inwardly shuddered at the forced brightness of her voice. And then did shudder when her mother—her makeup crystal clear despite a "crying" episode—swooped in.

"Yes, darling, we are. I have a restaurant picked out and everything. No expense spared for my Lila!"

"Mom, I really don't think we should be—"

"Nonsense. Now come here and give me a hug." Her mother cast a pointed glare at her dad.

Lila's hackles rose, but she obeyed. With something closer to a polite grimace than a frown, Lila fell into her mother's outspread arms. She stayed there for the two seconds etiquette required. Then Lila pulled away.

"I'm gonna be late if I'm not careful, Mom." *Lie.* Lila had fifteen minutes before she was due in the main office, but her mother didn't know that.

Still, she didn't let Lila go. No, she held Lila out at an arm's length with her fingertips digging into Lila's biceps.

Lila stared at a gilded earring darting this way and that instead of meeting her mother's moss-green eyes, the ones that Lila shared.

"Oh, my dear, darling Delilah," her mother gushed.

Lila cringed at the use of her full name. Her mother knew she hated it yet insisted on using it.

"I thought I had years before this day would arrive. And even then, I was sure I could convince you to go to a college just down the road!" Her mother's shiny lips spread into a grin that didn't reach her mascaraed eyes. She extended her arms again.

With her own chapped lips clenched together, Lila allowed her mother one final hug.

After what seemed like an eternity, her mother released her. Shielding her disgust with a raised shoulder, Lila hurried back to her bags. There, her dad waited with the suitcase's handle already extended.

While he settled the duffel bag's strap over Lila's shoulder, he whispered, "She can't help it, Lila, she's going through something. She'll get through it, and then she'll be right back to her old self."

Without conviction, Lila nodded. He'd been telling her that lie for nearly a year now. Lila was done believing it. If he wanted to play the fool, so be it. That didn't mean she had to watch.

"Okay, we'll see you for dinner, Lila. Just let us know when you're free?"

"Sure, Dad, see you then."

Conflict crumpled his broad features. Lila would have given anything to run to him and ask — no, *beg* — him to make it better. But he couldn't fix their family. He'd been trying to and failing to for ages. Instead, they each plastered on a fake smile and exchanged half-hearted waves. Then her dad descended into the passenger seat of her mother's cardinal red convertible, a car they couldn't afford.

As her parents disappeared down the road winding through the forest, Lila turned toward her new home. She'd escaped. Now it was time to learn what she'd escaped to.

A pebble beneath a boulder, Lila studied that front building—the Administration Building according to her crumpled map—once more. Dizziness threatened as she gazed up, up, up. Three rows of windows reflected an antlike silhouette alone in front of a deserted parking lot.

Lila's fingers tore through her hair until the tight braid stopped them. Her breath stalled in her chest. What had she done?

A blast of wind pushed Lila toward that archway. She used the momentum to place one foot in front of the other. Her free hand skimmed over the waist-high shrubs lining the cobblestone path. She focused on avoiding their inches-long thorns.

Too soon, Lila hefted open a wooden door emblazoned with another "Eversfield Preparatory Academy." Its groan sounded more like a scream.

Too soon, she rolled her suitcase down the immaculate hallway. Walls and floor alike glistened in the recessed lighting.

Too soon, Lila found the main office, a fish bowl of a room with a wall of spotless windows in eggshell frames.

Too soon, she shoved her swollen luggage through the final door.

Too soon, she stood in front of a U-shaped desk, staring at a bent gray head with an impeccable—if severe—bun. A floral scent with a hint of vanilla crept up her nose.

"May I help you?" a voice creaked from behind the desk. The woman did not glance up or pause her click-clack typing.

"Um, I'm new?"

"We do not say 'um' here, Miss..." The woman selected a single sheet from a crisp ivory stack. "Miss Lee. Eversfield students and alumni always know what they will say prior to speaking."

Lila's cheeks burned at the admonishment. She racked her brain for all the formal-ish words she'd ever heard. Her supply was inadequate, to say the least. "I'm…I'm sorry. M-ma'am."

The secretary's flinty gaze remained wary. "I am Ms. Pershing, Headmaster Flynn's and Eversfield's primary administrative assistant." Ms. Pershing stood, smoothed her pristine lace blouse, and offered Lila a hand with short shiny nails.

Lila grasped it and shook. Thoughts raced around and around her mind. Was she holding Ms. Pershing's hand too tight? Shaking it too fast? Had it been long enough to let go? "And I'm Lila, er, Delilah Lee. But I guess you already know that."

Ms. Pershing released Lila's hand. "Yes, Miss Lee, I thank you for your timely arrival. You may take a seat while I finish this task. I will then conduct an abbreviated orientation since you were unable to join our freshmen earlier this week."

Lila bit into her lower lip. Since Eversfield had only accepted her yesterday—giving her less than twenty-four hours to say goodbye to her home, let alone pack and prepare—there was no way for her to "join the freshmen earlier this week." Based on the hawklike eyes boring into her, that was not a valid excuse.

"I understand. Thank you…Ma'am." Lila flinched as she awaited another reprimand, but Ms. Pershing returned to her work, leaving Lila more or less alone. As much as she longed to crumple into one of those bowl-shaped chairs in the waiting area, Lila first set her bags next to a potted palm stretching toward the polished ceiling. Quiet as a mouse, she arranged her luggage into a neat pyramid with the suitcase on the bottom, followed by her duffel bag, then her backpack on its side. After balancing her messenger bag on top, Lila collapsed into the closest chair.

"Miss Lee, you may stow your luggage in the far corner by the umbrella tree." Ms. Pershing gestured to the corner opposite where Lila had already stashed her gear.

Lila swallowed a sigh. Apparently, one placed luggage next to specific types of rainforest plants and not next to others. While Ms. Pershing click-clacked away, Lila moved the bags across the room.

Although it was a small change, it crushed Lila's pea-sized confidence. Retreating to her chair, Lila tiptoed along a pit of despair. How was she going to get used to all this formality? She'd been an Eversfield student for five whole minutes, and already she didn't fit in. This had to be her most horrible idea yet.

Then again, what was the alternative? Go to the same lonely school, pretend that nothing was wrong while she watched her family crumble into bits and pieces, into shards and shrapnel? No, she hadn't had many choices. And Val had been so understanding, so willing to jump through any hoops needed. Lila would simply have to make the most of it. Everything would be…fine. She would adapt. She would survive. This was just a snippet of discomfort to be endured.

Her spine held rigid and straight, Lila counted the leaves of the potted palm across from her. Even with that distraction, she couldn't help wishing she was somewhere else, anywhere else—except, of course, for her parents' hotel room.

After several minutes, Ms. Pershing glanced at Lila over her frameless glasses. "Okay, Miss Lee, I'm ready for you." With shocking speed, Ms. Pershing spun around to select a shiny Eversfield-navy folder from the desktop behind her. By the time Lila reached the chest-high counter, Ms. Pershing already stood. The open folder faced Lila. "First, here is another map of our campus. I noticed yours has...seen better days."

Lila flushed. Her fingers rubbed against the bulge in her pants pocket where she'd shoved the map earlier.

"I took the liberty of highlighting your house, Miss Lee. You'll be in room 302 of Elizabeth Blackwell. Your roommate is Miss Marina Lazare. Of course, we won't have a...class...schedule...For goodness' sake, Miss Baker, just come in. All that pacing is giving me a headache."

A whirlwind by the name of Valerie Elizabeth Baker swept into the office. With every hop, skip, and jump, Val's high-waisted skirt swished around her bare thighs. Neither her striped tank nor her pixie cut—straight out of *Roman Holiday*—dared to move. Beneath defined brows, Val's catlike eyes gleamed with mischief.

Although joy radiated off her best friend, Lila's stomach sank. If only she'd known uniforms weren't required today, she could be in shorts and a T-shirt, instead of her stupid khakis and wrinkled blouse.

"Lila, Lila, Lila! I'm so happy, happy, happy that you're here!" Undeterred by their five-inch height difference, Val encompassed Lila in a rib-cracking hug. Her breath tickling from Lila's neck, she whispered, "You okay, kid?"

Lila nodded. Not even the stupid uniform mistake could block Val's bliss from cheering her up a smidge.

With a sunbeam of a smile, Val danced up to Ms. Pershing's lustrous desk. Balancing on the tips of her toes, Val rested her forearms on the chest-high counter and peered over it. "Well, Ms. Pershing, whatcha got for my dear friend Lila here? You wanna just hand it over, so we can start the *real* orientation?"

Val winked at Lila, then leaned over the countertop. She bobbed up and down, her heels kissing the floor with each bounce. Her nimble fingers poked and prodded the forbidden desk area.

Ms. Pershing swatted at them, but her slate gray eyes crinkled and her thin lips twitched toward a smile. She was the latest in a long line of Val-worshippers. And who could blame them? Val was the embodiment of a sunny day, one that infected anyone and everyone near her.

Ms. Pershing sighed. "First, Miss Baker, you know perfectly well that an Eversfield woman—"

"Yes, yes, I know. I hafta speak properly. But can't you see that I'm just so excited that my dear friend Lila is finally here?"

"Miss Baker, you know there are certain items I need to cover with Miss Lee—"

"And *you* know that I can cover those nearly as well as you. And I know that you are a busy woman, one whose talents go largely unappreciated at this school."

"Miss Baker, flattery will get you—"

"Everywhere?" Val interrupted, adding another wink. Then she widened her eyes and begged, "Oh please, oh pretty please, Ms. Pershing? Lila is my dearest friend in the whole wide world and I cannot bear to spend another minute without her running by my side!"

"Well, I suppose—"

"Wonderful! Lila, let's get your bags. Or actually, we should leave them here. I'm sure Ms. Pershing won't mind. And let me see where your room is. I hope we're in the same house! I mean, we should be, but you never know what—"

"Miss Lee." That hawklike gaze of Ms. Pershing's glued itself to Lila.

She shriveled beneath it. "Um, yes?"

"Miss Lee, since your dearest friend in the whole wide world is prepared to give you a complete," Ms. Pershing cast a pointed look at Val, who put on her best "I'm so trustworthy and innocent" face, "albeit colorful orientation, I will entrust it to her. But please, if you have any questions at all, do not hesitate to come to the office. And remember, your placement tests are on Monday. You're to arrive here at the main office promptly at eight a.m."

After separating a taupe envelope the size of an index card, Ms. Pershing handed the glossy folder to Val. She offered the envelope to Lila. "This, Miss Lee, contains your keycard. Do not lose it. It serves as your room key and provides all-hour access to Elizabeth Blackwell. It also provides access to the cafeteria, computer lab, and library during restricted hours and contains your meal plan, all of which Miss Baker can and will explain. Like I said, if you have any questions later, feel free to return to this office. Also, the uniforms you ordered wait in your room. If anything is missing, please let me know as soon as possible. You're dismissed."

Lila turned to fetch her backpack.

Val's hand caught her forearm and held Lila back. Val mouthed, "Just a sec," then approached Ms. Pershing's desk. "Ah, oh, Ms. Pershing?"

A charcoal eyebrow arched. Ms. Pershing's patience — even for the lovely Miss Baker — was failing.

"I'm sorry to bother you, but just one teensy favor if you don't mind. See, Lila here, she doesn't like her full name. Never has. I don't know why, Delilah is a perfectly lovely name."

Ms. Pershing continued her impassive glare.

Val fluffed her short locks with both hands. "Right, to the point, anywho, could you make sure to change 'Delilah' to 'Lila' on all Miss Lee's paperwork? And make sure the teachers all know to call her Lila from the start?"

"Miss Baker, that would be against protocol."

Below the high counter, Val nudged Lila in the ribs. Her chocolate eyes never left Ms. Pershing.

Oh, right, time to look pathetic. Lila put on her best sad puppy face with big eyes and pouty lips.

"But…I suppose I can make yet one more exception in this case. Now please, leave me to my work." Ms. Pershing waved them away.

"Thank you, Ms. Pershing!" Val sang.

Lila croaked, "Yeah, thank you."

As they exited the office, Val skipped with glee. "Oh, I'm so glad you're here. I mean, I know the situation that brought you here is just plain awful. But you're here! You're actually here! And I am so, so, *so* very happy." Val grinned up at Lila.

Lila reflected it. To her surprise, it felt almost natural. It turned out that Val's eternal sunshine could melt any ice, even that which had accumulated over several months. It was a welcome change.

CHAPTER 2

GABE

With a bead of sweat trickling down his spine, Gabe hurried along the path of woodchips through the forest. Not even eleven in the morning and humidity already thickened the air.

When the trail bent to the left, Gabe turned right. His feet sunk into the thick groundcover, swishing through leafy vines and snapping fallen twigs. In the daylight, there was no need for stealth.

As Gabe neared their clearing in the woods, something moved between the tree trunks. His pale eyes narrowed. About fifty feet away, tendrils of inky hair whipped in the wind like Medusa's snakes.

Gabe smothered a frown. That breeze had come out of nowhere. *Not nowhere*, he corrected himself, *from my sister*.

Crouching into a predatory stance, Gabe snuck through the trees toward her. One foot nestled into the underbrush, then the other. This time, he avoided those twigs and vines, moving through the noisy forest without a sound as only a Warrior could. Well, as only a Warrior and those they'd hunted for centuries—those soulless beasts called the Indestructible—could.

Gabe swallowed a sigh. Supposedly, the first Clan Warrior and Diviner had been conceived the moment the first member of the Indestructible had been created as a sort of magical balance to the world. The Warrior twin developed superhuman powers with superior strength, speed, and agility combining with a burning drive to kill the

Indestructible. The Diviner supported his or her twin—the gender changed depending on the story—by wielding first Elemental magic and later the less-defined Spirit magic that could heal or create more complicated spells or see the future.

Gabe shut down those folktales from his childhood. He didn't need to think about Portency right now. As far as he was concerned, it didn't exist. And besides, did it matter if it did? That ancient Diviner's Portency hadn't stopped either twin from dying to the Indestructible. Of course, both the Diviner and the Warrior had managed to live long enough to start families, thus passing down the curse of hunting the Indestructible—of *dying* to the Indestructible—through the centuries, right to him and Marina.

Steps away from his sister's turned back, Gabe hunched behind a shrub with pointy leaves. Locks of Marina's blue-black hair twisted in the wind that whirled around her. Her arms stretched out to either side. Even her fingers were outspread.

Marina rose onto the balls of her feet. Her fingertips twitched upward.

Marina's toes left the ground. The wind—*her* wind—lifted her up one inch, then two, then three.

That was enough. "Ahem," Gabe cleared his throat and stood, rising from behind the screen of bushes.

Marina's breeze died. Her feet slammed into the ground. Her arms fell to her sides.

A head snapped up from a figure sprawled out in the weeds. Its russet eyes found Gabe. *Lex. Of course.*

With her back still to Gabe, Marina's hands dug into her waist. One hip jutted out. "Lex, you were supposed to keep watch!"

Her cropped curls even wilder than usual, Lex leaned back on the heels of her hands. Her feet swayed in the violets lacing the ground. "Mar, it's just Gabe. It's not like he doesn't know all the gory details already. 'Sides, y' know I had no hope of spottin' him or hearin' him unless he wanted t' be spotted or heard."

"Still…" Marina's voice trailed off as she turned around to face Gabe.

He wasted no time. "Marina, you really should be more careful—"

"I had Lex on lookout! And I came all the way out here, to our spot. Plus it's early. The likelihood—"

"Still, Marina. If anyone but me had found you just now—"

Marina rolled eyes as dark as the ocean's depths. "Only members of our Cell come all the way out here."

"And do you want our entire Cell to know? Our entire Cell who is due to arrive here in fifteen minutes?"

The toe of Marina's sneaker dug into the tangled vines. "No."

"Because you know what'll happen if they find out. Someone will spill to someone else until the Bureau finds out that you can work with Wind and Earth in addition to Water. Between that and your Spirit Diviner affinities, Marina—"

"I know, Gabe, okay? I'll get carted off to headquarters for 'training,' but it'll really be all kinds of tests to figure out why I have more powers than any other Diviner for at least a hundred and fifty years, possibly ever. Then they'll never let me go to college, let alone have a career outside the Clan. I *know*."

Gabe arched an eyebrow at his little sister. "If you *know*, then you know to be more careful."

"I have to practice with my new talents if I'm going to control them, Gabe."

He snorted. "You were *not* practicing there."

A warm flush blossomed over Marina's cheeks.

Gabe's guts tied themselves into knots. Of course Marina had come out here to use her powers to hide from this day. He should have guessed that before now.

Better late than never. Pushing through the screen of shrubs, Gabe crossed the distance between them. He grasped Marina's shoulders, then ducked down to eye-level. "It's going to be fine, Marina. I'm sure the new roommate is nothing like Tasha."

"You don't know that." Marina's voice came out muddied, like she held back tears.

"Of course I do."

"Lex found those pictures, remember? She's friends with the same people Natasha was."

"With one of those same people, not all of them."

Marina crossed her arms and looked away. "Not yet."

Gabe set his jaw. Marina would not repeat one ounce of the horrors of last year, not on his watch. "Marina, even if she is another Tasha, it's not going to happen again. We won't let it. First, if it does start again—even a whiff of it— you're going to tell me immediately this time. Secondly, Lex and I are going to be with you when you meet her. We'll lay down the law, let her know that you're not alone, that you will *not* be a target again. Right, Lex?"

"Righto, Daddy-o."

Gabe squashed a sigh of exasperation. "Lex, how many times in these past two weeks have I told you not to call me that?"

Lex's ginger brows furrowed. She pretended to count on outstretched fingers. "Hmmm, I would say…eight, nine? Actually, no, I think we just hit double digits!"

"*Wonderful*." As Gabe shifted back to Marina, his pale gaze shot downward. Marina's fingers massaged her right wrist. She'd broken it last spring when she'd fallen while retrieving the underwear Tasha had thrown into the tree outside their bedroom window. That day, Gabe had found out that Tasha and her friends had been harassing Marina. That day, Gabe had put a stop to it despite Marina's protests.

Marina dropped her wrist and pressed her palms into her bare thighs.

"It's going to be fine. I won't let her hurt you, no matter who she is." A hint of a growl—of the predator lurking beneath Gabe's student façade—traced his words.

Marina nodded, although the corners of her mouth twitched downward.

Gabe wrapped his arm around Marina's shoulders, opting for optimism while he plotted protecting his sister from her new roommate. "Look, I've gotta do this Cell meeting first, but how about you, me, and Lex head over to your room afterwards? We can meet the new roommate, check things out…" *Intimidate her.*

"Sure." Marina's smile didn't reach her eyes.

Ever the energetic puppy, Lex bounded up to them. "You wanna practice puttin' out my fires while we wait for the others, Mar? Even *Gabe* can't object to that."

"Yeah, sure." Pausing on the outskirts of their Cell's ragged clearing in the forest, Marina peeked up at Gabe. "If you don't mind."

"'Course not. Just—"

"Be careful, we *know*. Geez, Gabe, don't be such a worrywart!" Lex skipped ahead to pick up a fallen twig. Not even a second later, a flame danced over the opposite end. Like the few Fire Diviners Gabe had known, Lex had nothing but enthusiasm for her craft and for killing the Indestructible. Unlike Marina and Gabe, she looked forward to her Cell assignment after high school. Which was good since Fire Diviners—like Warriors—seldom got to choose between life in a Cell and life as a civilian.

Lex held the branch toward Marina, fiery end first.

After extending her hands around the flames, Marina inched them closer together. A foggy substance between her palms grew more and more dense. Her hands hovered around the fire for a moment. In one fluid movement, Marina clapped them together.

The flames died with a sizzle.

Lex flashed a grin oozing with mischief, then scurried away beneath the towering pines. Every few moments, she nudged a creaky branch over or dug into a scraggly bush. Lex was looking for something.

Marina's shoulder bumped against Gabe's arm. "You okay?"

"Yeah, of course. Why wouldn't I be?"

Tucking her hands into the pockets of shorts, Marina placed a foot on one of the split logs that edged their clearing. "Just checking. I know last year wasn't easy for you either."

Gabe shrugged. "That was last year. This year…this year, I'm prepared. I know what to expect and what to do." *I know what I've given up.*

"Still…"

"I'm *fine*, Marina." Gabe's chiseled chin jerked toward Lex tramping toward them with a stick, this one still green and covered with leaves. A harder target for Lex, but easier for Marina to extinguish. "Looks like Lex wants to play some more." Gabe slid his phone out of his pocket, then wiggled it at Marina. "I've gotta check my notes anyway."

"Okay, just…make sure to have *some* fun this year." After throwing him a concerned look, Marina picked her way to Lex, avoiding clumps of fragile plants like any other Earth Diviner.

Gabe called after her, "I'm in Pasteur, is that even a question?"

It wasn't. His dorm, Louis Pasteur, was all about the fun. While Blackwell, Tubman, and Douglass battled it out for the house cup each year, Pasteur kicked back and relaxed. Gabe would get his moments of fun in this, his last year of high school and normal human life — well, as normal as someone like him got. Those moments might be few and far-between, but he was determined to enjoy them.

TEN MINUTES LATER, THE EVERSFIELD CELL GATHERED before Gabe on the split log benches of their clearing-slash-meeting-place in the woods. They clumped together in three groups. In the back, his fellow senior Warriors sprawled over the benches, Darius and Cosmina laughing over something Simon had said. To his left, the four Diviners huddled together, chatting in hushed voices. In the very front, his brand-new freshman Warriors sat, quiet and tense. As the Cell Second, Emilia stood to Gabe's right.

A gust of wind—one that had nothing to do with Marina or her late-blooming talents—blasted through the forest. While they'd waited for the meeting to begin, a storm had blown in. Branches now bent to the wind's will. The scents of pine needles, fresh woodchips, and rain swirled through the air.

Beside him, Emilia dipped her chin into a crisp nod.

Time to start. Gabe cleared his throat, verifying Emilia's count while the others settled down. Four Diviners and ten Warriors including himself and Emilia. That was everyone.

"All right, thanks for coming here on your final free Saturday. I hope you enjoyed the last few days because the *real* patrols begin tonight." No grumbles greeted his statement, but apprehension flashed through the cluster of freshman Warriors. In contrast, Simon, Darius, and Cosmina exchanged predatory smirks. Only the Diviners remained impassive—except for Lex, who smiled at flames flickering over a stone. The light cast shadows over her face, stretching her grin from ear to ear. She looked almost insane.

But that wasn't unusual for a Fire Diviner.

Gabe arched an eyebrow. "Lex, don't you think it's a bit dangerous to play out here?"

The flames continued to dance, darting to and fro in response to Lex's flitting fingers. "I've got it. 'Sides Marina can douse it easy if I have an accident. Which, by the way, hasn't happened t' me since I was six and definitely wouldn't happen with a rock."

"Still. Snuff it out," Gabe commanded in a low tone.

With an eye roll that she should have quashed, Lex collapsed her palms around the stone, extinguishing the fire.

"Like I was saying, we begin patrols tonight. Before we get into the details, I want to remind everyone of patrol protocol. Since we've been practicing with the Florence Cell for the past two weeks—you know, a full-fledged Cell versus the training Cell that we are—Emilia and I haven't been too strict about it. Now that we're on our own, that changes."

Gabe surveyed the Warriors in front of him. While the five freshmen watched his every move, the three seniors didn't bother to hide their boredom. Cosmina's hand even drifted down toward a rectangular lump in the pocket of her shorts.

Beside Gabe, Emilia shook her head, a quick, concise, *meaningful* movement. Cosmina frowned back, but she listened to her roommate and her Second. Her hand abandoning the pocket, Cosmina slumped forward to rest her elbows on her bare knees. Several of her beaded braids slipped over the bulk of her shoulder. Cosmina didn't dare fiddle with them under Emilia's stare.

Trusting Emilia to keep the others in line, Gabe began, "First, we start each and every patrol over in Juniper's downtown. Since that's the most populated area in our territory, it's the most likely place we'll find one of *them*. We expect you to turn on the location sharing app we all got from the Bureau by the time your patrol begins." Over his head, Gabe wiggled his phone back and forth. "That way, we always know where the others are, even if we have to split up. Of course, once your patrol is over, you can turn it off. Whether you do so is up to you." The minute the night's patrols were over, Gabe turned his off, savoring any bit of freedom he could get. In contrast, his roommate Darius left his on all the time. That way, Darius never had to remember to turn it back on. *But that's what phone alarms are for.*

"From Juniper, we'll head out along a predetermined route that your patrol leader—that's me or Emilia and sometimes Simon—" Gabe jutted his chin toward the bulky Simon sitting in that trio of senior Warriors, "has decided. Sometimes we'll meet up with the Florence Cell to the east or the Burley Cell to the south. Sometimes we'll do sparring practice or otherwise take a break in the middle. Sometimes we'll start late or end early. It's all up to your patrol leader."

That wasn't completely true. He and Emilia set the schedules in terms of Warrior rotation, route, and timing, unless they were contacted by the Florence or Burley Cell with a "request." Because Gabe was a fan of unpredictability, he and Emilia varied the route and timing each and every day without any set pattern to the weeks or months. Even if some *thing* was paying attention, it wouldn't be able to determine where the Eversfield Cell would be at any given time.

Of course, the Indestructible didn't pay attention. They were nothing more than hungry animals seeking their next meal. Dangerous: yes. Plotting, intelligent creatures: no.

"On the patrol itself, you know the deal. We stalk around waiting for the Cull and the Bloodlust to strike. And before I forget, a quick note for some of you: yes, these are different things. I know some of your Troupes back home might have used the terms interchangeably, but Cells do not. The Cull refers to our supernatural senses—you know, when suddenly we can see every little detail in the dark, hear every conversation for a mile, separate each and every scent. It lets us know that one of *them* is near us. The Bloodlust, on the other hand, prepares us to fight. It gives us the energy

29

and the drive to kill our immortal enemies. It also gives us an approximate direction of where to find them. If they're far away or in a crowded area, this might feel like a subtle tug. The closer *they* are — and the less crowded it is — the easier we can find them."

On the edge of the freshman Warrior clump, a boy with ice-blond hair, high cheekbones, and squinty gray eyes raised his hand. He could have passed for Simon's little brother, but they couldn't be related. Gabe and Marina were the only siblings — indeed, the only members born and raised in the same Troupe — allowed to attend the same boarding school. Gabe still didn't know how they'd gotten away with it. "Yes, Marius?"

"I've n-never felt that pull-thingy y-you described with my Bloodlust."

"Yes, that's something we'll be working on with you freshmen in the coming months. It can be difficult at first to feel that on top of everything else." It had taken Gabe himself almost half a year of training to separate that pull from the Bloodlust's demand to attack. It wasn't easy, but it was a skill they'd all need when they joined a regular Cell after high school.

"Once your patrol is over, you're of course free to return to Eversfield and go back to pretending to be a normal high school student." Gabe flashed a wry smile.

The entire group reflected it. They were all too used to pretending to be normal.

"Now, if something comes up," *like a body*, Gabe thought but didn't say lest he freak out his brand-new freshmen, "we have a few options. For any generic cleanup after *them*, we've got the Juniper Troupe — that's the group of retired Diviners, Warriors, and their spawn living just outside Juniper. For any school issues — like, for instance, a hall monitor gives you trouble about going out after curfew — your best options are Mr. Clarkson over in World History and Ms. Vasile, Tubman's house manager. Headmaster Flynn also knows about us and our mission, but he prefers to stay out of the supernatural drama. He *is* a regular old civilian after all. He's not used to it like the rest of us."

A few chuckles emerged from the senior Warriors and more experienced Diviners. They'd all had their run-ins with the overzealous hall monitor or house manager over the years. And they'd all found out that they were better off involving one of the retired Diviners-slash-Eversfield teachers over Headmaster Flynn.

"And that's pretty much it for patrols. The rest you'll get on the job." Gabe angled himself toward the huddled group of four Diviners on his left. Marina and Lex sat in the front with their gazes glued onto him. Behind them, Diana nestled into Luke's side, his arm tight around her plump shoulders.

Gabe's stomach clenched. A Cell First — and Second for that matter — had to be devoted to his or her Cell. There was barely room for friends, let alone significant others. While he was in the relative safety of a training Cell in one of the Clan's boarding schools — or rather one of the boarding schools the Clan had infiltrated with retired Diviners and the occasional Warrior — he could make an exception here and there for the former. He could make none for the latter. And neither could Emilia. Even Simon was in a similar bind. Since the Augurs had labeled him as having "leadership potential" too, Simon was destined to become the First or Second of a regular Cell, the same as Gabe and Emilia.

Simon's future was no different from theirs, even if his present was.

Not that Simon or Emilia minded if the Clan hijacked their future. Both were willing to give up their lives in more ways than one.

That glorious gene must have skipped Gabe. But at least he wasn't alone. Marina and Cosmina also wanted lives outside the Clan's never-ending war with the Indestructible. Gabe suspected Luke and Diana did too, along with at least one of his freshman based on numbers alone.

But none of them had been sucked into the next generation of Cell leaders by the Augurs. None of them had had their future ripped away from them in the blink of an eye. None of them were as trapped as he was.

Gabe shoved the dark thoughts back into their lockbox. What was done was done. All he could do now was enjoy the freedoms he did have while he still had them.

"Diviners, you know the deal. While we Warriors are out hunting them down, you take care of the border protecting Eversfield. As long as those spells are fresh — or intact or whatever, I don't pretend to know the hocus-pocus side..." Gabe wiggled his fingers in a mock spell.

A chuckle or two wormed its way out of the Diviners' cluster.

It was about the best Gabe could hope for. "Anyway, as long as those spells are good to go, any one of *them* who dares to cross it will be maimed long enough for us Warriors to get to them and put them down. You'll also maintain the spells on our weapons, although..." Gabe shifted back to the freshman Warriors. "It's our responsibility to take our weapons to the Diviners for regular checks on the spells. Marina and Diana are the best choices since they're our resident Weavers, but Luke or Lex will do in a pinch, at least to check whether the spells need refreshing. I recommend you take your weapons in on a rotating schedule, so you never have to borrow one from someone else." Gabe's gaze flicked over to Cosmina hunched between the hulking figures of Simon and Darius.

She winced at his reminder. Twice last semester, Cosmina had borrowed his backup cutlass since the spells that enabled their weapons of steel to injure the Indestructible had faded away to nothing on hers.

"And I think that's about it. Any questions before we get into what's happening tonight?" When no one raised a hand or a voice, Gabe dove right in, "All right, this month's schedule has been posted, and you all should have reviewed it already. As a reminder, Diana and Luke, you're assigned to the border tonight."

The lovebirds nodded as one.

Gabe squashed his frown. He still doubted Marina's claim that she, the less experienced Diviner, should handle young Fire Diviner Lex. Then again, Marina's Water should be more than enough to quench any accidents from Lex's end. And Lex did appear to be as well-trained as he'd expect the daughter of the head Augur to be. Giving Diana and Luke as much time together as possible before Diana headed off to assist a Cell next year was the right thing to do. Wouldn't he do the same if it was an option?

But it's not, Gabe reminded himself. With Emilia's help, he'd accepted his grisly fate months ago. His purpose was to kill the Indestructible and protect his Cell until a member of the Indestructible killed him. No more, no less.

Gabe turned back to the two Warrior clumps seated before him. "Since it's the weekend, the Warriors will split into two patrols to cover the entire night. The first shift is Emilia leading with Darius, Cosmina, Simon, Marius, and Teddi patrolling with her. I'll lead the second shift with Emilia, Cosmina, Simon, Sandy, and Victoria. For those of us pulling doubles—that's Emilia, Cosmina, and Simon—it's your responsibility to catch up on sleep either before or after your shifts. We might need less sleep than regular humans, but we still need some," Gabe pointed out for the benefit of his freshmen. Too many freshman Warriors—himself included three years ago—tried to rely on their supernatural abilities to pull all-nighter after all-nighter. It didn't go well for any of them. "And that's it. Any questions?"

Marius raised a freckled hand. "Any n-new casualty reports?"

Crap. After weeks of summer freedom, Gabe was out of practice. While all the Warriors in his and Marina's family had long died out, that wasn't true for everyone. "No, sorry. I'll double check when I'm back in my room and let you know."

"Thanks," Marius squeaked.

"Anything else?"

Head shakes surrounded Gabe.

"All right, go about your business, enjoy your day, try not to get run over by moving carts. First patrol will meet in the student parking lot at eight p.m. And in case I forget to remind you tonight or tomorrow, daily workouts for Warriors begin Monday evening, seven p.m. sharp. You're dismissed." While his Cell rose to head back to Eversfield, Gabe turned to Emilia. "We'll chat about workout plans tomorrow?"

"Sure." Emilia gestured to the game trail of dirt and pebbles peeking through the underbrush. "You headin' back?"

"Not quite yet." Gabe's gaze flicked to Marina slumped in her seat alone, memorizing every inch of her worn sneakers.

"Ah, gotcha. How 'bout you take care of her and I'll take care of them?" Emilia tilted her head toward the group of freshmen at the edge of the clearing. In the center, Lex detailed a story that had everyone laughing.

"Sounds good."

"All right, see ya later." Emilia's ponytail swayed from one toned shoulder to the other as she strode to the freshmen. With swinging hands, she herded them onto the trail. "C'mon, c'mon, y'all can continue this enlightenin' discussion back on campus. We gotta get back." Emilia's voice trailed off. All but Lex disappeared into the evergreens.

How many of them would live to see an old age? No matter how hard they fought, they never exterminated the Indestructible.

But maybe that was the point. If their magic had been born with the Indestructible, would it die with them too? Maybe the Bureau thought it would and so maintained a careful stalemate regardless of the cost of human lives.

Or maybe the General, his Second, or even a Bureau Diviner or two was like him, Marina, and Cosmina. Maybe they too wished for a different life. And maybe they didn't do as good of a job leading the Clan because of it.

No, that wasn't right. The Augurs selected each General and Second using their Cyphering and Portency. As such, the Augurs *knew* who the best option was. And so it didn't matter if the Clan's leadership was more like him or more like the "I live to hunt the Indestructible" Simon. They were the best ones to lead.

Arriving at Marina's side, Gabe shook off his doubts. "You ready?"

Marina raised her head. Her dark blue eyes were as big as boulders. Her lower lip jutted out.

But Gabe couldn't let her out of it. She'd have to meet this new roommate sooner or later. "Marina…"

With a sigh, Marina peeled herself off the bench. "I know, I know, it has to happen at some point, so it might as well be now," she grumbled.

Skidding to a stop next to Marina, Lex looked from Marina to Gabe and back again. Her shoulder bounced off Marina's upper arm. When Marina glanced askance, Lex nodded. Her fluffy ginger halo echoed the movement.

Gabe narrowed his eyes. What did they have planned?

"Although," Marina adopted a wheedling tone, "it *is* close to lunch time…"

Gabe shook his head in mock dismay. "If I didn't know better, I'd think you were procrastinating, Marina."

"Just this once. Pleeeeeaaaase?"

Gabe peeked at the silent Lex. For once, her bright gaze was focused away from the action without setting anything on fire. "Fine, but only if Lex comes too."

Lex's attention snapped back to them. "Yes, please, I'm already so sick of the cafeteria food!" She rolled her eyes like eating the Eversfield food was torture.

It reminded Gabe of his terms. "But there's one condition for you, Lex. No more rolling your eyes at me unless I really deserve it."

"What if I always think you really deserve it?"

"Then I suggest you raise your bar."

Lex crossed her arms over her chest. "Fine. Deal."

That settled, Gabe turned back to Marina. "All right, it's your idea, why don't you pick the place?"

"Hmm, I don't know. What are you in the mood for?"

Debating their lunch options, Gabe, Marina, and Lex picked their way down the game trail toward one of the woodchip paths that led back to Eversfield. After a quick lunch, they'd evaluate Marina's new roommate.

Gabe's jaw clenched. This new roommate had better not mess with his sister.

CHAPTER 3

Val walked on air. Her best friend in the whole entire world was by her side. First, she would give Lila the grand tour. A few stops here, a few stops there, and Lila would meet all the right people. And all the right people would meet Lila. From there, they'd go to Lizzie to find anyone she might have missed, including Heidi and Sara.

Val's stomach twisted. Heidi and Sara—the president and vice president of Elizabeth Blackwell and Val's supposed friends—had stopped by her room this morning. Was it to congratulate Val on her success sneaking Lila into Eversfield in the wake of Tasha's expulsion?

No, of course not. They had nothing but threats for Val. "Lila better get us house points," and "Lila has to fit in with us," and "If she doesn't, it's your neck on the line, Val." Blah, blah, blah. Of course Lila would fit in. She was Val's best friend! How could she not?

But as Val's fingers brushed the handle of Admin's back door, she glanced askance at Lila. *Those clothes! That wrinkled shirt. Those awful khakis.* All would have to go before Lila could meet her new classmates. While Val was at it, she might as well fix that wild mane of Lila's and add a little makeup. At least cover up those rings under Lila's eyes. She'd have to borrow concealer from Cheri, but Cheri was only a text away.

Yes, that was it. She'd have Cheri deliver the makeup straight to her room, then take Lila the back way to Lizzie. With any luck at all, they'd avoid meeting anyone before Val got Lila presentable…which may or may not involve pouring a gallon of coffee down Lila's throat.

Swinging around, Val pressed her back into the door and barred the exit.

Lila scrambled to a stop. Her brows rose, asking an unspoken question.

Val answered it, "Actually, why don't we go straight to Lizzie? You know, drop off your stuff and everything before the tour?"

"Lizzie?"

"Oh, I'm sorry, I didn't tell you. Lizzie is what we in the know call Elizabeth Blackwell."

"Oh, um, okay. If that's what you want."

"It is, Lila dear." Val linked arms with her best friend and trotted them back to the office. "Anyway, like I was saying, Lizzie is what we call Elizabeth Blackwell."

"Uh huh."

"And we have fun names for the other dorms as well, but I'll tell you all about them during our tour this afternoon." Val lowered her voice as she re-entered Ms. Pershing's territory and headed straight for the pile of bags. Val knew when she wasn't wanted. While Lila stooped to collect her backpack, Val scanned the waiting room for the rest of her things. "Um, Lila, where's everything else? Already in your room? Still with your parents?"

"Nope, this is it." Her backpack and messenger bag secured, Lila began to heave the duffel bag over her shoulder.

Val reached for it. "Here, I'll take that." She settled the polka dotted strap over her shoulder and across her chest while Lila collected the lone remaining suitcase. As Val led the way out of the office and toward one of Admin's side exits, she whispered, "But seriously, how is this all your stuff? I mean, why? I know for a fact you own more clothes than this."

"Oh, um...I just...I just thought it would be easier for my parents. You know, if there was evidence I was coming back. I don't have any plans to go back—at least not for more than a couple weeks—but they don't know that yet. So, I only packed what I needed and left the rest."

"Oh, sweetheart, but all your beautiful things! Dresses and jewelry. Shoes. Makeup!" Val's hip nudged the back door open. She stepped onto the cement sidewalk that grazed the student parking lot then curved toward the girls' dorms. Visions of her bursting closet, her packed dresser, and her desk-turned-vanity danced before her eyes.

A nudge in the ribs broke Val's reverie.

Lila's lips quirked. "I think that's you, Val. You know I've never been that girly. And honestly, it wasn't that hard. I just picked my favorites and left everything else. Besides, aren't we in uniforms the vast majority of the time?"

"No! Not the 'vast majority' anyway. Only Monday through Friday, breakfast through dinner, with Friday night dinner as an exception."

On the sidewalk next to Val, Lila shrugged. "Sounds like the 'vast majority' to me. Uniforms pretty much all day during the week, then T-shirts and jeans or sweatpants at night and on the weekends. And Val, it made packing easy and fast, instead of a never-ending chore. It's not like I had a ton of time."

Alarm tied Val's stomach into knots. "But...but...my friends and I, we dress up for Friday night dinners! And we go out on the weekends definitely not in jeans. You can't wear jeans and T-shirts to JCC parties."

Lila's brow furrowed. "JCC parties?"

"Juniper City College. But don't let that get your hopes up about Juniper. It may only be fifteen minutes away or so, but it's not anything close to a city. It's more like a town really. I mean, it's the closest thing we've got to a city out here in the boonies, unless you include Florence, which is almost an entire hour away without traffic. And Juniper does have a cute little downtown area. JCC..." Val arched an eyebrow at Lila.

"Ummm, Juniper City College."

Val beamed. "Right. See Lila dear, you're gonna do so well here. Anyway, JCC is nestled right next to that downtown area and has simply the *best* parties. But we have to dress up for them or they won't let us in."

"That's not me, Val. College parties and dressing up...I'd rather just hang out here and watch movies in jeans and a T-shirt, y' know?"

Determination dethroned Val's dismay. Val could make jeans and a T-shirt work for everything but JCC parties. And Lila would compromise for them. She just needed the right clothes and accessories, something Val could provide. "Either way, Lila dear, don't you worry about it. I'll take care of everything."

"I wasn't worrying — wait, who's that? Coming toward us?" Tension raised Lila's voice.

Val peeked over her shoulder. A group of three students walked along the edge of the student parking lot, making a beeline for her and Lila. "Hmm, the redhead in front I don't know. Behind her is Gabe Lazare, a senior — and a real cutie, if you ask me. Fun fact: he used to date Lizzie's current president, who you'll meet later. Next to him is his younger sister…who also happens to be your new roommate. Looks like they wanna meet you."

Lila's fingers picked at her dreadful outfit like they could fix it. "But I'm not ready. I'm not prepared."

"Guess you should've thought about that before you dressed this morning."

Lila rolled her eyes. "Not helping, Val. Besides, *someone* forgot to tell me that I didn't have to wear an Eversfield uniform today. Or more accurately, something resembling a uniform."

"It's Saturday! I didn't think I needed to tell you. Either way, it's too late now." The trio were but feet away. Val squeezed Lila's trembling hand. "Breathe, Lila. She's the last to criticize you about clothes anyway. I mean, look at what *she's* wearing."

"Val, don't."

"I'm just sayin'. Okay, here they come. Bright smile, straight spine, chest out, chin up. Here we go."

LILA

LIKE A BOA CONSTRICTOR, APPREHENSION WRAPPED around and around Lila's stomach. It tightened its hold with every step of the group approaching her. The moment to meet her roommate and her first non-Val Eversfield classmates had arrived.

If only she'd worn normal clothes today. If only she fit in, just a little.

But she hadn't and she didn't. She'd have to do this with her khakis and her wrinkled blouse branding her as an outsider while the others paraded about in normal tanks and T-shirts, in shorts and skirts.

I can do this, Lila told herself, *and if not, Val's right here to bail me out*. Her fingers dashed upward to rake through her hair.

Val's glare stopped them in their tracks. Confidence, Lila was supposed to exude confidence.

The stocky girl in front — a hair taller than Val but with a ginger halo that added at least an inch — stopped first. Her stance was wide and powerful. When she thrust a sun-kissed hand toward Lila, her copper eyes crinkled. "Hi, I'm Alexandria Wilmer, but everyone calls me Lex. New Freshman and all that."

"Lila, Lila Lee. New sophomore transfer." Lila offered what she hoped was a winning smile.

"And I'm Val Baker, old sophomore. Nice to meet you, Lex." Val and Lex shook hands.

By now, the two in the back had caught up. Lila shifted her attention to her roommate. Glistening blue-black waves surrounded a heart-shaped face with wide eyes, an aquiline nose, and rosebud lips. Lanky legs emerged from what Val surely considered to be too-long shorts. A worn navy T-shirt hung loose around her lean body.

"Hi, I'm Lila." Lila extended a hand toward Marina. It hung in the air.

"Yes, um, I guessed as much. I'm Marina Lazare, your roommate." Marina's hand slunk in and brushed against Lila's. Not even a second passed before Marina pulled it away.

Lila plastered on a fake smile. "Nice to meet you, Marina."

"Uh huh, I mean, y-you too." With her hands shoved into her pockets, Marina stepped to the side, making way for the stranger lurking behind her.

Lila met his icy blue eyes.

Her heart thundered in her ears. Her breath hitched. Her thoughts scattered like dandelion fluff on an unruly breeze.

Lila's gaze slid over the Adonis standing before her, from the ebony locks swept back from straight, serious eyebrows, along the cheekbones that could cut glass, down to the chiseled jawline. Ivory teeth peeked through full lips while he spoke.

While he spoke.

Lila hurtled back to reality. She'd missed everything he'd said. And now he waited for a response.

With a gulp, Lila gathered her far-flung wits. "Sorry, what was that?"

"Oh, I just said that my name is Gabe and that I'm Marina's older brother." Gabe's deep voice threatened another swoon.

Lila adjusted the strap of her backpack, though it needed none. If she wanted to talk like a normal human being, she'd have to avoid eye contact with him. Possibly forever. "I'm Lila...but I guess you already knew that. Um, hi, nice to meet you." Lila offered her hand first despite silently cursing Eversfield for assigning her a frosty roommate with a too-handsome brother.

Gabe clasped Lila's hand.

Her insides plummeted past her toes. Her lungs battled for a breath. Blackness invaded her vision.

Blurry images swirled before her sightless eyes.

GABE

ICE FLOWED THROUGH GABE'S VEINS. HIS FINGERS AND toes were numb from it. Chunks of it sat in his stomach. It crusted around his lashes, sealing his eyes shut. Forcing him to watch the visions.

They played on a loop, all centered on this girl—this plain, boring girl. One moment she smiled up at him, her gaze a more vibrant green than the forest after a storm. The next she giggled and spun in a dress that matched those eyes. At a Pasteur party, she sang on a makeshift stage and pride swelled within him. His fingers tangled in her soft curls as he pulled her closer beneath a starry sky. A door slammed in his face, leaving him lost and alone.

Gabe ripped his hand away. The visions stopped.

Who was this girl, to bring the visions back? For months he'd escaped them. Then one handshake and it was last winter all over again.

Gabe's anger thawed his ice from the outside in. Power thrummed along his limbs. He could kill any one of *them* right now and enjoy it.

Yet when he peeked down at her, his frozen heart stuttered. Confusion—and maybe pain—wrinkled her forehead. She stared at her hand like it held the answers. Her front teeth worried her lower lip.

She's not my problem. But the urge to comfort her surged.

Gabe had to get away. "Ahem. Marina, Lex, I'm sorry, but I forgot I have to…I have to chat with Emilia. I'll see you later. Nice to meet you, Lila."

Not daring a backward glance, Gabe spun on his heel and rushed away.

CHAPTER 4

KANE

Still as any statue, Kane perched on the edge of the ripped sofa. Her followers gathered around her, staring at the black and white TV spouting nonsense. While her blood pulsed with impatience, her hands folded together in her lap, creating the vision of tranquility.

Here, we're finally here. The woods called to Kane, begging her to start her mission, to begin her victory.

But Kane would not yield. She and her lackeys had arrived at this decrepit cabin outside Juniper no more than an hour before sunrise. Daylight now trapped the five of them inside their new home. It was enough to drive any vampire crazy, let alone ones who hadn't fed in weeks.

To do something—*anything*—Kane rose. With three brisk strides, she entered the kitchen. Distaste curled her upper lip. Nothing but stained counters and empty slots for appliances greeted her. *Such is the price of lying low.*

Kane twisted the faucet of the kitchen sink. Bursts of rust-colored water shot through the air bubbles. A full minute passed before it ran free and clear.

Having verified that the plumbing worked, Kane approached the cardboard box filled with her favorite cleaning products. Her slender fingers fiddled with a tear in the corner while the list of tasks assigned to this week cycled through her mind. After the fourth round of reminders, Kane dismissed them, suppressing a sigh lest the others notice. Not that they would, sprawled throughout the living room watching that TV.

Well, no longer. While the sun trapped them here, they might as well get some work done.

Kane marched to the center of the living room and turned off the TV. Three of her vampires — all except Fang — glowered at her.

Annoyance crawled up Kane's throat like bile, setting it afire. Her hands flew to her hips. "Look, I know you want to relax after all that driving, but we need to get some things straight." Kane ignored the glares of those who were supposed to obey her every word. "First, you will not feed within a hundred miles of this location."

On the floor below impassive Fang, Ramrod crossed her arms over her chest. Toulouse's black gaze narrowed from his half of Kane's couch. Brock dared to bare his canines.

Red-hot fury coursed through Kane's veins, but it would not control her. She would not let it. Her powers were reserved for rebellions, not complaints. "Secondly, you will feed no more often than once a month."

From between his thin lips, Brock exhaled useless air in a burst. "Are ya kiddin' me? We're here for a mission, maybe fight the Clan, and ya want us to only feed once a month? How are we supposed t' keep our strength up, only feedin' once a month?"

Kane's silver eyes turned to cold steel. She growled, "First, we're not dealing with the Clan, but one of their training Cells. Secondly, if we do our job *correctly*, we won't interact with them until we're ready to kill them all. And finally, our illustrious sire feeds once every three months. Even I feed only every other month despite my additional energy expenditures. Be thankful I do not hold *you* to the same standard."

Grumbles abounded, but Kane raised her voice over them. "The good news is that I'd like everyone to feed tonight. We have two cars, so Fang and Toulouse, you'll go in one direction, and Brock and Ramrod, you'll go in the other. I'll stay here, as *I* have no need to feed. Remember to be quick. I expect you back before sunrise, even with driving at least a hundred miles each way and being discreet. Perhaps you should use this time to plan your trip."

"Why do we need to be back before sunrise?" Unlike the others, Fang hid no hint of anger behind his words. His question was nothing but innocent curiosity.

Kane showed her teeth in that expression of sinister excitement unique to vampires, something halfway between a snarl and a smile. "Because tomorrow at sunset we begin." It was a half-truth — Kane would begin tonight in secret — but it had the intended effect. The defiance of Kane's vampires morphed into determination.

At least there was one thing they could all agree on: the vampire hunters of the Clan must die, starting with those at Eversfield.

CHAPTER 5

LILA

With every step down the cement sidewalk, a new question twisted and turned in Lila's mind. What had happened back there? How could a simple handshake cause the world to swim before her eyes? Was it because she'd gotten up too early after going to bed too late? Or maybe it was because she'd hardly eaten anything this morning.

"You're quiet." Val poked Lila in the ribs.

Lila rubbed at her upset stomach. Her temples throbbed. "Yeah, um, I just…I just don't feel very good."

"Oh, no, what's wrong?" Val stopped in the middle of the path and tucked a loose curl behind Lila's ear.

"I dunno. My head hurts and my stomach's upset…"

"Well…" Val shoved Lila's bag behind a slim hip, then resumed their stroll toward a line of identical brick buildings. "Fortunately for you, I've got some delicious espresso back in my room. We'll get you changed, get some coffee in you, then some food, then—"

"Val, can…can we not? I barely got any sleep last night between my nerves and getting ready and leaving early. What I'd really like to do is take a nap, then unpack, then have dinner with my parents. You know, stay low-key."

Val's brows furrowed. Her rosy lips twitched toward a frown.

Guilt flooded Lila. "I know I promised, but—"

Like the sun on a cloudy day, a gentle smile broke through Val's concern. "No, no, no, it's okay, Lila. We can do your tour tomorrow if that's better."

"Thank you, Val."

"No problem, Lila dear. We'll get you settled and then I'll leave you to your nap."

"Great…" Lila sucked in a breath before making her final request, "And Val, can we maybe do the tour first thing in the morning? Before everyone's up 'n about? Say…nine a.m.?" Whether her fellow students would be up and about at nine in the morning, Lila had no idea. It sounded early enough to at least reduce the amount of people Val could force her to meet.

"Lila…"

"Pleeeeeaaaase?" Lila begged without shame.

"Fine." Val's index finger wagged at her. "But don't think this gets you out of meeting my friends and being social."

"I wouldn't dream of it." Lila transferred her suitcase handle to the opposite hand, then linked arms with Val. "Thank you."

"You're welcome. So…what didja think of your new roommate?"

Lila couldn't respond. The path had become quicksand. Her feet struggled to creep forward.

It — her new home — stretched before her. Four rows of iron-framed windows glared down at Lila. The red of the bricks flickered through the ivy, seeking to touch her. To *burn* her. The same menacing bushes from out front clung to every side. The sunlight filtering through the storm clouds landed on their inches-long thorns.

Goosebumps prickled up Lila's forearms. She was not welcome here.

An elbow jutted into her side. Lila jumped.

Val snickered. "You may close your mouth at any time, Lila dear."

Clamping her jaw shut, Lila stumbled toward a response. "Sorry, I...I didn't expect it to be...quite so..."

"Grand?"

"Not exactly. I mean, that too, but I guess...angry?"

"Angry? Lila, you're not making any sense."

"I know, I just..." Lila shook her head as if to clear it of the foreboding thoughts. "I dunno, I guess it's not what I expected."

"Didn't you look at the brochures I sent you? Lizzie featured in at least one of them."

"Yes, well, I guess..." Lila bit her lower lip. "I suppose I mostly looked at what I had to do to get the scholarship and not so much what it would be like to go to school here." Her cheeks on fire, Lila offered an abashed shrug as an apology.

"Oh please. I don't care whether you looked at them at all. Besides, if you *had*, I never would have seen that shock of yours, which I've enjoyed thoroughly." Val laced her arm back through Lila's, then herded her down the winding path leading to the far end of the dorm. "Don't worry, Lila, you'll get used to it in no time. Let's just go in and get you settled. Then you can take a nice long nap and wake up feeling better about everything."

When Val opened Lizzie's back door, Lila gulped. This—not the rushed goodbyes with her parents nor the "orientation" with Ms. Pershing—marked the start of her new life. Uncertainty rang loud and clear.

Lila crossed the threshold.

Plain concrete steps and a metal handrail welcomed her. Aside from being clean enough to eat off and deserted, this back stairwell could have been in her old school. Lila's shoulders relaxed a smidge.

With her toe resting on the first stair, Val clutched Lila's duffel bag to her chest. She shot a mischievous grin at Lila. "Last one to the third floor's a rotten egg!"

Before Lila could ask if they were allowed to race up staircases, Val took off. Like the world's tiniest football player performing a quick feet drill, she darted up the steps. About halfway to the second floor, she stopped. Over her shoulder, Val arched an eyebrow at Lila.

At the bottom of the steps, Lila's fingers dug in and out of her suitcase's plastic handle. She should be the responsible one, the one who said "this is not a good idea."

But this time—just this once—Lila didn't want to be that person.

She wrapped her arms around her suitcase, then leapt the stairs two at a time, chasing Val. Giggles reverberated off the whitewashed walls. Twice Lila almost smashed her kneecap into a cement step.

Val beat Lila by a stair, but Lila didn't care. She and Val collapsed on the third-floor landing, a pile of limbs and bags against a wall of buttercup yellow marked with a script "3."

Once her breath slowed enough to speak, Lila pulled herself into a seated position. "Thanks. I needed that."

"Any time, Lila dear." Val stood and offered a hand. "You ready?"

"No...but I suppose it's now or never." Lila grasped Val's hand. Together, they hauled her up. After collecting her bags, Lila followed Val through the polished door, then down the empty hall.

Val's heels clicked against the wooden floor. Lila's flats slapped against it. Stress knotted Lila's stomach tighter and tighter for each gilded nameplate that passed by. 316…314…312…

"There are roughly sixteen rooms per floor, though sometimes that shifts, depending on how many singles there are. Unfortunately, each floor has only one bathroom area and one shower area. That's a single bathroom for thirty or so girls to share. I recommend getting up early to shower, do your makeup, all that jazz."

Lila had no intention of getting up early to do her makeup before classes. And she might take her showers at night to avoid the rush. Her hair would be a mess no matter when she showered anyway. But Val didn't need to know all that.

"And yeah, usually all or most of these doors would be open to be social and all that, but today's the main move-in day. So that means long drives and lots of parents to amuse. Don't worry, it'll be bustling by the time you wake up from your nap."

Lila nodded. Her drive had begun at five this morning to make sure they wouldn't be late for breakfast with Headmaster Flynn and the sophomore and junior grade leads. If Lila had been a normal student and not a transfer, they might be just arriving too. Given the anxiety coursing through her veins at the mere thought of all those open doors—of all those strangers staring at her—deserted halls ranked low on Lila's list of worries.

"All right, here we are, room 302." Val gestured to the last door on the left, then stepped back to wait for Lila.

Lila approached the door—*her* door. Her hand stumbled through her backpack's front pouch, searching for the keycard. By the time the envelope's coarse paper brushed against Lila's fingertips, Val leaned against the pair of oak doors marking the end of the hallway. Her fingers tap-tap-tapped at her phone.

The crinkled envelope trembled in Lila's hands. She pulled the plastic keycard out, then slid it through the slot above the door handle.

Nothing happened.

Lila gulped. Of course she needed help even with this one itty bitty thing. She raised the keycard to try a second time.

Ka-thunk! The lock unlatched. A green light blinked at Lila.

Pushing the door inward, Lila stepped forward and into her new home. Two lofted beds were shoved against the back wall on either side of a central window showing nothing but green leaves and bark. To her right was a bookcase full of textbooks, binders, and pristine notebooks. In case there was any doubt, precise lettering on aqua tape identified it as "Marina." A battered loveseat squished between the bookcase and the edge of the lofted bed Lila assumed was hers based on the naked mattress. To her left were two doors, one labeled with more tape. *Closets, probably.*

Lila rolled her suitcase past the doors and into the office area beneath the bed on the right. Opposite her, more "Marina" tape labeled a matching desk, dresser, desk chair, and even the bed frame itself. At least Lila knew what wasn't hers.

As Lila unloaded her backpack and messenger bag onto the bare desk, Val strolled through the open door. Her jaw dropped. So did Lila's duffel bag from Val's limp fingers. Stepping in a circle, Val surveyed the room with her hands on her hips. "I can't believe she did this."

"Did what?"

"Labeled everything! Like you're gonna steal her stuff or somethin'." Val stomped over to Marina's office area. Her desk was almost as bare as Lila's. The only items on it were a roll of aqua-colored tape, a calculator, a potted succulent, and an Eversfield mug containing a horde of pens and mechanical pencils. Val dumped them out.

"Val! Leave her stuff alone!"

Val raised a pencil and wiggled it back and forth. The Marina tape stretched from its tip to the eraser. "Lila, she labeled every single pen and pencil. Who does that?"

"Val, just put it back. It's fine, I promise."

"Hmmph, this is why I don't have roommates."

"That and your parents paid bunches to make it happen."

Val shrugged. "It helps me study."

"Uh huh." While Lila hadn't *thoroughly* reviewed the Eversfield pamphlets, she had caught a few relevant details. "Speaking of which, how'd you move in early? I thought that today was the first day regular students could move in."

Val lifted her chin, her tone haughty. "Lila, don't pry. It's unbecoming."

"Unbecoming, huh? Been brushing up on your eighteenth-century vocab?"

"Lila."

"Val."

Val's brows dropped and her arms crossed. "Okay, fine, you win. I may have...I may have had some difficulty last year...you know, with my grades. But it's all better now, or at least, it should be! I took the summer school classes they told me to."

"Class*es*?"

Val's fingers picked at her perfect hair. "Yeah, um, just Algebra, English Comp, and —"

"*And*? Val!"

Val rushed to Lila. Her eyes wide and glossy, she wove their fingers together. "I know. I haven't been the most studious. But now that you're here, I'll be so much better! And you can help me!"

"Listen, Val, I don't know. I feel like I'm gonna have my hands full managing my own grades."

"Lila, Lila, Lila, you'll be fine. You're a genius, remember? You'll get all A's in your classes no problem!"

Lila suppressed a snort. Val only thought she was a genius because Val excused herself from the vast majority of Lila's studying. Asking Val to sit still for more than five minutes amounted to the most heinous of crimes in her world.

"If it's really a problem, this new freshman sat in on some of my summer school classes. Mary or Megan or something. Anyway, she helped me this summer, and I'm sure she'd be willing to help this semester too."

"Uh *huh*. And how does she help you when you can't remember her name?"

Like a toddler caught with a hand in the cookie jar, Val stared at the ground. "She helps me with my homework."

"How does she 'help' you? *Exactly*."

Val examined the hem of her black skirt. In the smallest of voices, she admitted, "She does it."

"Val!"

Val's arms flew up in self-defense. "What? At least then I get good grades on the homework!"

"And you think the teachers won't notice you acing the homework and failing the tests?"

"See, this is why I need you, Lila dear. I just don't think things through, not like you do."

"Uh huh. You do know that if I help you—and I'm not promising that I can—you will be doing all your own homework."

"Yup yup yup! I'll be a good li'l student, I swear. And of course you'll be able to help. You're my genius friend who knows all! Now," Val stepped back to look Lila up and down. "I know you want a nap and all, but let's find your outfit for tonight first."

"Can we maybe…*not*? I mean, don't get me wrong, I wanna change out of these clothes, but…I mean, the dinner with my parents is gonna be uncomfortable enough as it is, can't I just wear, I dunno, whatever?"

"But Lila—"

"Please, Val? You know what they're like right now. I promise I'll let you dress me later."

"All right, I suppose."

That one problem solved, Lila flopped onto the unlabeled sofa, then tossed an arm over her poor fatigued eyes. "Ugh, why did I promise my stupid parents that I would go to stupid dinner with them tonight? I'm such an idiot."

"No, you're not. You're the smartest person I know. You're just…you're not very good at saying no when you need to."

Sensing Val had more to say, Lila peered around her forearm.

Beside Lila's desk, Val fiddled with the aqua tape attached to a stolen pen. "Hey, here's an idea: what if I go with you? Regale them with tales from my parents?" Val's chocolate eyes flicked to Lila's.

"No, that…that'd probably be worse. They pretend to be happy about your parents' success, but…"

"Oh, yeah. Right." A frown twitched Val's lips downward. She looked away from Lila, preferring to gaze at the open doorway rather than at her best friend. There wasn't much on this planet that could embarrass Valerie Elizabeth Baker, but monetary discrepancies were one of them.

"Okay, well, I'll leave you alone then. Take your nap, go to your dinner, then we'll hang out tonight. Just let me know when you're back." Val's sunshine-y smile squashed all memories of her frown. "Besides, by then everyone you need to meet will be out 'n about. It'll be perfect, Lila dear!"

Lila stifled her eye roll. What she considered to be perfect and what Val did couldn't be further apart.

CHAPTER 6

GABE

The lapping waters of the lake reflected the storm clouds in the sky above Gabe. His arms wrapped around his shins. His thighs pressed against his torso. His toes dug into the sand.

Two years ago, he and Simon had stumbled on this secluded beach during a paired patrol. At the time, he'd joined Simon in scoffing at its small size, barely big enough for even a handful of people. A year later, it'd become a refuge. At least once a week he'd hidden here, seeking to escape his present as the Eversfield Cell First and his future as nothing more than another dead Warrior. By winter, he'd recovered enough to function, and his visits became less and less frequent. He hadn't been here since the last time his Portency had flared up.

A shiver crawled up Gabe's spine. In this very spot, he'd vowed never to act on the visions again. After months of silence, he'd hoped they'd abandoned him. Evidently not.

It wasn't fair. He hadn't asked for this. All he wanted was a normal life—or at least as normal as anyone in his family could have. He knew his duty: grow up, go to school, train hard, fight until he was killed. That was his destiny, as much as he may pretend it wasn't. He didn't want or need this…*complication*.

All ten of Gabe's fingers tugged at his hair. In the lake stretching out in front of him, a few ducks floated up and over a wave, napping with their heads tucked under a wing.

Maybe that's what he should do. Tuck the visions away, forget that they'd ever happened. After all, that's what he should have done last spring.

But no, Marina would never allow that. Ever since she'd found out about his "gift," she'd bugged him to tell their parents. Since Marina had her own secrets *he* could expose, she'd backed off any outright threats. *For the time being*, she'd said.

Still, Gabe had overheard Marina quizzing Lex about Portency just last week. With more tenacity than a bulldog, Marina almost certainly recognized the sign of an incoming vision by now. There was little chance she didn't know what had happened back there and less that she'd let him off the hook. He'd just have to convince Marina that she didn't need to inform their parents, who'd inform their Troupe leader, who'd inform the Bureau, who'd collect Gabe for testing. Even a short life fighting *them* was better than a long one as a lab rat.

A figure plopped down beside him. Gabe flinched.

"You must be deep in thought not to hear clumsy old me sneak up on you." Marina wore a wry smile.

When Lex sat in the sand next to her, Gabe smothered a grimace.

Marina's shoulder bounced off his, a signal for him to explain everything, just like that.

Gabe debated pulling rank on her. He could say that he wasn't obligated to tell her anything. That she wasn't the boss of him. That it was quite the opposite. But his little sister would never accept any of those excuses.

He could protest Lex's presence. She wasn't needed for this, and it would distract Marina, giving him a few more precious minutes of freedom.

But that was pointless. Marina wouldn't back down with or without Lex. Besides, Lex could prove useful. A second opinion could only help, especially from the daughter of the lead Augur. And Lex already kept Marina's secrets. What was one more?

"I take it you noticed then, Marina?" Her nod answered him quicker than Gabe could find the words to explain. "Um, well, I don't know what happened exactly."

A gust of wind tossed Lex's untamed curls as she darted forward to peek around Marina. "Seemed like somethin' happened when you and Lila met?"

"Yeah, when we shook hands." At that memory, the visions resurfaced, playing before him like an old-fashioned silent movie. His blood rushed in his ears, but Gabe stretched out his legs and leaned backward as if he didn't have a care in the world. As if his Portency didn't own him.

After only twice through, the visions faded away. Despite his rigid control, Gabe's shoulders dropped with relief. To disguise the movement, Gabe shifted back toward Marina. He flicked his eyes at Lex, asking the unspoken question.

Marina's pointy chin dipped twice to confirm it.

Of course she told Lex. Gabe sighed. "That was when my super special 'gift' made an appearance."

"Okay, so your Portency showed up. I assume it involved her?" Marina doodled in the sand like she longed to take notes.

"Yes."

"And?"

Unwilling to face his Portency just yet, Gabe grasped the final straw. "Hey, how's Lila? Is she okay? She seemed, I dunno, affected by the visions too. I've never had them about a civilian. I don't know if they could affect her." *If they could hurt her.*

Marina's brows knitted together. "I don't know. She and Val hurried away right after you left." Her lips pressing into a thin line, Marina rubbed at her upper arm. "I *suppose* I can check on her later today."

"Thanks," Gabe answered too quickly.

Marina's frown deepened for a heartbeat, then disappeared. Her shoulder bumped against his again. "You're procrastinating."

"Ugh, fine. I saw a series of images, okay? Moving images, I suppose." Later involuntary rewatches included an artist's palette of emotions, most of which Gabe was ninety-nine percent sure didn't originate from future-him. But he wasn't about to admit that to Marina. She'd force him to tell their parents about his Portency for sure. And then he'd end up trapped in headquarters, the Bureau Diviners' lab rat.

"And what were these images?"

"Marina," Lex scolded in a low tone.

"What? We need to know the details to figure out what's going on."

"But sometimes visions are personal — "

"No, Lex, she's right." Gabe rubbed his hands over his face, shielding him from their prying eyes. He knew, he *knew* that he would feel a whole lot better once he told them. As usual, Marina would be the brains, him the brawn. He wouldn't have to worry about any of it, not with his sister on the case. But the act of expressing them, of describing those visions, was difficult. More than difficult. Near impossible.

After a deep breath, Gabe forced himself to begin, "I saw a series of four images." A white lie, but somehow Gabe couldn't share the most personal of the five visions. "They all centered on her—Lila—and no one else. In the first, she…" Gabe squeezed his eyes shut like he struggled recalling the images tattooed across his brain. "She just kinda looked up and smiled." *Beamed, more like.*

"In the next, she was dressed in a green dress that swung out around her when she twirled. She was dancing, I guess." Gabe rushed forward lest they ask who she was dancing with. "In image three, she was singing on a stage or something and in image four she slammed the door in someone's face." *In my face.*

Finished, Gabe glanced up, expecting shock or disbelief. Instead, Marina chewed the inside of her lip, lost in thought. An unimpressed Lex picked at the dirt underneath a fingernail.

After an eternal two minutes of silence, Marina initiated the discussion, "Well, we always knew that your gift could grow and develop. It appears that it has. Perhaps we should revisit—"

"No. We are not telling anyone beyond the two, er, three of us. It has yet to provide anything of use." In fact, it had only done the opposite thus far.

"To be fair, you don't really know that. Not for sure." This from Lex, which, okay, her mother was an established Portent, not to mention lead Augur. But it didn't give Lex the right to tell him what to do.

Gabe crossed his arms over his chest. "It's not happening. I don't want this, so as far as I'm concerned, it doesn't exist. Not until something forces my hand."

"But it's our duty—"

Marina placed a hand over Lex's freckled forearm, stopping her mid-sentence. "Lex, it's fine. Okay, Gabe, we won't say anything until there are no other options. And even then, we'll go to our parents first."

Lex scowled at Marina's rebuff but held her silence.

Marina turned back to Gabe. "So, you had this series of visions, all of this one girl. It's got to mean something."

"It's pretty clear, isn't it?" When both Gabe and Marina hurled incredulous looks at Lex, she shrugged. "Most Portents — 'specially the weak or untrained ones, no offense, Gabe — have visions about those they're close to. Gabe has a massive crush on this girl, so his Portency gave him a glimpse into her future."

"First, I do not have a 'massive crush' on her. Secondly, I don't even know her."

"Okay, to your second part, Portency has no concept of time. Close to her now, close to her in the future, it's all the same. At least that's what my mom says."

"Lex, being 'close to her' isn't going to happen now or ever, not with who I am. Not with *what* I am."

"Fine, but if you were 'normal,' you'd go for it, right?"

Gabe ran both hands through his hair in exasperation. The obvious "no" died in his throat. "I don't know. I'm not normal, so I haven't considered it."

"And all I'm sayin' is that your Portency considered it for you. Sounds like you two'd be happy for a while, but then you wouldn't be. Easy peasy." Lex dusted off her hands like the matter was closed.

"Lex, that makes absolutely no — "

Ever the mediator, Marina leaned forward, intercepting the twin glares of Gabe and Lex. "Gabe, let's examine all our options before we discount any. As much as I may hate to admit it, Lex's theory is possible."

Gabe narrowed his eyes at Marina, communicating how "possible" he thought Lex's theory was. A butterfly wing tickled his ribs.

"How about something a little less direct? For example…" Marina sifted a handful of sand between her fingers. "Maybe Gabe's Portency is trying to highlight Lila for some reason."

"What? Like she's a Latent?" Gabe scoffed.

The rest of the sand dropped from Marina's hand in a clump. Her somber face brightened. "Maybe! I mean, I thought those were urban legends—at least after age ten or so—but just last month Lex's mom found one in a high school, so I guess not."

"But she's an Augur. If anyone could spot a Latent…"

"True, but none of us Diviners here at Eversfield are ever going to be Augurs. None of us have Cyphering *or* Portency." Marina's gaze flashed up to Gabe. "Except you. So maybe the only way to get the message was through your Portency."

"That's assuming there's some organization to this chaos," Gabe grumbled.

"Maybe there is, maybe there isn't. Either way, I think the visions could mean Lila's a Latent…which means I have to find a way to smuggle her back to Mom. I don't want to invite her home, but if I could get Mom here…" Marina chewed on her lower lip.

Gabe racked his brain. He was missing something.

The image of Lila twirling in that green dress popped up in his mind's eye. Gabe's stomach flipped. "The dance. At the end of the semester. Mom and Dad always help out. It'd be easy to introduce them. I mean, I know Dad's no help since his Healing won't tell him anything about Lila, but Mom's Cyphering should do the trick."

"True, but the Masquerade Ball is four months away. What if we need something sooner? Latents can be a danger to themselves and those around them." Marina sounded like she was quoting from a textbook.

"You're her roommate, you'll be able to look out for her. You know, watch for any obvious signs. Plus Mom and Dad might visit earlier."

Marina's brows collapsed over her navy gaze. She crossed her arms. "I suppose…but it's not like I'll have a bunch of free time once classes start up again. I'll have stud —"

"Yes, yes, Marina, we all know you'll have studyin' to do." Lex elbowed Marina, a smile twitching the corners of her toad-like mouth. "Gabe and I can keep an eye on Lila when you can't." Lex winked at Gabe.

His fists clenched around the sand on either side, but Gabe swallowed his rebuke. He did not need or want to get to know this girl any more than he had to.

No matter what Lex or the butterflies thought.

CHAPTER 7

"Val, you're going to lose this battle, no matter how many shiny dresses you wave in my general direction." Lila's hands smashed into her hips.

"But, c'monnnnn. It's your first night here. At the very least, we should go into Juniper and pick up some bubble tea. I know you wanna talk about tonight's dinner, and I won't even make you late for curfew!"

"First, no, I do not in fact want to talk about tonight's dinner. My parents were civil, so dinner was bearable. Then we said goodbye, and that was that." A lump swelled in Lila's throat. Not fifteen minutes ago, both her parents had walked through sheets of rain to accompany her all the way to Eversfield's entrance. Huddled beneath the shelter of that brick arch, Lila had hugged her mom, then her dad. Despite months of dreaming of this escape, she'd struggled to let them go—even her mom. As long as she was clutching one of them, the moment couldn't pass.

But pass it had. Her parents had climbed into that cardinal red car of her mother's, bright even in the gray gloom. Then they drove down the tree-lined road winding away from Eversfield. Winding away from Lila.

A dark figure in the archway, Lila had lingered long after her parents' car had disappeared. Unexpected tears had rolled down her cheeks. For the first time in her life, Lila was alone.

Only when the tears stopped did Lila trudge back to her room. She'd thought only of the comfort of slipping into a bed — even an unfamiliar one.

She should have known better.

When she'd arrived at her door, Val sat outside with her chin resting on a stack of dresses. This time, Val hadn't taken no for an answer, not that Lila had put up much of a fight. Her loneliness wouldn't let her.

But when selecting a dress for Semester Start tomorrow had morphed into picking one for tonight, Lila's compliance had shattered. "Secondly, curfew is in an hour, Val."

"Exactly, Lila dear, one whole hour! That's more than enough time to pick up some bubble tea. I'm sure Rudi'll let us borrow her car. Then we can watch a movie or something."

"If that's the plan, tell me why I have to get dressed up."

"Well...I thought that...if we were out 'n about already..." Val glanced up at Lila. Hope gleamed in her catlike eyes.

Lila cut it off without mercy, "No, definitely not."

Val's face fell.

After a sigh, Lila joined Val beside the leaning tower of dresses on her desk chair. "Look, Val, you know you're my best friend and that I'd like nothing more than to hang out with you tonight, preferably in something less glittery." Lila hooked her pinky finger under a spaghetti strap as if afraid the dress might bite, then put it back on its pile. "But it's been a long day — even with my nap instead of the tour this afternoon — and I still have to unpack. Plus, I'd like to get a good night's rest before you make me meet everyone in the world tomorrow."

"Fine, deal, you don't have to dress up. Let's go!"

"Val, I'm sorry. I just…I just really want a night in. Decompress, y' know?"

"I guess…but I hate to leave you alone on your very first night…"

Now Lila understood. The plan had never been for only Val and Lila to go out. It was to join Val's friends and probably stay out far too late. "It's okay. I'll finish unpacking, then curl up in bed with a book or something."

Val's eyebrow arched. Never in a million years would Val choose a book over a night on the town.

"Really, Val. Go. Have fun." Lila shooed Val toward the door with both hands. The sooner Val left, the less likely Lila would find herself "accidentally" getting bubble tea and more tonight.

In the doorway, Val turned around. With an expression sadder than the saddest hound dog, she whispered, "Lila, you have to go. If you don't, all my friends will think that you're d-u-double-l."

Lila snorted. "Let them. If they can't understand why I wouldn't want to go out after a long day and when I haven't even unpacked yet, I don't care what they think."

Val's glossy lips parted to argue.

Lila beat her to it. "Val, you're the only person in this whole darn place that I care about. I want to be a good friend to you, but first, I'm here to get an excellent education. I don't know what's gonna happen with my parents, so I need to be able to pay for college on my own, preferably through scholarships."

"I know…but it doesn't feel right! You should be meeting people, making lifelong friends. Definitely not hiding in your room alone."

"Val, I know. And I will later, I promise, no matter how much I want to 'hide in my room.' Okay?"

"Okay, fine. But you will come out with me next weekend, all gussied up in one of those dresses over there. And you'll wear one of them for Semester Start tomorrow."

"Deal. I'll even figure out the final contenders tonight, just for you. Now, you go have fun. I'll see you in the morning for the tour."

"All right. You have fun too, if reading a boring ol' book can be called fun." Val scrunched her face in mock disgust, then waved an elven hand around the room. "And don't forget to get rid of all her stupid labels."

"Val..."

"Or not, up to you. I'll see you tomorrow, Lila dear." After a rushed hug, Val skipped through the open door. Her steps echoed down the deserted hallway. Although the rain had cancelled tonight's bonfire, it hadn't stopped Lizzie's residents from abandoning campus.

All except Lila, anyway. Even Marina had disappeared after that initial meeting.

Lila's stomach clenched. She did not want to think about that again. Not her roommate's icy greeting and not *him* lurking in the background.

Shoving the memory away, Lila confronted the heap of dresses standing between her and her latest book. Promise or no promise, Lila wasn't in the mood to try on a bajillion outfits. Besides, if she waited until Marina got back, she could ask her for a second opinion. Maybe that would thaw Marina's chill. If not, at least it was an excuse to procrastinate.

Lila stepped around her unopened suitcase. *While I'm at it, I might as well put off unpacking too.* She reached toward the navy cover peeking from underneath the flap of her messenger bag.

Green flashed in the window.

Only it wasn't fair to call it simply "green." No, there was lime and olive, kelly and jungle, moss and emerald. It was a rainbow composed only of shades of green.

Lila couldn't stay away from it. Her mesmerized feet carried her to the window. There, an ancient oak welcomed her. Its younger branches swayed with every gust. Below her, the bushes—now more leaf than thorn—clumped together. Kelly green grass shimmered in the rain, stretching from those hedges to the start of the forest surrounding Eversfield. Where the thistles and wildflowers took over, more trees bent to the wind's will. In the distance, olive-green willow boughs lashed at each other. Between their trunks, dark waters peered. Farther away, stalwart pines awaited Lila.

Lila's hand moved on a nameless urge. She wanted to get closer. She wanted to *see*.

Knock knock

Lila's fingers clasped the window's latch.

Crrr-reak

Lila twisted the lever.

"Um, Lila?"

Lila jumped. Her hand slammed the lock closed. All thoughts concerning the wilderness outside her window bolted. Lila flipped around.

Of all people, Gabe stood in her doorway. A stray lock danced over his forehead. Those stupid pale blue eyes of his shone.

Lila's mind muddied all over again.

She fought for control. *He's not that cute. No, he's not. Even if he is — which he's not — he's a senior and he's Marina's brother, which means he's not for me. He's just another Eversfield student, that's all.* With that rant circling her mind, Lila dared to look at him.

Her heart stuttered. Her breath hitched. But her brain moved, albeit at a snail's pace.

"Sorry, I didn't mean to startle you. The door was cracked open, and when I knocked…" Gabe shoved his hands into his pockets. His gaze darted to the window behind Lila. "Anyway, yeah, sorry about that. I thought you would be off with Val."

"It's okay. Val's busy, so here I am alo—" Lila bit her lower lip at the accidental reminder of the loneliness she'd been fleeing all day. She waved toward the window. "Anyway, I was just checking out the storm."

Gabe's eyebrow arched.

Lila's cheeks burned at his attention. Lest she lose her words all over again, Lila focused on her thumbnail scraping against the windowsill's fresh paint. "I'm guessing you're looking for Marina?" *Since there's no way you're looking for me.*

"Yeah, I need to talk to her about…a family thing. Do you know where she went?"

"No, I haven't seen her all day." For reasons unknown, Lila leapt toward the truth. "I kinda feel like she might be avoiding me." When the blush spread down her neck, Lila scolded herself for being so honest with someone she barely knew — especially about the sister of said someone.

With a sigh, Gabe sank onto the loveseat. When he patted the cushion next to him, Lila couldn't refuse. She perched on its edge and angled her body toward him.

Avoiding his heart-stopping gaze, Lila fiddled with the hem of her shorts.

"Listen, just be patient with Marina. Tasha…let's just say that Tasha wasn't a great roommate for Marina."

"But Tasha was—or I guess *is*—one of Val's friends."

"I'm not gonna get in the middle of you and Val, but if you wanna know about it, ask Val. My point is: give Marina time and she'll come around. Provided you treat her well." A hint of a threat laced Gabe's final sentence.

Confusion wrinkled Lila's brow. During their tour tomorrow, she'd have to ask Val all about Tasha and Marina.

Gabe's arms stretched backward like he owned the place. "Anyway, if I know Marina, she's probably in the library, studying like a…a…" His arms fell back down. A whisper of a flush dusted his sharp cheekbones. "A banshee. Or something."

"Already? Classes haven't even started yet!"

"Well—and you'll find this out for yourself—some classes have summer assignments. That said, I'm sure Marina finished *those* weeks ago. She's just…a little intense, especially about her grades. She had more trouble with math last year than she'd like to admit, so I'm guessing she's brushing up on that right now."

Lila brightened. "Oh, yeah? I actually…I like math, so maybe I could help her. I mean, depending on where she's at and if she even wants my help."

"She's in Algebra II this year, and—"

"I took that last year! I mean, I'm sure it's not the same, my being in a regular, I mean, public school and all…"

"If you end up with time, offer. If I know Marina, she won't reject your help. I'd help her myself, but I'm pretty busy. You know, applying for college and all that." Gabe slid his palms down his shorts.

"Yeah, I'm definitely not looking forward to that in a couple of years."

"Oh, I'm sure you'll be fine. You don't look like the procrastinating type."

A snicker burst from Lila's lips.

One of Gabe's eyebrows cocked. When his gaze collided with hers, the butterflies rioted.

Clinging to her wits, Lila gestured toward the still-packed luggage scattered among Val's stack of dresses, Ms. Pershing's box of uniforms, and the backpack exploded over her desk. "Have you seen this room? This evening, not only am I supposed to unpack, but I'm also supposed to try on my new uniforms and figure out which of those...*things* I want to wear to Semester Start tomorrow. Instead, I got totally distracted by the storm, right befo—"

"Yeah, what were you doing over there anyway?"

The blush's fire returned, though Lila didn't know why she was embarrassed. Gabe's tone...it was almost like he was accusing her of something. "Oh, I dunno. I guess...I guess I've never had nature so close to me like it is here. You know, living in tamed suburbia. So I got a little distracted by it, especially with the storm tonight."

"Fair enough." Gabe hunched over and rested his elbows on his knees. He stared at his clasped hands. His accusatory tone remained.

Apparently, it was not "fair enough."

Lila rushed to find another topic, any topic at all. "Anyway, I'm supposed to be doing all that, but instead I decided to read my book and wait for Marina, at least to try on the dresses, although..." Lila surveyed the neat room that she was already ruining with her stuff strewn everywhere. "I suppose I should straighten up before I go to bed tonight. But yeah, I've pretty much been procrastinating in one way or another all day." Lila offered the tiniest of smiles.

A tight nod answered her.

Lila's confidence, brief as it was, crumbled. She could not understand him. One minute Gabe advised her on how to win Marina over, nearly as friendly as Val herself. The next he was as cold as his sister. It made no sense. *He* made no sense.

On instinct alone, Lila summoned her most cheerful voice. "Listen, if you wanna hang out until Marina gets back, you're welcome to. I'm not doing anything special." The words tumbled out of her mouth, but now that they were out there, Lila couldn't believe she'd said them. *Val must be rubbing off on me already.*

"Oh, um…" Swinging into a more relaxed position, Gabe settled his back against the couch's. "Sure, I guess. It's not like I'm gonna stop procrastinating any time soon. But I don't wanna keep you from unpacking or anything else…"

Lila dismissed his concerns with a wave of her hand. "Don't worry about that. I can always do it later."

This time, a crooked smile met hers.

Lila's stomach flipped. Perhaps she preferred Gabe all weird and aloof. With a gulp she prayed Gabe didn't notice, Lila turned toward him and tucked an ankle beneath her bare knee. "Besides, I hate unpacking. It can definitely wait until tomorrow. As for the frilly dresses from Val and company…" The realization that Gabe may like frilly dresses — specifically, *girls* in frilly dresses — hit Lila like a slap to the face. Before her cheeks could redden and her mood plummet, Lila declared, "I don't mind putting that off either." *And I don't care what kind of girl you like.*

Gabe kicked off his shoes and folded his legs beneath him. His cobra-like eyes transfixed her once more. Lila couldn't breathe.

"How are you feeling by the way?"

"How am I feeling…" Lila's voice trailed off. What was Gabe talking about?

"Yeah, Marina said something about a nap this afternoon?" Gabe prompted. A hint of uncertainty edged his words.

"Oh, um, *that.* Yeah, I had a headache earlier, probably from not getting enough sleep last night." Lila shrugged. "It's all better now."

"Okay, good." Gabe stared at Marina's side of the room for a moment. When he returned to Lila, he was all charm. "So, Lila Lee, what's your story?"

"Oh, um…" *He's only being nice to me because I'm his little sister's roommate,* Lila repeated to herself like a mantra. "I dunno…I mean, I guess I came here because Val's here."

"And you and Val have been friends for a while?"

Lila's head bobbed up and down. Finally a subject she could discuss without overwhelming her poor brain. "Mmhmm. Our parents met each other in college. After school, my mom and Val's parents started a company, so Val and I pretty much grew up together."

"Until Val came here."

"Yup." Lila's hand squeezed her upper arm. Her mom had quit the company and sold her stock two years before it made it big. When Val's parents earned their fortune, her family hadn't received a single cent. But Gabe didn't need to know any of that.

"And you, Lila? How did you get here? My understanding is that Eversfield doesn't take a lot of transfers, if any."

The blood rushed to Lila's cheeks. "Oh, well, I mean, I…I didn't want to stay home really. So, late last year, Val suggested I transfer here. I never thought anything would come of it, but I tried anyway. I don't know how well you know her, but once Val gets an idea in her head, it's useless to oppose her. She figured out the whole process, and I completed each task she gave me. Submitting my grades, online tests, teacher recommendations, the whole shebang. Midway through the summer, Eversfield notified me of…" Lila debated what to tell Gabe. She hated bragging, but it *was* the truth. And she hated the idea of someone thinking she was another spoiled rich kid more. "Of my scholarship offer. And of my placement on the waitlist, noting exactly what you said, that transfers are few and far between. So I abandoned what little hope I had and enjoyed my summer. Then, yesterday, first thing in the morning, Headmaster Flynn calls and says that I've been accepted and that I should report to him in the afternoon."

"That's not much notice."

"No kidding! And my parents are about three hours away—more if there's traffic—and I had to pack and order uniforms, and my parents had to take time off work. So, yeah, we managed to stall him off to first thing today, which meant hitting the road at five this morning."

"So what you're saying is, the past two days have been a little crazy?"

Lila snorted. "Understatement of the year right there. Especially since I'd thought I had two more weeks of summer. Anyway, yeah, that's my story." Lila pulled at her index finger, then dared to peek up at Gabe. "What about you, Gabe Lazare?"

Gabe tightened his crossed legs. "Me? Not a whole lot. Eversfield is sort of a family tradition, so that's how Marina and I got here."

"And it's just the two of you?"

"Yup. You have any siblings?"

"No, only child here. Though, like I said, Val and I were raised practically as sisters."

"Mmhmm." Gabe's gaze flashed away. His lips flattened into a thin line, almost like he disapproved of Lila.

She dove back to the safety of a previous topic, "So, Marina studies a lot?"

Whatever had bothered Gabe disappeared into thin air. Crooked smile and all, he returned to Lila. "Now that gives *your* understatement a run for its money. But...I can't blame her. She wants to be this world-famous, life-saving chemist. So she's doing what she has to do to make it happen." Gabe's eyes shifted to his folded hands. His voice quieted. "Me, on the other hand, I have no clue what's ahead of me."

"Well, that's easy." Lila bumped her shoulder against Gabe's beefy biceps. Her traitorous heart skipped a beat. "College."

Gabe shook his head in mock dismay. "Ha ha. Very funny."

"I thought so."

"Anyway...not to change the subject, but to change the subject, have you thought about what you'll do for the talent show?"

The blood drained out of Lila's face. "Who the what now?"

"You don't know? The talent show. It's every year before the Masquerade Ball at the end of fall semester. It's a long way away, but I could've sworn competitive houses like Blackwell start planning for it over the summer."

And Lila could have sworn Gabe was making it all up just to see how far her jaw could drop. "You're. Kidding."

Gabe's ribs shook with stifled laughter. "Nope, definitely not. Each performance is awarded house points, with the top three results getting extra poin—"

Lila raised her hands. Nothing he said made sense. "Wait, wait, wait. Start at the beginning. With the house points?"

Gabe whistled. "Did no one tell you yet? Not even Val? Word is she's going out for Blackwell's treasurer, you'd think—"

"Wait, Val? Val. My friend, Valerie 'I don't know the meaning of the word budget' Baker, is treasurer for Elizabeth Blackwell? As in, in charge of money for Elizabeth Blackwell?"

"Not yet. We officially hold nominations tomorrow, but given how Blackwell works, Val'll win easy."

Lila crossed her arms in disbelief. "They're going to be in some serious trouble."

"You. *You're* going to be in some serious trouble. Hate to break it to ya, kid, but you're one of 'em now."

"Yeah, I guess so…" Lila chewed on her lower lip, both at her visions of Val's "creative" accounting and at Gabe's "kid."

The door creaked.

Gabe's and Lila's heads snapped toward it.

"Um, hi guys…" Marina took a cautious step into the room. A flurry of tangerine-tinted hair and rust-colored eyes bright with curiosity peeked around her shoulder. *Marina's friend Lex.*

Gabe sprang up from the sofa like it was a bed of hot coals. "Yeah, hey Marina, I, *we* were just waiting for you. Mom called me earlier. She had a message to pass on."

Marina's hand swept her midnight waves over to one side, then fished her phone out of one of her backpack's many front pockets. "Hmm, I don't have a missed call or anything, but okay, we have a few minutes before curfew."

A single ground-devouring stride delivered Gabe to the doorway. "See you later, Lila."

With that hurried goodbye, Gabe, Marina, and Lex vacated the room, leaving Lila alone — and maybe the only person alone in all of Elizabeth Blackwell. Lila dragged her feet toward the suitcase. *Guess I'll start the torture now.*

CHAPTER 8

MARINA

L ex's and Marina's shoes padded against the wooden planks. Marina fought to keep up with her brother. Down the hall he marched, then down the back stairs, out of Blackwell, and into the forest, all without a single word.

Curiosity swelled within Marina. While Gabe trampled through wildflowers and pushed through shrubs, Marina picked her way through the underbrush with Lex tracing her footsteps. A stream of her Floral energy trailed them, mending the damage they — mostly Gabe — wreaked.

When Gabe stopped, the brick façade of Blackwell still peered between the tree trunks. So did the woodchip path winding through the woods. Good thing no one would walk it on a rainy night like tonight.

Crossing his arms, Gabe leaned against the pale bark of a birch tree. One ankle rested over the other, but Marina wasn't fooled. Gabe was trying too hard to look nonchalant. Something was up.

"So Mom didn't actually call me."

"I figured since I had no missed call and you didn't shoo Lex away." The wind whipped Marina's hair across her face. Its power surged within her, radiating down her arms and legs. Her Wind and Water snapped and fizzed with excitement. Marina's fingers throbbed with the ache to release them, to call the storm looming on the horizon closer.

Not everyone shared her enthusiasm. Beside her, Lex glared at the clouds that dared to peek through the leafy canopy, as if that would burn them away. She tightened the hood of her raincoat, even though not a drop had fallen in at least an hour.

Marina's lips twitched toward a smile. *Fire Diviners, always hating my lovely water.*

"Emilia called me."

Marina's attention jerked back to Gabe. While he and Emilia stayed in touch during patrol hours, it didn't usually involve Marina or actual phone calls. "And?"

"She says that she feels weird, almost…wired or something. She can't explain it, just more urgency and restlessness than normal. And that it's not only her. All of them feel it out there." A hand pushed through wavy locks matching Marina's own. "I'm going out to join them on the first shift tonight, just in case. But first—"

"You want Lex and me on the border?"

"Yeah, you know how Diana and Luke are, especially after being apart for most of the summer. You'd think that after two weeks back together already…" Gabe shook his head as though freeing it from an objectionable thought. "Anyway, if something's happening out there, I'd like to be positive that the border and Eversfield are secure."

Marina nodded. This was the typical Warrior response. Something happened out there, so the Diviners got stuck spending their entire night double- and triple-checking every inch of the border. Most of the time, not a single spellstream needed refreshing. Even when one did, the spell guarding the border would maim any member of the Indestructible that crossed it to enter Eversfield territory. The injuries just wouldn't be as severe or as sustained as usual.

But even a night of wasted effort wasn't worth a fight with Gabe. If it allowed him to concentrate on what was going on out there, she and Lex could devote their night to the border. With the bonfire cancelled, it was a small price to pay. Plus, it provided an excellent excuse to avoid Lila—not that she could speak of said excuse with anyone outside the Clan.

At least Lex's roommate was a freshman Warrior. Marina could sleep over there without any uncomfortable questions. No Portency was required to foresee her using— and abusing—this strategy as long as Lila was her roommate. All Marina had to do was tell retired Diviner Ms. Vasile. As the house manager for Lex's dorm, Ms. Vasile would handle the logistics with Blackwell.

"Unless…Marina, if you and Lex need to keep an eye on Lila with the storm and all, I can tell Diana and Luke to get on the border and hope they can focus on it and not each other."

"No, it's fine," Marina answered too quickly. Between Gabe getting all comfy-cozy with Lila earlier and Lex pointing out how Lila—with her ill-fitting clothes, wild hair, and distinct lack of makeup—didn't fit in with Valerie and her cronies, Marina had had enough of her new roommate. Of course, she wasn't allowed to have enough, not with "Lila the potential Latent" sleeping in Marina's bedroom.

It. Was. Exasperating. Here she was, forced to not only live with another adversary, but to watch over her due to her stupid supernatural inheritance. Even if Lex's repeated observations were true, the best-case scenario was that Lila was Valerie's puppet, which was only a hair better than last year's Natasha situation.

No, Marina chided herself, *no matter Lila's intentions, I will not let it happen again. They cannot — they will not — hurt me. I will protect myself this time.* The wind brushed against

Marina's fingers, a reminder that it was there for her, that it could make Lila pay. Not that Marina would ever use her powers against a civilian. But it was comforting to know that she *could*, if push came to shove.

"Lila will be okay. With the rain blowing in," Marina gestured to the sky while Lex shivered beside her, "I'd only be concerned if she was a Wind or a Water Latent, either of which I would have sensed by now."

"But…when I got to your room, she did seem, I dunno, entranced by the storm."

Marina shook her head. "Like I said, with all that extra power, I would have felt her respond to Wind or Water. *If* she's close to manifesting. As for the others, manifestation of Earth or Spirit Divining usually isn't sudden or destructive. And the rain should keep any emerging Fire talents in check." Her head tilted toward Lex. "I mean, look at her."

"Hey, I don't look that bad!" Lex protested.

Marina knocked her elbow against Lex's upper arm. "I didn't say you looked *bad*, just unhappy. Do you disagree with my assessment?"

Ginger eyebrows crouched over dull eyes. Lex crossed her arms over her chest. "No."

"That's what I thought. Anyway, based on Lex's displeasure and my lack thereof, we're not getting any lightning tonight, just wind and rain. Which means that, if Lila's a Fire Latent, she's safe from any manifesting powers for tonight. And…" Marina took a deep breath, then plunged forward. She fought to hide her irritation behind a cold, clinical demeanor. "She might be crabby, grouchy, or easily annoyed right now, you know, if she's a Fire Latent. Gabe, since you were…with Lila earlier, did she seem like that then?"

"No, she seemed fine, though it's not like I would know what crabby looks like on her."

"Then I'm guessing Fire Divining's out for the time being. If she is close to manifestation, we're pretty much down to Earth or Spirit Divining. Neither of which are particularly dangerous for Latents in general, nor do storms introduce extra risks. Of course, both options present an additional difficulty in that my own Earth and Spirit abilities are too weak to sense oncoming manifestations, but that's a problem for another day."

"So, long story short, Lila should be good for tonight?" Lex shifted her weight, one toe of a wet sneaker rubbing against the other. The earlier rain had washed away Lex's normal cheery sarcasm, even though she'd hidden indoors. The sooner they escaped from Gabe and any potential civilian eyes, the better.

"Yup. Gabe, anything else for us?"

"Nope. And you two are good, right?"

"Mmhmm. We'll be on the border. Let us know if anything happens."

"Will do. See ya." Gabe launched into a sprint, disappearing into the woods within seconds. He didn't even bother to pick up his car in the student lot.

"C'mon you, we might as well get started." The scent of rain on the wind emboldened Marina. With a flick of her fingers, a breeze swirled around Lex, ready to repel any droplets that ventured too close.

Lex's lips spread into a wide toadlike grin. "I knew I picked the right partner."

"Indeed. Now let's get to work."

GABE

REBELLIOUS THOUGHTS RACED ALMOST AS FAST AS Gabe's legs. No matter how he tried to drown them out in Clan concerns, still they resurfaced. Had it only been this morning that he'd looked forward to a straightforward senior year? Now there was this girl tied to a new, unique set of visions. And she was a potential Latent, which meant he couldn't escape her. After one measly chat, he wasn't sure he wanted to.

But there was no hope for him. He had but two duties: to keep his Cell's territory clear of the Indestructible and to graduate high school. No girl, no matter the visions, no matter…*who*, could interfere with those. He could not allow her to, whether he had to babysit her as a potential Latent or not.

At least for tonight she wasn't in any danger, from her own emerging powers or otherwise. And at least for tonight he wouldn't have to interact with her further. He could hole up in the shelter of the Clan and its eternal battle. He could forget that this day had ever happened. He could pretend that she didn't exist. *Any port in the storm, right?*

Just past Juniper, Gabe's heart began to beat with an urgency that had nothing to do with *her* and everything to do with *them*. His feet longed to slam to a halt, but Gabe didn't dare let them.

This was what Emilia had called about. It had to be. Every pine needle separated from its siblings as far out as twenty feet ahead, even at his supernatural speed. Weak moonlight peeked through the clouds, highlighting each and every obstacle in his path, whether it be fallen log, rock, or thorny shrub. Although Gabe refused to slow, his fingers skimmed the wooden stake rigid against his back. He would be ready if one of *them* attacked.

No, that wasn't right. Owls hooted. Crickets chirped. A rodent cracked open a seed. If a member of the Indestructible was near, all those forest animals would hide in their homes, the first clue that something dangerous lurked.

A murmured discussion from the east reached Gabe's sensitive ears.

He headed straight for it. Two minutes later, he skidded to a stop in one of the meadows they used for combat practice during slow patrols. Under Emilia's and Simon's watchful eyes, two groups sparred. On his arrival, Emilia broke away, gesturing that Simon should continue on his own.

"Y' feel it?" she whispered.

"It's more than you said. This is activated Cull."

"Yeah, the restlessness or whatever shifted to full-on Cull a few minutes after we talked."

Guilt strangled Gabe's stomach. That was when he'd been with Lila, claiming that he waited for Marina. But he could have texted or called Marina to give the order. He hadn't needed to tell Marina in person. *No, I had to stay with Lila, in case her powers were manifesting. Right?*

"Still no Bloodlust, though." Emilia frowned. Her dark gaze swept the forest behind him.

Partners through and through, Gabe mirrored her. His Cull lit up the clearing behind Emilia, transforming night to day. The scents of his Warriors' sweat, of the night-blooming flowers, of their steel weapons, of the pine needles, all rose distinct from the others. Blood throbbed in Gabe's fingertips.

He clenched his hands. His reflexes would surpass a cat's right now.

Yet that craving for violence, his Bloodlust, was absent. The few times he'd experienced this phenomenon he'd either been part of a crowd or too far away from *it*. The former didn't apply to an empty forest, and a subtle tugging always accompanied the latter, directing him where to go. After a few minutes of following it, the Bloodlust would hit him full force.

But tonight there was nothing but the nervous energy and enhanced senses of the Cull.

Gabe pushed a hand through hair wet with sweat. "Have you contacted the Florence Cell? Given where we are, it seems like *it* would've come from their territory."

"Yeah, and it's been quiet out there. Whatever's causin' this, 'snot from the city."

Gabe nodded, staring at a dying pine. Its tawny boughs stuck out against the olive-green branches of the rest of the conifers ringing the meadow.

A member of the Indestructible couldn't last outside a city for long. Less people meant less food and an easier task for Warriors to track *it*. In fact, a large portion of the Clan's strategy consisted of flushing the Indestructible out of cities and into open space where the nearest Cell would hunt them down. Sometimes, that meant using their Bloodlust in a deadly game of hot and cold.

There, that's it.

"Okay, here's what we're gonna do." Gabe accepted one of a paired set of cutlasses that Emilia extended toward him. It wasn't his favorite blade, but he hadn't taken the time to stop by the main weapons cache on his way here. While the others gathered around him, he attached its scabbard to his belt.

"There're seven of us, so we'll split into three groups and head in opposite directions. The goal is to pick up the trail, not to engage. I repeat, *not to engage*. I'm hoping there's only one, but even so I'd like our numbers against it. When the Bloodlust hits, stop where you are and text the group. We'll come to you. Everyone's got their location shared, right?" Gabe waved his phone at them. To his relief, everyone nodded. Not one person scrambled to turn on the app, which was pretty good for their first real patrol. Under the guise of tucking his phone back into his pocket, Gabe assessed the Warriors clustered around him. *Better pair the seniors together and have the freshman in the group of three with me.* "Emilia and Darius, you're together, then Simon and Cosmina. Marius and Teddi, you're with me."

Terror twisted Marius's sharp features.

Gabe squashed his judgment. Most likely, this was Marius's first time hunting one of *them*. Controlling the fear would be one of his earliest lessons here. His other freshman, Teddi, met his gaze with more determination than fear, but her hands trembled at her sides.

"All right. Let's head out."

Like a well-oiled machine, the Warriors trotted away, one group forming each point of an equilateral triangle.

Once the others had fallen out of sight and earshot, Gabe slowed. His index finger pressed against his lips, their signal to choose stealth over speed. His hand drifted to his hip, where his fingers wrapped around the worn leather hilt of Emilia's sword. Although his feet continued to move forward, confusion tainted every step as if his body didn't know where to go without the Bloodlust.

Soon, Gabe reminded himself, *soon there'll be a text telling us where to go. Soon we'll know.*

A rustle spoiled the silence.

The silence.

Gabe's blood rushed in his ears. How had he not noticed the silence — the oppressive silence — before? Spreading his arms out, he stopped Teddi and Marius behind him. He braced for the onslaught of his Bloodlust, ready to fight against it, ready to force his body to wait for Emilia and the others.

It didn't come.

Gabe narrowed his eyes. Something had created that rustle. Based on his supernatural hearing, the source hid behind a rotting log about fifty feet ahead. Not only did that log provide too much cover on its own, but it had fallen into a thick shrub. While the parts of the bush beneath and in front of the log had died back, behind it was nothing but layers and layers of pointy green leaves covering woody branches. Together, they could mask any *thing*.

The metallic scent of blood curled up Gabe's nostrils.

He should stop where he was. He should text the others. And yet…where was his Bloodlust?

No, he was overreacting. The forest was just a little quieter than normal. And the blood was a natural smell around here. It only loomed large due to his Cull. If one of *them* were near, he wouldn't be able to debate like this. The Bloodlust would hit and it would require all his self-control to text the others and wait for them.

An animal had caused that rustle. An animal hid behind that log.

Curiosity drove Gabe closer. Teddi and Marius followed on his heels. When they were still twenty-five feet away, the muffled sounds of a predator enjoying its prey — all satisfied snarls and growls — came from behind that fallen log. Without thought, Gabe withdrew his cutlass from its scabbard. Years of practice resulted in not a whisper of noise.

Now fifteen feet away from the carnivore devouring its dinner, Gabe glanced down at his weapon.

Filtered moonlight speckled the wicked blade.

What am I doing? If this is dangerous enough for a sword, it's dangerous enough to call for backup. Isn't that what I told the others to do? We have to go back. I'll text Emilia, then we'll wait for the others. It's probably nothing, but we can't be too careful. Gabe swung his free hand upward to signal for retreat.

A sword's cross-guard clattered against a metal scabbard.

Gabe froze. So did the unseen creature behind the log.

Silence beat against Gabe's eardrums. His nails bore into the smooth leather of the sword's hilt. On his left, Marius twisted his sword — a saber of sorts — one way, then the other. On his right, Teddi stuck close. An empty hand hovered over either hip, ready to select her blessed sword, dagger, or wooden stake.

But nothing happened.

Gabe scanned the woods ahead. Most likely, Marius had spooked the animal. Most likely, it now cowered behind that log, terrified of a larger predator.

Gabe had to know for sure. With the fingers of his free hand spread wide, he shot a look rife with meaning at Teddi, then Marius. They'd stay back here — safe — while he moved forward alone. A breeze promising rain tickled the pine needles above them.

With his cutlass unsheathed at his side, Gabe stepped toward the log. He nestled each foot into the groundcover before beginning the next stride. It — whatever it was — would not hear him coming.

After ages, Gabe could peek over the log's edge. He lifted himself onto his tiptoes.

Behind the log, a human body lay sprawled over the crushed branches of the bush. His limbs splayed out at unnatural angles. Bloody shreds of flesh were all that remained of his lacerated throat.

Gabe swallowed his shock. Now was not the time to panic. His lips flattening into a thin line, he scanned the silent forest for movement. *Where are you?*

Another body — this one as hard as steel — dropped onto Gabe. Its knees collided with his shoulders, then slid down to his chest. Under their guidance, Gabe crashed into the ground. His cutlass spun away.

Perched on top of Gabe, the beast darted forward and snarled. Its razor-sharp canines shone in the darkness a handbreadth away from Gabe's face.

Too close. On his back, Gabe dug the heels of his hands into the creature's windpipe. With that thirst for violence singing in his veins, Gabe forced *it* farther away. He locked his elbows, holding the beast at an armlength above him.

The demon narrowed its eyes, then leaned into Gabe. It pressed down, down, down.

Gabe's elbow buckled.

The creature fell forward. Its black eyes swallowed every speck of moonlight. Its jaw snapped, seeking purchase on any part of Gabe it could find.

It found Gabe's forearm. It ripped into him.

Blood poured out, but the beast didn't stop there. No, it had its eye on the prize.

It dashed toward Gabe's throat.

Gabe caught the creature's face an inch away from his jugular, an inch away from death. The heels of his hands bored into *its* cheekbones. Blood dripped from his bent elbow, but there was no pain. There was only the beast's emaciated face between his hands. Gabe drove the creature up and away.

Again the demon countered Gabe's supernatural strength. Millimeter by millimeter, its fatal fangs neared Gabe's jugular.

Gabe ground his teeth. He pushed harder.

So did *it*.

A muscled arm slashed across *its* chest. It hauled the monster off Gabe, then hurled *it* into a tree.

Crrrr-ack! The beast slid down the trunk of the one ancient oak in this forest of pines.

Gabe scrambled to his feet, his good hand pulling out his stake, his gaze searching the underbrush for his cutlass. Her jaw clenched, Teddi joined his side.

The creature crouched at the base of the oak opposite them. Its glittering ebony eyes challenged Gabe.

But Gabe knew better. He'd do this on his terms, not the beast's.

A few strides to his right, something shimmered in the vines.

Gabe gnawed on his lower lip. Retrieving Emilia's cutlass would leave him vulnerable to an attack.

But not having it might be worse.

Keeping one eye on the beast, Gabe slunk over to his cutlass, ripped it out of the underbrush, and returned to Teddi. Through it all, the creature didn't move one muscle. *Must be its first time fighting a Warrior. The experienced ones never let you regain a blessed blade. Good thing those are few and far between.*

In front and to the left of Teddi, Gabe muttered, "Marius?"

Teddi shook her head.

That's a problem for later. If there is a later. Gabe wiped his forearm against his T-shirt. The wound was ragged and ugly, but the bleeding had already stopped. He swirled the cutlass, testing its weight on his injured arm. It was fine, at least while his Bloodlust and Cull were active. *Time to get this show on the road.*

Sensing that, Teddi dipped down. Her lower lip shook, but her jaw jutted out with determination. She extended her arms, her short sword in her dominant hand and her wooden stake in the other, just like they practiced. The sword provided extra reach, allowing them to fight from a safer distance. The blessings laid upon it by the Diviners would injure the Indestructible, even with the barest of touches. With luck, the spells would distract the beast long enough to provide him or Teddi the opening they needed, whether that was for a stake to the heart or a sword to sever the neck.

Teddi cried out.

Gabe's head whipped around. The demon surged toward them on all fours.

This time, Gabe was ready. An instant before the creature could land on his shoulders, Gabe spun around and dropped to a knee. He drove his cutlass up, up, up. With the help of the Diviner spells lacing the blade, it cut through the beast's iron flesh, gashing *it* from chest to navel.

The monster skidded over the ground. Before it could recover, Gabe charged. Talons shot toward him, but he ducked beneath the creature's arm. As he dashed by, his cutlass sliced into *its* hip.

Impatience joined pain, making the beast reckless. It lunged toward him.

Gabe hopped backward, the flat of his blade knocking its desperate hands away.

Its blood-stained mouth opened into a roar of frustration.

Gabe never heard it. Before the demon could utter a peep, its eyes widened in shock. Its scarlet lips created an *O* of surprise. The creature turned to dust.

A trembling Teddi stood before Gabe, her wooden stake hovering where *its* heart had been a moment before.

No time for relief, Gabe shoved the sword into its scabbard and his stake into the waistband of his shorts. His blood still thumping with adrenaline and Bloodlust, he covered the distance between them in a single stride. *Teddi first, then Marius.*

Gabe grasped Teddi's still-outstretched arms and dropped down to gather her unfocused gaze. "Teddi. *Teddi.* Are you okay?"

Slowly, her mouth closed. Shining eyes rose to his. "Was that real?"

Spasms of shame erupted throughout Gabe's body. What had he done? Teddi and Marius's first experience shouldn't have been this. If Teddi hadn't rescued him when she did, he might have—no, he *would have*—gotten all three of them killed. "Yes, Teddi, I'm so sorry. It shouldn't have been like that."

Teddi shook her head. Her lips slipped into a weak smile, but a tremor crept into her voice. "No, it had to...it had to happen sometime, right?"

"Yes, I suppose so." Gabe forced a sunny smile and a cheerful tone. "And hey, you got your first kill, right? That's something to celebrate! Now, where's Marius?" Gabe turned to search the woodland stretching out in front of them.

Teddi tugged his arm backward. "Gabe, is this normal?"

"Is what normal?" Gabe continued to scan the forest ahead of them. A shadowy figure hunched in the underbrush about fifty feet to the north. It had to be Marius.

"To still feel...to still feel the Bloodlust, even after?"

Gabe's head jerked back to Teddi. With Marius off hiding in the shrubbery, he hadn't noticed. His own nerves still teetered on a razor's edge. His own blood still pumped with energy. His own fingers still throbbed with power. He still craved violence.

Gabe clenched his hands into fists that shook. Identifying Marius's form in the distance and the dark had to be due to the enhanced sight of active Cull. All of it could only mean...but no, there couldn't be *another*. It would have attacked when they were vulnerable. Yet his Cull and Bloodlust should have dulled by now. Gabe shifted back to the woods ahead of them, but the figure shrouded in shadows had disappeared.

"Hey, guys. Um, sorry about that, but I thought I saw something..." Marius's voice trailed off. It came from *behind* Gabe.

Gabe whipped around. About ten feet away, Marius's ice-blond hair shone silver in the moonlight. His head bent down while he picked his way through the groundcover, weaving between tree trunks and saplings alike. Marius came from the south.

A shiver crawled up Gabe's spine. Panic rose like bile in his throat. Out there in the forest — out there too close to them — that shadowy form had vanished. *Where did you go?*

"Behind me. Defense only. We might not be out of this yet," Gabe growled.

The muscled shoulders of Marius and Teddi brushed against his as they set up the defensive triangle. Not daring to look away from the forest, Gabe flipped his phone out of his pocket. He texted Emilia three letters.

SOS

CHAPTER 9

KANE

The Warrior's eyes seared through Kane. Like a deer caught in headlights, she couldn't move, couldn't think.

Only when he shifted toward his companion did her limbs thaw. Staying low to the ground, Kane rushed away with all the supernatural speed she could without risking a twig snapping or a leaf rustling. She would have concealed herself in a tree, but after that other vampire, the Warriors would look for it. Besides, the odds of her shaking a branch and signaling her position were too high. Biting her lip, Kane hunkered down behind a shield of bushes twice as far away from the Warriors. Their tangy scent stung her nostrils.

Perhaps I should have gone back.

With her ears alert, Kane tugged on the spell clinging to her body, checking it from head to toe. Every spellstream was intact. The Weave was flawless.

So how had that Warrior sensed her? Her Dampour was supposed to disrupt their Cull and Bloodlust, allowing her to walk among Warriors undetected. Yet here she was hiding from them. *I should have run.*

No. First, it could have been mere coincidence, the Warrior staring in her direction. Secondly, she was not in danger yet, not at this distance. Even with the expense of her Dampour, she had enough juice left to flatten the three of them with a hallucination. If she did so, she'd have to feed tonight or tomorrow night, but that was a price Kane could pay. Better to feed early than die a permanent death.

Kane closed her eyes and listened to the Warriors a hundred feet of dense forest away.

"Hey, guys. Um, sorry about that, but I thought I saw something…"

Ah, the deserter returns.

"Behind me. Defense only. We might not be out of this yet."

Kane frowned. Unless there was another vampire in the area—which was *highly* unlikely—the Warrior's words confirmed it. He'd sensed her through her Dampour.

Kane squashed the urge to run. Based on their fiasco with the other vampire, she'd hear the Warriors coming long before they reached her.

After a brief moment during which clumsy feet crushed weeds and twigs alike, silence reigned.

Kane opened her silver eyes and peered through the leaves. A defensive triangle of three Warriors stood beneath the trees, each one wielding a stake in one hand and a sword in the other. Even from a hundred feet away, the tangle of spells laid over the blades shone.

Kane smirked. That was inept Weaving, a world away from the ordered symmetry of her own spells.

::*A world away, huh?*:: The too-familiar voice echoed through Kane's mind. A shimmering teenage girl materialized out of the shrub in front of Kane.

Crap. Not here. Not now. Kane squeezed her eyes shut like it would make the girl disappear.

It didn't.

The girl tossed ebony waves over a translucent shoulder. Blue eyes so light they verged on white scrutinized Kane. ::*You screwed up again.*::

::*I miscalculated, Grace, that's all.*::

The girl was a figment of Kane's imagination, a twisted consequence of the barrels of magic Kane could access at any time. Ignoring her was useless. Grace would have her conversation when and where she wanted. Fortunately, she only appeared when Kane was alone. Unfortunately, she preferred times of distress. Grace was not a sympathetic soul.

::*Uh huh.*:: Grace's slim arms crossed over her chest.

Malice turned Kane's mental tone harsh. ::*Listen, Grace. Yes, okay, this Dampour apparently does not work as anticipated. But it is my first attempt. The next one will be better.*::

::*Will it?*::

::*Yes.*:: Kane spat the word out.

::*How?*::

::*First, everything was fine until that other vampire showed up. Perhaps…*:: Licking her chapped lips, Kane evaluated several theories, then selected the most likely one. ::*Perhaps my Dampour doesn't disguise me as much as interrupt the Clan's Cull and Bloodlust as a whole. Not that the specific way matters right now. In the future, I'll just have to account for vampires not protected by my Dampour.*::

Grace's fine eyebrow arched.

::*Or…*:: Her forehead furrowing, Kane examined her words. What was Grace hinting at? ::*I mean, and we can wipe out the other vampires in this area, so there's only me and those I control.*::

Grace nodded. Her lips stretched into a rare smile.

::*I'll still want to modify –* ::

Body after body crashed through the underbrush from the west, all haste and no stealth. Her heart in her throat, Kane abandoned her thought and peeked through the shrub Grace had stood in a moment before. As usual, Grace had evaporated into thin air at the first hint of others joining Kane.

A group of four exploded out of the trees to the west. Whether they couldn't sense Kane or ignored her, she couldn't tell. They charged toward the triangle. The shoulders of those Warriors—along with Kane's own—slumped with relief. The two younger ones holstered their stakes and swords. The older one, still scanning the woods in front of Kane, did not.

"Gabe? Gabe! You okay?" A girl at the front of the reinforcements sprinted to the older Warrior's side. A tight braid streamed behind her.

"Yeah, we're fine…just…" The Warrior who'd seemed to detect her—Gabe apparently—did not turn away from his post. No, he continued to stare right at where Kane had been hiding minutes before.

Anxiety tossed and turned Kane's stomach. Her fingers dug into the dirt beneath the bush. She should have run when she had the chance. Seven Warriors were too many to fight on her own. All Kane could do was watch, listen, and wait for her chance to flee.

Gabe inclined his head toward the girl with the braid, now stopped at his side. "Do you feel it, Emilia?"

"Feel what?"

"The Bloodlust. It's still—"

Emilia shook her head. The knotted end of her braid slapped against her toned shoulders. "Nothin', I got nothin'."

Gabe shifted toward the cluster of five Warriors behind him. "What about you, Teddi? Marius?"

Two of the Warriors nodded, their lips set into firm lines.

Kane grimaced. Although they confirmed what she'd already guessed, a part of her had hoped that it wasn't true, that it was only a coincidence. At least she had their first names and faces. Assuming she survived this, she'd google this "Teddi" and "Marius" later—and "Gabe" and "Emilia" too.

Emilia's fingers brushed against Gabe's arm. "It's pro'ly nothin'. I'm guessin' you fought?"

"Yeah." Gabe flashed a gleaming grin that rang false to Kane. He slapped the younger girl on her shoulder. "Teddi here got her first kill!"

Congratulations surrounded Teddi while Emilia and Gabe dropped away from the group. Kane strained to hear Gabe's whisper.

"Seriously, Emilia, you're getting nothing? Not even the weirdness from before, coming from back there?" His head tilted in Kane's direction.

"Nope, nothin'."

Gabe ran a hand through his hair. The gash along his forearm—and the dried blood edging it—glinted red in the moonlight.

Kane's fangs throbbed with longing. Her throat burned, reminding her of all the weeks that had passed since she'd last fed.

"All right, it must just be left over from the fight or something." Gabe's chin cut toward the rotting log. "By the way, we've got a victim back there. Do you wanna call the Juniper Troupe or should I?"

With a critical gaze, Emilia scanned Gabe from head to toe. She gestured toward his wound. "After you visit Diana and get *that* taken care of, I'm guessin' you could use some sparrin'?"

"I could, but it's not about me."

Emilia shrugged. "That's pro'ly enough excitement for t'night anyway. I don't mind placin' the call if you wanna lead the tourney."

"Sure."

Emilia snapped back to the other Warriors. "All right y'all, that's 'nuff celebratin' for now. Semester Start's tomorrow, so we can all continue congratulatin' Teddi then. For now, let's get back t' Eversfield for a li'l workout till shift change."

Kane remained frozen in her leafy bush until the noise of the Warriors smashing through the underbrush had long faded away and her heart had stopped its pounding. Curiosity getting the better of her, she picked her way through the weeds, the shrubs, the saplings, and the trees, toward that mossy log where it had all begun. Based on Duncan's map, she had at least half an hour before the Juniper Troupe could arrive, even with cars and Warrior super-speed.

Kane sat on a — relatively — clean area of the log. Her index finger traced patterns in the drying blood splattered over its back. With her Dampour still in place, Kane reviewed all she had learned tonight.

::And what have you learned?::

Kane expelled a sigh. Of course *she'd* returned. *::Plenty, Grace.::*

::Care to share?::

Kane's hackles rose at Grace's snooty tone. *No.* But Grace would never let her off the hook. She might as well detail her observations for Grace, rather than waste time fighting her for the same result. *::Well, first, we've got some* names and faces. Emilia, Gabe, Teddi, Marius. No last names yet, but the internet can help with that.::

::And?:: Grace prompted in that annoying older sibling know-it-all way.

After racking her brain for a few moments, Kane remembered something Adara had taught her long ago. ::Gabe and Emilia, they're the leaders of the Eversfield Cell. The "First" and "Second" in terms of Clan vocabulary.::

::Yes. What else?::

Kane supplied the easy answer. ::They fight with stakes and swords, both having spells laid upon them. Like we thought, the spells are a mix of Elementals, with Fire dominating the effects and Earth and Wind enabling Fire. The wooden stakes have a different spell than the metal blades.:: A light bulb flickered in Kane's mind. ::The spells are tangled and I thought lazy, but….::

::But?::

::But it may be on purpose. The more tangled the spell is, the harder it is for me to undo it.:: Kane sucked in a breath. ::Do you think they know about me?::

Her glistening tresses swinging from side to side, Grace shook her head. ::No, I don't think so. Based on our history lessons from Adara, I'd guess it's a remnant from centuries ago. It's likely more a lucky coincidence for them than anything else.:: Grace's upper lip curled with distaste. She despised the Clan as much as Kane did.

::Regardless, I won't be able to undo those spells on the move. The others will have to defend themselves from the Clan's bespelled weapons.::

::Which they trained to do back at Duncan's base anyway.::

::Yes, I suppose.:: Kane reminded herself to ensure Fang and the others restarted their training when they returned from their feeding escapades. ::Anyway, yes, the weapons could be a problem, but not one that we can't prepare for. Similarly, the

Warriors fought better than I'd like. When that vampire caught Gabe unaware and Marius ran off, I thought for sure they were done for. But no, that little girl Teddi came out of nowhere to save him. Then the two of them – Gabe and Teddi – killed it with ease despite Gabe's injury.:: Kane's hand rose, staving off Grace's predictable refute. *::Yes, yes, I know. We have no idea how well that particular vampire could fight given that it wasn't one of our own. Still, I would have liked the Warriors to struggle a bit more, especially with only two who aren't fully trained yet and one of those wounded.::*

Even Grace couldn't disagree with that argument. Not that it stopped her from digging her hands into her waist and jutting one hip out. *::And what about your Dampour, Kane?::*

Kane sighed. This was the topic she'd been dreading. *::It doesn't work.::*

::Mmm, I wouldn't say that.::

Kane's silver eyes flashed up, almost hopeful. *Almost*, for Grace never said anything positive. *::What do you mean?::*

::Well...:: Grace pulled herself taller, a specter looming over the sitting Kane. *::The other Warriors – the ones not involved in the fight against the vampire – couldn't feel you at all, so that's something. Also, Gabe mentioned "weirdness from before," which implies that your Dampour did disrupt their Bloodlust, possibly their Cull too. And Gabe practically walked on top of that vampire before it attacked. That too may indicate that your Dampour confused their Bloodlust. I would say I'm surprised you didn't notice all these things, but I'm not.::*

Ignoring the barb, Kane reviewed Grace's notes. Her dark brows drooped. *::Hmm, I'll have to think over this further.::*

Grace snorted. *::Obviously.::* Her ghostly blue eyes narrowed as she extended a translucent finger toward Kane.

::And don't forget. That vampire back there almost killed the leader of this Eversfield Cell with the element of surprise alone. We have many more tools in our toolbox, but we shouldn't overlook that one.::

::No, Grace, we should not.::

CHAPTER 10

*M*ip. Mip. Mip-mip. Mip. Miiiiiiiip. Mip. Mip. Mip-mip.

Lila's fingers stumbled through the sheets, following the vibrations until they found her too-loud phone. She shut the alarm off by feel, then peeled her bleary eyes open. Despite being more tired than she'd been in weeks, it had taken her ages to fall asleep last night. Her mind had whirled like the ceiling fan above her, cycling between Val's budding expectations, the stress of meeting all these new people today, her roommate's icy demeanor, and her stupid crush. That inner voice had reminded her over and over again that she was the lonely loser in an empty dorm, the only one going to bed early on the Saturday night before classes started. Curfew or no curfew, not even her frozen roommate had come home before Lila had fallen into a restless slumber.

At that thought, Lila propped herself up on an elbow and glanced toward Marina's lofted bed opposite her. It was still made. Unless Marina had somehow snuck in and back out again while Lila slept, she hadn't come home last night.

Lila fell back onto the creaky mattress with a groan. *Great, my roommate's avoiding me.*

After a minute or two of feeling sorry for herself, Lila dragged herself out of it. Today was a new day with new challenges. She just had to put one foot in front of the other. First a shower, then Val's tour. Then this whole Semester

Start thingy, then house bonding. Just one foot in front of the other.

Too bad Val—apparently—had other plans. After her shower, Lila waited forty-five minutes for her. At first, it didn't bother Lila. After all, Val being late wasn't anything new. To keep her eyes off her phone, Lila futzed with her hair, attempting to control her wild curls with a variety of creams, gels, and other potions. Then she did as much makeup as she dared: a sweep of mascara, a dusting of gold eye shadow, and lip balm galore. She finished unpacking her suitcase and tucked it in the bottom of her bare closet. She read her book—or tried to anyway. Only after her eyes had roamed over a full chapter without Lila comprehending one word did she give up. By then, Val was almost an hour late. It was time—past time—for Lila to accept the truth. Val had stood her up.

But that wouldn't stop Lila. No, it would not. Lila grabbed her crumpled map and her keycard, then slipped on her flip flops. Lila would give herself the tour.

She stomped to the door, but when her hand clasped the doorknob, Lila bit her lip and peeked over her shoulder. Her phone laid on the arm of the loveseat, next to her battered book.

No. If I can wait for Val for an hour, she can wait until I get back. If she even cares.

Lila whipped out the door, down the hall, and down Lizzie's back stairway. She'd just have to figure things out on her own. Alone.

MARINA

THE LIGHT FLICKERED ORANGE ON THE BACKS OF HER eyelids.

Marina groaned. She was not ready to wake up. All night she and Lex had checked the spells wrapping around Eversfield, napping between their randomly scheduled visits. She'd told herself that she would wake at seven this morning—her normal weekend routine—but her body had decided differently. She should have set an alarm.

Since she was late anyway, Marina arched her back into a stretch. Her arms reached over her head and her legs extended off the bean bag's edge. She rolled out either shoulder, then her neck. Her toes flexed up and down, loosening her calves and ankles. Once the kinks were sorted out, she opened her eyes.

"Hey there, sleepyhead. It's 'bout time." Lex, her ginger hair every which way, peered down from her lofted bed.

Marina yawned. "How long have you been up?"

A graphic novel, its colors too bright for Marina's sleepy eyes, rose in Lex's hands. "Two chapters worth."

"What time is it anyway?"

"Phone says..." Lex rolled over and tossed a few pillows to the foot of her bed, exposing a kinky cord. Her fingers traced it back to her phone, tucked beneath yet another pillow. "Almost ten."

"Really? Oh no, I gotta go." Marina hadn't thought it possible for her to sleep in *this* late. Ten in the morning, on her last day of freedom! She should be out relaxing, out doing something. Not wasting time sleeping.

Marina rolled off the overstuffed bean bag and collected yesterday's clothes along with the few things she'd snuck out of her room. With Lila's arrival, she'd planned to sleep over at Lex and Teddi's long before Gabe's surprise request had forced her hand.

"Mar, you have things to do before Semester Start?"

"No, but I...I had planned to—"

"Get an early start?" The corners of Lex's lips twitched up and down.

Marina scowled up at Lex. Her hands pressed into her narrow hips. "I want to enjoy my last day before school starts. Is that so bad?"

"No. Guess that didn't include sleepin' in?"

"No, it did not." Marina jammed the last of her things into her backpack. While Lex climbed down the ladder at the foot of her bed without a retort, Marina's jaw clenched. People were always telling her that she was too tightly wound. She didn't need it from Lex too.

Lex raised her hands with her fingers spread apart. "Okay, okay, I'll stop. You just enjoy your day. Let me know if you wanna hang out before Semester Start."

"Thank you. And I will." Marina hefted her backpack onto a shoulder, then waved goodbye. "See you later."

After a pit stop in Tubman's second floor bathroom—Marina couldn't very well walk back to Blackwell in her pajamas, after all—she hurried toward the back exit. By the time her sneakers touched the path between the dorms, Marina was scheduling her day of relaxation down to the minute.

Marina was so deep in her plans that she didn't notice *her* until it was too late. Woodchips skipped over each other as Marina skidded to a halt before Lila, the very roommate she'd spent most of yesterday avoiding. "Oh, um, hi there."

Lila's empty hand picked at her weighed-down curls. Her other hand clutched a brochure in Eversfield navy and cream. "Hi, Marina…you just getting back?"

"Yeah, um, I stayed over at Lex's. I thought that maybe you could use a night with the room to yourself." Marina rubbed sweaty palms against yesterday's shorts.

"You didn't have to do that."

"Yeah, well, it's okay." On either side, Marina's fingers curled into a fist of frustration. Why couldn't she ever come up with anything intelligent to say when facing an enemy? "So…what are you doing up so early?"

"Well, it's not *that* early, but yeah, I guess it might be for a Sunday around here." Grass-green eyes shifted away from Marina and toward the crumpled pamphlet. "Val and I were supposed to have our tour this morning since I was too tired yesterday. We were scheduled to start an hour ago, but…I guess Val's busy." Lila shrugged. "At least I got some unpacking done this morning."

A rush of undesired sympathy bloomed in Marina. She beat it back down.

"Anyway, I thought I would do it myself, but it turns out I'm not very good with directions. Or maps." Lila offered a tentative smile as she unfolded the flyer to display a color-coded map of Eversfield.

Like a glass of spilt milk, memories of Natasha's treachery splashed over Marina's mind. She did not return Lila's smile.

"But no worries, I'll figure it out, even if I get lost a few times." The forced cheer in Lila's voice failed to reach her eyes.

Marina smothered a sigh. Lila clearly wanted help, and Marina was right here, literally on Lila's path. She *was* supposed to observe Lila as a potential Latent. And the sooner they figured out what Lila's talents were, the sooner Marina could ignore her, at least until Lila joined their Cell. Even then, the Bureau could assign Lila to another boarding school since Eversfield was already at capacity for Diviners. Which meant Marina could get her precious single back.

"Um, well, I can help you. If you want." *Please say no, please say no.*

"That would be great! If you don't mind, that is. I know you're probably busy."

"Nothing that I can't delay for an hour or so." Marina gestured to the door behind Lila. "Just let me drop off my stuff and change, okay?"

"Okay, but I think I'll stay down here. Study this map of mine." With a wry smile, Lila wriggled the map back and forth.

When Marina passed by, a hand grazed her forearm. Her head snapped back to Lila.

"And…thank you, Marina." Lila's tone was low, sincere.

Too sincere.

"No problem." Marina heaved Blackwell's back door open with a gulp. She almost preferred Natasha's overt rudeness to this pretend politeness. With Lila, she kept waiting for the shoe to drop. It was giving her a stomachache.

MARINA CONTINUED WAITING, THROUGH THE ENTIRE tour and then an impromptu visit to Snack Station in the gym. Lila never even hinted at being like Natasha and Valerie and Audrey, but Marina refused to trust her.

112

But that didn't stop Marina from pretending like she did. After all, she had to monitor Lila as a potential Latent. If Lila wanted to pretend to be a nice person, Marina could pretend Lila was too. Marina had even paid for both their cookies and drinks.

"So that's pretty much it. It's not too bad, right?" Marina swallowed her last bite of oatmeal raisin cookie.

Lila scowled around her mouthful of chocolate chip cookie. "I dunno about *that*."

Marina's lips twitched toward a sympathetic smile.

She shut it down. *All of this is just an act to convince me to trust her*, Marina reminded herself. But Marina would be polite even to a serpent disguised as a mouse. "C'mon, Lila, you've got this. Tell me about Eversfield's layout. No looking at your map."

Leaning over the blond cocktail table stamped with the Snack Station logo, Lila ticked off her fingers. "Let's see. First, every single building looks the same from the outside, all bricks and ivy and bushes."

"Technically hawthorn hedges, but yes, that's true. That said, every single building has a sign out front. It might take you a bit at first, Lila, but you'll get the hang of it. I promise." Memories of her own confused wanderings a year ago swelled. Marina smushed a crumb against the polished tabletop and transferred it to her empty paper plate. "What about the dorms?"

"Well…" Lila's face scrunched in thought. "Blackwell is the one in the middle behind the cafeteria."

"And what's connected to the cafeteria?"

"The library," Lila answered without hesitation.

"See, Lila, you're getting it."

"I guess…" The storm raging over Lila's features cleared, replaced by the creepy sincerity Marina refused to believe. "Thanks again, Marina, for the tour and the cookie. I know you didn't wanna spend your last day of summer teaching me everything there is to know about Eversfield."

The metal legs of Marina's bar chair scraped against the tile. Avoiding Lila's suspiciously honest gaze, she scooped their trash onto her plate and stood. "No problem. After all, I was hungry too. But I do think we're done here, so we should head back."

"Sure, I don't wanna use up any more of your time."

Marina's teeth ground together. After sorting their trash into the color-coded containers next to the side exit, she shoved her hands into the pockets of her shorts. Why did Lila have to be so nice all the time? Marina wished she would just come out with it already, just attack her like Natasha had.

But Lila didn't. Docile as a lamb, she followed Marina through the side door.

Outside, humidity caressed Marina's agitated fingers. While they cut across the freshly mowed grass between the gym and the girls' dorms, the scent of it called to her, as did the water-laden air. But Marina couldn't obey, no matter how indulging in her powers would comfort her. If someone noticed, Gabe would never let her hear the end of it. And that was the best-case scenario. Marina's hands curled into fists.

Behind her, the silent Lila traced Marina's footsteps. Now *that* was something an Earth Diviner would do. By following in another's footsteps, they could minimize the damage to the vegetation around them. Perhaps if Marina tugged on her Floral affinity, Lila's latent powers would respond.

No. Marina could not test Lila out here where anyone could see. She'd have to wait until they were alone in their room. Which meant Marina had to occupy their room for more than a few minutes.

With a sigh pressing against her clenched lips, Marina passed through Blackwell's back door, returning to air-conditioned safety. Usually it irritated Marina to be indoors without a single window open to nature. In this case, it was a relief.

A relief that died the moment Marina reached her— *their*—room.

With two iced coffees dripping onto the polished floor, Valerie sat outside their closed door.

CHAPTER 11

L ila followed Marina down Blackwell's noisy third-floor hallway. Through open doors on both sides, she peeked at her new housemates. Some were clad in exercise shorts and tanks, others in sundresses, and the rest in everything in-between. They unpacked. They appeased hovering parents. They flung cheerful jabs between rooms. One thing remained constant among them: no one gave Lila a second look. She didn't know whether to feel relieved or disheartened about it. She opted for relieved.

Until her jaw dropped in shock.

Val hunched over her phone outside Lila's door like nothing had happened this morning. Upon Lila's arrival, she sprang to her feet and rushed to enfold Lila in an embrace that Lila did not share. Behind Val's back, Marina slipped into their room without a word. Lila frowned.

Val pinched one of Lila's curls between her thumb and forefinger, then tugged. "An excellent try, m' dear, but definitely too much gel. We don't want your lovely curls all crunchy!"

Lila swiped Val's hands away. "What are you doing here?"

"I brought you coffee, see!" Val bent to retrieve the twin plastic cups.

"Yes, but—"

The door opened, interrupting Lila. Marina exited in a gray robe, her full shower caddy hooked over a wrist. A beach towel displaying a diving sea turtle in an ocean alive with brightly hued coral and striped fish slung over her shoulder.

"Marina, you don't have—"

Marina waved away Lila's protests. "I have to shower before Semester Start anyway."

As Marina's form faded down the hall, Lila turned around, only to witness Val flounce into their room uninvited. Her short skirt bounced with every perky step.

Lila sighed. Val acted like she hadn't abandoned Lila hours ago.

Now standing beside Lila's desk, Val wiggled Lila's phone at her. "Lila dear, you really must keep your phone on you at all times. I tried calling you *over* and *over* again."

"Oh yeah? I left my phone in my room once I realized you weren't coming." The door clicked shut. Lila placed her hands on her hips. Her chin jutted out. Her brows crouched over her narrowed gaze. Val would not blame this on her.

Val's sunny smile didn't budge a millimeter. "Weren't coming? Lila, of course, I was! I just needed a li'l extra sleep after a long night of fun. Fun that, by the way, you could've joined."

"First, I enjoyed my night off, thank you very much." That wasn't completely true. Once Gabe and Marina left, the loneliness had hit Lila full-force. But Lila wasn't about to admit that to Val. "Secondly, it didn't occur to you to tell me you were going to be late? You know, before I waited for an *entire hour*?"

"Lila, I—"

Lila rounded on Val before she could invent an excuse. "You what, Val? You didn't care? You didn't think? What?"

Val's eternal sunshine disappeared behind a cloud of anger. "I'd *thought* you would be with me, so I didn't worry about it. You were supposed to go out last night—"

"Supposed to go out? Refresh my memory, exactly when did I agree to that?"

"When you accepted the invitation to Eversfield! Do you have any idea how hard I worked to get you in here? And now you're mad at me when *you* couldn't even be bothered to meet my friends!"

"How hard *you* worked? If I remember correctly, I was the one submitting grades, taking scholastic merit exams, gathering teacher recommendations, breaking the news to my parents."

"And I was the one explaining what to do, making it as easy as possible for you. I was the one convincing my friends that you were the right fit for Lizzie. My friends who are the president and vice president of Lizzie and therefore have a *significant* voice in the admission process, particularly for any prospective Lizzards!"

"So that gives you the right to stand me up whenever you want?"

Val's expression softened. "No. It does not. But it does give me the right to ask for forgiveness. I *am* sorry, Lila. I had my alarm set and everything. I just got back so late last night, I must've slept through it. I felt terrible as soon as I woke up. We can do the tour now if you'd like."

Like water out of a bathtub, Lila's indignation drained away. This *was* Val after all. "No, it's okay. Maybe it's better this way. I ended up running into Marina, and she gave me a tour."

"Hmmph, I doubt she did it as well as I would have."

Gabe's words from last night echoed in Lila's mind. "Speaking of which, what's up with you two? You don't seem to like her very much."

Val dismissed Lila's concern with a wave of her hand. "It's not that I dislike her. She's just boring. You could do so much better, Lila dear."

"She seems nice. Maybe a little quiet, but nice."

"Yeah, like I said, b-o-r-i-n-g."

Lila rolled her eyes. "You know excitement isn't all there is to life."

"Sure it is! Speaking of which, you should've come out last night." Val handed Lila one of the forgotten iced coffees, then settled onto the couch. She patted the cushion next to her.

After slurping up a swallow, Lila obeyed and sat sideways on the sofa to face Val. With her legs crossed beneath her, she cradled the iced coffee in both hands. "Oh really? And what happened that was so exciting?"

Val grinned. "Well, at first, it was simply *beyond* terrible. Sara and Drey are going after football players now, who happen to be the most boring characters in the entire world."

"More boring than Marina?"

"Oh, for sure! All they wanna talk about is football, their workout routines, and whatever it is they eat. Nothing of interest at all. But, Lila dear, they sure make good eye candy. Speaking of which, have you noted anyone of interest yet?"

"Val, I've hardly been out of this room." But Lila's cheeks burned.

Val bounced up and down, as did her plastic cup. The coffee sloshed back and forth. "You have, Lila dear, you have!"

"Val, please…" Lila didn't want to admit her crush to herself, let alone to Val.

"Okay, okay, you don't have to tell me now. But I *will* figure it out. Anyway, to make a long story short, Rudi and I danced the night away while Sara and Drey chatted to the most dreary boy toys I've ever seen and—"

"And Heidi?"

Val beamed at Lila. "Good memory! Yes, Heidi was there too, only *she* was busy with someone else…" Val's shoulders shimmied like a cat preparing to pounce.

Why Val was so excited, Lila had no idea. "And?"

Val's grin stretched from ear to ear. Her chocolate eyes sparkling, Val leaned forward and whispered in Lila's ear, "Okay, okay, stop badgering me, I'll tell you. Just promise not to tell anyone else, okay?"

"Okay, I promise." After all, who would Lila tell?

"Heidi is dating Joe Rodriguez, who was a senior here last year and about the geekiest geek you've ever seen."

"Wait, I thought you said Heidi and Gabe dated?" Lila cursed the blush curling around her neck.

"Good memory again, Lila dear! See, you're gonna be a whiz at this whole school thing, remembering random details like that. Yes, they did date, back before my time when they were sophomores, so two-ish years ago. Anyway, Joe tutored Heidi for years before she finally realized she had feelings for him and *voila*! Of course, she kept it a secret and still does, though I'm not one hundred percent sure why. No one would dare to care anymore. Besides, Joe already teaches over at JCC, so you just know he's gonna *be* someone. Regardless, it is a secret, so you absolutely cannot tell anyone, Lila dear."

"And I won't." Even if Lila hadn't promised, it was no business of hers who dated who.

"*Anyway*, Rudi and I danced the night away, eventually finding some superb partners. Although I suppose my judgment may have been off, if you know what I mean." Val winked. "Then all of us went out to this twenty-four-hour pancake place in Juniper and had a simply marvelous time. Until, that is, we got thrown out for 'disturbing the other customers,' which of course didn't happen until after we paid our bill. Once they got our money, we were suddenly too loud for the three whole other people. At that point we came home and went to bed. The end. Now, Lila dear, about your hair." Val's elven hand stalked toward her curls.

Anxiety's icy fingers wrapped around Lila's stomach. "What about it?"

"Like I said earlier, that's too much gel. I mean, valiant effort and all, but it simply won't do for Semester Start." Val leapt to her feet and collected the mint green robe from inside Lila's closet door. She extended it toward Lila. "Off to the shower with you."

Lila stayed planted on the slouchy sofa. Her arms crossed over her chest. "Val, I just showered a few hours ago."

"And you pro'ly got all sweaty during your tour."

"No, not really."

"No arguments, Lila dear. Now go shower while I figure out what you're gonna wear tonight." Val tossed the robe at Lila. It landed at her feet.

Lila gathered it off the ground, curiosity dimming her resistance. She'd failed at trying on anything last night, but she hadn't admitted that to Val. "How did you know?"

"Because I know *you*, silly. You've never been any good at picking out outfits. Now go shower!" Val turned around to face Lila's closet.

With a grumble, Lila collected her shower caddy from the bottom of the now-open closet. Once Val made up her mind, resisting her was futile.

CHAPTER 12

With Lila out of the room, Val set to work, but not on the task she'd claimed.

Ignoring the dresses piled high on Lila's desk, Val focused on the interior of Lila's closet. It was worse than she expected. Not even half full and mostly uniform attire! And all that was cheap and ill-fitting, whether it be khaki or navy pants, plaid skirts, Eversfield sweaters, or the dreaded polo.

Fortunately for Lila, Val had begun scheming the moment she'd picked Lila up in Admin. Val had already delivered new plaid skirts to Lizzie's Future Fashion Designers. With Val's position in the Lizzard inner circle, they'd been more than happy to alter the skirts even on a short timeline. The rest she'd begun replacing using her emergency credit card last night. When—and if—her parents asked, she'd just claim it was for books or tutoring or something else school-related. After all, wasn't getting her best *genius* friend equilibrated to Eversfield good for Val's grades? Yes, of course it was.

But even Val couldn't get everything together in time for Lila's first day tomorrow. She'd have to tell everyone that, due to Lila's late acceptance into Eversfield, these were the only uniforms left. With a little luck—and more than a little determination—Val would fix Lila's wardrobe before the end of the week. Then Lila would fit right in with the rest of the Lizzards.

At the end of the sparse rack, Val found the only non-uniforms in the entire closet: a couple of coats and three dresses, all chosen by Lila's mom. Val's fingers slid over a marigold frock with lace trim. *Perfect for tonight.*

"What are you doing?" a voice accused from the doorway.

Val rolled her eyes. *Marina.* As if *she* had any right to comment on her or Lila. Val didn't bother turning around. "Do you know where Lila keeps her makeup?" That was the next thing on Val's checklist.

"No. Don't you think you should wait for Lila before you paw through her things?"

Val rounded on Marina, gulping down surprise at Marina's boring — but cute — dress. "I think *you* should mind your own business. 'Sides, I know Lila, and *she* wouldn't mind me looking through her stuff, not if it's to help her."

"Fine, whatever, I don't care." Marina grabbed a worn backpack and stormed toward the door. Her wet hair swung with every rushed step. In the doorway, Marina's fingertips pressed into the wooden frame. She shifted back to Val. "If Lila asks, tell her I'll see her at Semester Start." Only then did Marina stomp out the door. Her footsteps echoed down the hallway.

Pssh, as if my Lila cares about seeing Marina *tonight.*

As if summoned by that thought, Lila entered the room, her eyes wide with surprise. Her head tilted back toward the hallway. "What was that about?"

Val leaned against the wall and checked her cream-colored nails for any last-minute touch-ups. They needed none. "I dunno. She just came in, grabbed her stuff, and left."

"Huh. You'd think she'd at least finish getting ready here…" Lila's voice trailed off. Her gaze fastened to Val. "Why's my closet still open?"

Snapping to attention, Val whipped out the yellow dress and wiggled its plastic hanger back and forth. The frock jumped from side to side. "Well, Lila dear, it turns out that you have a few dresses worth wearing after all!"

"Do I have to? My mom made me bring that dress," Lila whined.

"Now, Lila dear, you saw Marina. Even she dressed up."

"What do you mean by 'even she?'"

Val ignored Lila's comment. "Okay, here's what we're gonna do. Tonight you'll wear this *lovely* dress your mom made you bring. Then, later this week, we'll pick out a few of the others for you to borrow on a more permanent basis." Val waved toward the sparkling garments heaped on top of Lila's desk.

With a scowl, Lila crossed her arms over her chest. "And why do I need to borrow them on a more permanent basis? I thought tonight was the only night I have to dress up for. Besides, I have two other dresses."

"Lila dear, you didn't forget, did you? For Friday night dinners of course!"

Lila rolled her eyes. "I thought we already talked about this."

"Lila, please? It's just one itsy bitsy night. Surely that's not too much to ask for your ol' gal pal Val?"

Lila's frown deepened. Her wet curls swung to and fro as she shook her head. "Fine, Val, you win." Lila wagged her finger at Val. "But only Friday nights."

"Yes, Lila dear, of course." *For now anyway.* "We'll even get you some dresses that you love! I know just the place."

"Val, I don't have any money —"

"But I do!"

"I can't let you do that."

"I want to. Just consider it a nice li'l reward for playing dress up with me on Fridays, okay?"

"Okay, fine."

It wasn't the enthusiasm Val craved, but it was an agreement. "Now that *that's* settled, why don't we both change into our outfits for tonight?"

Lila's frown softened and her fingers ran through her locks. She eyed the window where the late afternoon sunbeams wheedled their way through the leaves. "Yeah, I guess it's about that time."

"Now don't you worry about a thing, Lila dear. We're gonna have such fun tonight!" Val danced over to the nook between the sofa and Lila's lofted bed where two neglected cups waited. After retrieving their iced coffee — now more like kinda-cold coffee — she pressed a drink into Lila's empty hand. "Don't forget about this. You'll want to be all perky tonight." Val gulped down a full third of her remaining coffee as a good example.

"Val, I shouldn't. It's already late for so much caffeine, and I have those placement exams tomorrow. I need to get a good night's rest. Honestly, I'll probably be too nervous to sleep well as it is —"

"So you might as well be happy and caffeinated in the meantime!" Val waited for Lila to take a sip.

After a sigh, Lila complied. "I *guess* it won't hurt, and it is pretty good."

"Well, Lila dear, I did get it from the best place in Juniper. I'll take you there soon, I promise. Anyway, you change, drink your coffee. Oh! And be careful! Don't spill it on your dress or you'll be in one of those borrowed ones."

"I don't need to be reminded not to spill, Val." Nevertheless, Lila grabbed a handful of tissue from the dispenser on the windowsill and wrapped them around her plastic cup.

"Okay, I'm gonna run up to my room and change. Don't you *dare* do anything with your hair or makeup until I'm back. And should I bring my straightener? I think we have time to straighten your hair, though I do remember that it takes approximately forever…"

Lila shook her head around another mouthful of coffee. "No, I don't really like it straight. Never feels like me, y' know?"

Val did not know as she dreamt of switching her hair from short to long, from straight to curly, from bangs to no-bangs, on a whim. "Okay, sounds good. You change. Drink coffee. Relax. I'll be back in a jiff!"

Val rushed down the hall, up the stairs, and into her fourth-floor single, waving to others as she passed open doors framing her housemates putting on the final touches for Semester Start.

With a practiced hand, Val hurried through her preparations. Her pixie cut only required a bit of freshening, and she went with her old standard for makeup: winged liner and scarlet lips. She'd selected the lacy dress, stilettos, and jewelry this morning.

In fifteen minutes flat, Val raced back down the stairs heedless of her towering heels. One arm pinned her neon makeup bag against her side and the other clutched the curly hair products she'd borrowed from Heidi. Nearly all those open doors were closed now.

Val's stilettos clicked against the wooden floor as she slowed down to approach Lila's room. Alerting Lila to the late time would just cause another argument, one that Lila had no hope of winning.

Within the room, Lila stared at the full-length mirror attached to the back of the closet door. Her brows crouched over a narrowed gaze. Her mouth pursed. "Val, you're sure this dress isn't too bright?"

With her free hand, Val tore Lila away from the mirror, then pushed her into the desk chair beside the window. Natural light—albeit filtered by the oak tree outside—spilled onto her canvas. Val sprayed detangler over Lila's wet mane. "No, definitely not. First, this color looks *gorgeous* with your complexion. Secondly, we want you to stand out." Val pretended not to notice the grimace crossing Lila's round face. They'd have to work on *that* later. "Thirdly, it brings out the golden flecks in those lovely emerald eyes of yours." Val worked potion number two through Lila's thick hair. "Now, why don't you tell me about your tour?"

"Well, as I was leaving, I ran into Marina. Apparently, she slept over at her friend Lex's last night, and—"

"No, no, no. Not about your tour itself. What you learned *during* the tour. I wanna fill in anything Marina might've missed."

"Oh, okay. Well…" Lila bit her lower lip. Her forehead wrinkled in thought. "First, there's the central courtyard with the fountain and picnic tables and benches and all."

"Uh huh."

"And clustered around the courtyard are all the classroom buildings."

128

"Which are?" Val scrunched Lila's curls.

"Well…behind the Administration building—"

"Admin," Val corrected. Her fingers skimmed over containers of makeup spread over the windowsill. One day, she'd convince Lila to try something bold, maybe the pin-up girl style Heidi preferred. Today was not that day. Val settled for understated with a hint of gold.

"Okay then, behind *Admin*, there's the math and science building."

"Smience."

"Then the arts and music building—"

"Marts."

"Then the literature and language building—"

"LnL."

"Across from that is the cafeteria and the library—"

"No cute shortening for that atrocity." Stepping back, Val surveyed her handiwork. The brown liner on Lila's right eye didn't *quite* match her left. She stooped over Lila's upturned face to fix it.

"And in the back is the gym, complete with a pool and various courts for sports. The theater's kitty corner to it and the outdoor sports fields are behind it."

"Excellent job, Lila dear! Now just remember their actual names and you'll be fine."

Lila's brow furrowed. "Their actual names?"

"The ones I just said. You know, Smience, Marts, LnL." Val extended a tube of rosy lip gloss toward Lila. "You're done. And in record time, I may add. Now don't forget to reapply this gloss as needed. And leave your hair alone, except for *maybe* finger-combing it if absolutely necessary."

Lila nodded as she shoved the lip gloss into a boring black wristlet.

Just another item to replace. "All right, you're all set, so let's head downstairs."

Lila rose from her desk chair and began collecting Val's smattering of beauty supplies off the windowsill.

"Leave it, Lila. We're already a *teensy* bit late," Val admitted.

Lila whirled around. Panic widened her eyes. "Why didn't you tell me? We coulda skipped all this." She gestured from scalp to shoulders.

"Don't worry about it, Lila dear. These things never start on time." Val wrapped an arm around Lila's waist, the leather of her brown belt smooth against the inside of Val's wrist. As she guided Lila toward the door, Val caught their reflection in the mirror.

Pride swelled within her. She and Lila were the most adorable pair. Lila in her lace-trimmed marigold dress complementing her curves with its scooped neckline, belted waist, and loose skirt; Val in navy lace clinging to every nook and cranny — not that she had many of those. Lila with her just-tamed-enough curls; Val with her sleek pixie cut. Lila in natural makeup hinting of gold; Val in liquid liner and crimson lips. Lila in her precious flats; Val in sky-high stilettos boosting her to Lila's height. Yes, tonight they made a statement. New sophomore transfer Lila Lee *belonged* with Valerie Baker.

Val peeled her gaze away from their reflection to focus on Lila. "Besides, we'll have seats saved. Only the Blackwellians arrive now. Lizzards have more flexibility."

"Blackwellians? Lizzards?" Lila asked while fumbling in her faded purse. Only after verifying her keycard was present did Lila allow the door to shut behind them.

"Oh, sorry, Lila dear. Those are the terms we Lizzards use." Val trotted down the empty hall with Lila a step behind. "Don't worry, you'll get used to it in no time. Lizzards are those in Elizabeth Blackwell who are…well, more fun than your typical member. And who have the power, we can't forget that. So that's me, you, Sara, Drey, Heidi—you know, the house officers and those they're friends with. And then there are the other members, the Blackwellians. They're the ones who study instead of actually enjoy life. So that would be Marina, for instance. Of course, there're others, but they're not important."

A frown tugged at the corners of Lila's full lips.

Seeking to distract Lila from whatever had upset her, Val switched to tour guide. "Like I said yesterday, the top three floors of Lizzie are all dorm rooms, so nothing exciting. But on the bottom floor we've got all kinds of good stuff. First," Val waved toward the bottom of the stairs they descended, "there's the back door in and out of Lizzie, which I'm sure you're used to by now. Next to us are the common rooms where—"

"Where we'll be hanging out tonight, right? For the house bonding?"

"Correct, Lila dear! Yes, where we'll do the house bonding tonight." *What Lila doesn't know can't hurt her.* "The first and bigger room has a TV, some couches, a bunch of movies, pretty much everything you can think of to relax. We call it Beechy. The second room—Louie—is a bit smaller, but it has some exercise equipment along with another TV. Of course, for serious exercise you're supposed to go to the gym, but Louie is great for quick study breaks." Or so Val had heard.

With her heels clicking against the marble floor, Val led Lila down the first floor of Lizzie. Chandeliers spotlighted paintings hung on glossy walls. A line of burnished wooden doors on either side of the broad hallway reflected their yellow light. Whiffs of potpourri wafted from crystal bowls set on low silver tables.

Val didn't so much as glance at any of it. "After Beechy and Louie, we have an assortment of soundproof rooms. First, there's a game room, filled with exactly what you would expect—you know, video games, a pool table, foosball, table tennis, the usual. Then there are the group study rooms. All the way down by Lizzie's formal entrance…" Val pointed at the distant end of the lobby. The crowd of Blackwellians and Lizzards gathered for Semester Start blocked her view. "Is the music room, which is where some people practice rather than walk all the way down to Marts. Across from that is the house manager apartment, which, as you would guess, is where our house manager— Ms. van Straten—lives. Got it, Lila dear?" Val twisted around to check on the quiet Lila.

She'd frozen a few feet behind Val. On either side, Lila's fists clenched a handful of marigold skirt. She stared at the mass of sitting students ahead.

Val backtracked to link arms with Lila. She steered her forward. "*Relax*, Lila dear. Like I said, we Lizzards always have a seat saved, no matter how late." Besides, they were intentionally late. *Fashionably* late. Val stepped around Blackwellians seated on marble tiles that looked like swirled cream. At last she arrived at the empty chairs Heidi had saved for her and Lila.

"Nice of you to join us, Miss Baker," croaked Ms. van Straten, stationed at the head of the congregation. Despite her words, her wrinkled lips wriggled like a pair of excited earthworms. Amusement crinkled her beady eyes.

"No problem, ma'am. And everyone," Val commanded the crowd with ease, "this is our new member, simply my bestest best friend, the *lovely* Miss Lila Lee."

After a grimace and an awkward wave, Lila plopped onto her chair. She watched her fingers pull at each other.

Val smothered a wince. "Back to you, Ms. van Straten." With a bright smile pasted onto her face, Val tucked one foot behind the other. Her knees bent into a *plié* as she sank onto the chair's cushion. Her feet crossed at the ankle. Her hands folded in her lap. Her spine straightened into the perfect posture. In her peripheral vision, Lila rushed to mimic her. *Good.*

"Thank you, Miss Baker, and welcome to Elizabeth Blackwell, Miss Lee." Ms. van Straten glanced down at the translucent clipboard resting on a forearm. A rounded nail traced the top sheet, stopping a few lines down. "Now, as I was saying, the house rules are the same this year as every year and are noted in your student handbook. Any and all guests sign in with me. Male guests must remain on the first floor at all times."

Val suppressed a snort. That was hardly true. Even the strictest hall monitor would turn a blind eye if the door stayed open and it wasn't too early or too late or for too long. Of course, what constituted too early, too late, or too long varied by the hall monitor.

"Curfew is ten p.m. Sunday through Thursday and midnight Friday and Saturday, after which all members are restricted to Elizabeth Blackwell, along with pre-approved female guests. As you know, the Arts and Music Building, the computer lab, and the library are open from six a.m. to eight p.m. for all students. Extended hours are restricted by house and rotated on a weekly basis. I will post each week's schedule outside my office on Monday mornings. Are there any questions regarding house rules?" Ms. van Straten surveyed the crowd for only a moment. "If you have questions later, either consult your student handbook or ask your hall monitors. As a reminder, they are Miss Cohen on the second floor, Miss Hernandez on the third floor, and Miss Jackson on the fourth floor."

Although each member stood in turn and waved, Val paid no attention. They were, after all, lowly Blackwellians. She could buy herself out of any scrape with them, whether through actual cash, social favors, or outright threats.

"Without further ado, I'll hand it over to your house president." Ms. van Straten extended an arm toward Val.

Val's heart pounded. Had she missed something while giving Lila her tour? Had she become president over a year earlier than planned?

Beside Val, Heidi rose. The seated Blackwellians crushed together, parting like the Red Sea before Heidi's slingbacks. She strode through them without a downward glance, her skirt swishing with every step. The metallic roses painted on Heidi's dress shimmered beneath the light of the chandeliers.

Val swallowed her disappointment. Of course that had been impossible. Heidi would never resign this close to the end of her term. Even if she did, Sara would have to surrender before Val could ascend. And with such an unconventional election, Drey was sure to challenge Val despite last year's agreement. No, it had been an impossible hope from the start.

An ebony tendril slipped over Heidi's round shoulder as she turned to face the crowd. "It is my great honor to begin our nominations. As outgoing president, my duty is to facilitate this process, not to nominate. So I open the floor to you, the members of Elizabeth Blackwell. We'll begin with president."

A row behind Val, heels tapped against the marble. Drey stood, then gathered her chocolate-hued waves to one side. Her hazel eyes shone more green than gray, reflecting the beading swirling over her bodice. "I, Audrey Diaz, nominate Miss Sara Howland."

On cue, Val bounced up. "I, Valerie Baker, second the nomination."

"All right, Sara Howland has been successfully nominated for president. Are there any other nominations?" Heidi scanned the mass of students assembled before her.

Most of the Blackwellians squirmed in their seats on the floor. A few seniors poked at their phones, but Heidi wouldn't scold them for now. After all, this process wasn't about them.

"Nominations for president will close in 5...4...3...2...1...the nominations for president have closed. Miss Sara Howland will become the next president of Elizabeth Blackwell pending meeting quorum during October's elections. The floor is now open for vice president nominations."

Normally the vice presidency would go to Val, stationed as she was to inherit their clique from Sara. But last year's truce stipulated that Drey become vice president and Val become treasurer. It wasn't ideal, but the compromise had stopped them before they tore each other—and Sara and Heidi—apart. Although Val didn't trust Drey in the least, she wouldn't be the one to break the peace. Val rose to her feet again. "I, Valerie Baker, nominate Miss Audrey Diaz."

"And I, Sara Howland, second the nomination." Sara glanced at the seated Drey next to her. Her chin dipped down, then back up. The nod was so subtle that the golden locks trailing down Sara's back only twitched.

Pretending to have missed the exchange, Val stared at Heidi. Her expression didn't budge an inch away from neutral, but Val's brain worked a mile a minute. Drey imitated Sara in every way from makeup to hair to clothes to speech, something that Sara more than appreciated. While Val could do the same — and better — that was not a sacrifice she would make. Last year, she'd won her throne. This year, she'd defend it.

"Miss Audrey Diaz has been successfully nominated for vice president. The nominations for vice president will close in 5…4…3…2…1…" Again, Heidi searched the crowd for additional nominations.

Again, Lizzards and Blackwellians alike held their silence. Everyone but the freshmen knew how this worked and freshmen didn't run for office.

"The nominations for vice president have closed. Miss Audrey Diaz will become the next vice president of Elizabeth Blackwell pending meeting quorum during October's elections. The floor is now open for treasurer nominations."

Val's heart thumped. This was hers. Yet doubt wriggled in the back of her mind. What if this was Sara and Drey's plan to unseat her? She should have talked to Lila and maybe that mousy girl who did her laundry. She should have forged a backup plan.

"I, Sara Howland, nominate Miss Valerie Baker."

"I, Audrey Diaz, second the nomination."

Val squashed a sigh of relief while Heidi counted down the nomination period for treasurer. With Sara and Drey on her side, no one dared challenge her.

"Miss Valerie Baker will become the next treasurer of Elizabeth Blackwell pending meeting quorum during October's elections. The floor is now open for secretary nominations."

The mousy girl who did her laundry — *Elspeth "Elsie" Adams, that's right* — gazed at Val through lenses that magnified her pale blue eyes.

Val ignored her. *Some promises are made to be broken.* "I, Valerie Baker, nominate Miss Lila Lee."

CHAPTER 13

LILA

L ila's jaw dropped. Beside her, Val sank into her chair, all confident smiles. From one of the seats on the floor, a girl with frizzy brown hair glared at Lila through thick glasses. Someone murmured "second the nomination."

It was all too much. Lila lurched upward. "No." The stares of her new housemates seared into her. Lila's cheeks burned as if tongues of flame lapped over them. Her arms wrapped about her stomach. If only she could shrivel up into nothing. If only the ground would swallow her whole. "I, um, I decline. Or something." Lila's voice trembled.

Val yanked on Lila's elbow. "What're you doing?"

"I don't want it, Val. I can't. It's…it's too much." Lila studied the padded arm of her chair rather than meet Val's gaze. Val's disappointment could not change her mind.

Val pitched her voice an inch below the hum of a crowd sprung to life. "Lila, don't do this. *Please.*"

"Miss Lee," the girl with the perfect curls called from the front.

Miss Malik, Val's friend Heidi, Lila reminded herself.

"Please confirm. Do you decline your nomination for secretary?"

Lila straightened her spine and banished any quakes from her voice. "Yes, I confirm. I decline my nomination for secretary." Refusing to even peek in Val's direction, Lila retreated to the safety of her seat.

Heidi's jet-black eyebrow arched for a moment, then she returned to the mass huddled before her. "All right, Miss

Lila Lee has declined her nomination. Are there any other nominations for secretary?"

All eyes remained trained on Lila. She twitched under the pressure.

After a sigh, Val leaned toward Lila and hissed into her ear, "Just nominate Elsie already."

Lila started. "Huh?"

"Nominate Elsie, so I can second her. Elspeth Adams."

"Um..." Lila's guts clenched at the prospect of speaking in front of this horde of strangers once more.

"Just do it, Lila, okay?"

"Fine, okay." Lila rose to her feet. Her breath hitched on what was supposed to be a deep, calming inhale. "I, um, I, Lila Lee, nominate Elspe—*Miss* Elspeth Adams." She collapsed back into her chair. At least the girl who'd glared at her before now grinned.

"I, Valerie Baker, second the nomination."

"Lovely." Heidi's smile cascaded over the crowd, her teeth shining stark white against wine-red lips. "Nominations for secretary close in 5...4...3...2...1...Miss Elspeth Adams will be the next secretary of Elizabeth Blackwell pending reaching quorum during October's elections. And that wraps up nominations. Please rise and form our double line. Current officers first, then our newly nominated officers, then in descending grade. Remember we stay in step with the girls next to us and in front of us. We keep our postures tall and proud. We are Elizabeth Blackwell, after all."

Without a backward glance—let alone a goodbye—Val bolted from Lila's side.

Lila's lips pressed together while she searched the line forming in the middle of the lobby. Not a single familiar face greeted her. When she reached the end of the line, she joined it. *Alone.* A couple of girls chatted in front of her. Maybe no one would notice the one girl amid all these pairs?

"Miss Lee, where is Miss Lee?" Ms. van Straten boomed over the mob. A mechanical pencil hovered over her clipboard.

Lila poked her head out. "I'm right here."

"Why are you all the way back there? Did you not hear Miss Malik's instructions? Get your bum up here."

Lila squeezed her eyes shut, battling the tears pricking at them. *Too much humiliation for one day.* At least now she looked forward to the solitude of tomorrow's placement exams.

When she reached Ms. van Straten, a liver-spotted hand waved Lila toward a girl with blue-tipped inky hair. Although the vast majority of students wore a dress of one kind or another, this girl sported a button-down shirt with the sleeves rolled up. Her navy shorts were embroidered with sharks baring their teeth.

The girl turned to Lila. Her mouth stretched into a wide smile. A hand, its nails cut short, shot out of her pocket. "Hi, I'm Izzi."

Lila grasped Izzi's hand. "Lila."

"Oh, I know that. Val's been tellin' everyone 'bout you for ages."

Lila's stomach flipped. "I'm sorry, what?"

"Well, not everyone, I s'pose. Just everyone at summer school." Izzi flipped stick-straight locks over a shoulder, then angled her dark gaze toward Lila. "So why'd you decline your nomination?"

Lila sucked in a breath. There was no easy answer to Izzi's question.

140

From the front of the line, Heidi's voice rang out, "All right, here we go. Remember: no talking, not even whispers, until I dismiss you in the cafeteria."

A surge of thankfulness welled in Lila. To answer Izzi's question, she shrugged.

Dipping down to Lila's level, Izzi murmured, "Don't worry, y' can tell me all 'bout it durin' dinner." Izzi straightened, then began whistling a tune despite Heidi's instructions. Her hands slapped against her bare thighs like they were drums.

Lila dreaded the coming dinner.

CHAPTER 14

MARINA

Alone rock in a sea of chatting, sipping, and munching students, Marina rubbed the sole of one flat against the toe of the other. Clusters of her happy classmates crowded the back third of the cafeteria. A screen of Eversfield-navy curtains hemmed them in from the front. A brick wall bordered the back, interrupted by double doors opened wide to the hallway behind them. On either side, spotless windows stretched from the floor to the ceiling. Through one set, a lawn divided by a cement path peeked. The ivy-covered girls' dorms rose in the background. The opposite end framed the green grass, pruned trees, and cobblestone lanes of the courtyard. In front of either set of windows, teachers served appetizers and drinks of every hue from behind carved wooden tables.

Marina retreated into the shadow of one of those open doors. Her free hand pressed against the loose skirt of her dress. The other clutched a glass of strawberry lemonade. Its condensation pooled over her index finger and thumb.

Alone, she watched her classmates talk and laugh in their cliques. Alone, she drank her lemonade while pretending to be content. Alone, she searched the hundreds of assembled students for Lex, Teddi, or any of her non-Eversfield Cell friends. She found no one.

A throat cleared behind her.

Marina jumped. Her strawberry lemonade swished toward the top of her glass. Before it could splash over the

142

edge and stain her sky-blue dress, Marina pulled the pink liquid back down.

Her relief lasted only a moment. Then dread wrapped its icy fingers around her stomach. Had anyone noticed her use magic? With her breath caught in her throat, Marina scanned the groups of students around her.

No one glanced at her. *Sometimes it's good to be invisible.* Hoping *he* hadn't noticed, Marina turned around.

Gabe wore an abashed expression like a mask. "Sorry, I didn't mean to startle you."

"It's okay. Um…what's up?"

Gabe twisted the striped straw in his drink. Ice cubes clinked against the glass. "Oh, um, I thought that maybe you could use dinner to check on Lila? As a potential you-know-what."

"I already did that today." Marina's voice neared a whine.

Gabe arched an inky brow. "Oh, yeah?"

"Yes, this morning I gave Lila a tour of Eversfield when Valerie ditched her."

Gabe's lips twitched toward a frown, but only for an instant. "And?"

"And nothing. We were outside and nothing. I mean, Eversfield's campus isn't exactly full of nature, but I still would expect *something* if she's a manifesting Earth Diviner. Not that I tested her or anything."

"Can you test her tonight? During dinner?"

Marina's jaw dropped. "And how do you expect me to do that without anyone noticing?"

"Oh, right. Yeah, of course…" Gabe's fingers tugged at his messy locks. "Just keep an eye on her tonight, okay?"

Marina flattened her lips into a thin line. Lex's theory from last night swirled through her mind. She did not like this…this *focus* Gabe — her brother and the First of her Cell — had on Lila. Before he could walk away, her free hand darted out and squeezed his bare forearm. It was steel beneath her fingers. "Is there something I should know?"

Gabe's head tilted back toward her. "What do you mean?"

"I think you know what I mean."

Gabe jerked his arm out of her light hold. "It's nothing, Marina. We decided to look out for her is all. I can't do it tonight and neither can Lex since we're both stuck with our houses for the next few hours. That leaves you. Besides, all three of us should get into the habit of watching out for her whenever we can. That way, if and when her abilities manifest, we're ready."

Marina raised her hands with her fingers outstretched. "All right, all right, I'll keep an eye on her. *Sheesh.* But I don't think her abilities are anywhere near manifesting if she is a Latent. But you're right. That could change overnight."

"Exactly." Gabe scanned the crowd, then thrust his stubbled chin toward the tables in front of the courtyard-side windows. "She's over there."

Indeed, Lila — clad in a canary yellow dress — had tucked herself into the corner preceding the floor-to-ceiling windows and appetizer tables. Her drink perched on a row of overhanging bricks while she picked at the appetizers heaped on top of an Eversfield-navy plate. She was alone.

Gabe didn't wait for Marina to confirm. Over his shoulder, he called, "Thanks, Marina. I gotta go." Light on his feet, he weaved through the tangles of students, returning to his usual group without a backward glance.

144

Marina, on the other hand, dragged her feet, scuffing her way to Lila. Just like that, Gabe had handed her all the responsibility, so he could run off and enjoy his night without Cell duties to distract him.

But he deserves a break. Per tradition, Semester Start was one of the few times they cancelled all patrols. After tonight, patrols would start in earnest and Gabe would work at least four nights per week in addition to leading their Cell. Emilia helped him with all the organizing, planning, and communicating as an equal, but it still was a hefty amount of Cell work and far more than Marina's.

Besides, it wasn't like Marina expected to have fun tonight. None of her friends lived in Blackwell. If she could find them, she'd tag along with Sandy and Victoria — two new freshman Warriors and fellow Blackwellians — if only to look like she belonged. Perhaps adding Lila to the mix wasn't the worst idea. After all, she and Valerie appeared to be on the rocks between Valerie missing this morning's tour and Lila declining Valerie's nomination.

Then again, it could all be a trick to convince Marina to trust Lila so Valerie and company could repeat last year's antics. No, she wouldn't trust Lila any more than she would a cobra or maybe a baby raccoon.

Clinging to that vow, Marina approached Lila in her corner. "Hey."

Lila's green eyes flashed up from her half-full plate. Her lips spread into a wide smile with a dimple in either cheek. "Hi, Marina!"

"No Valerie tonight?"

Lila slid her plate onto the brick ledge, exchanging it for a glass containing more melting ice than pop. "No, um, I think she's mad at me. You know, for not accepting the nomination."

"Yeah, why did you decline?" Marina's stomach twisted. She shouldn't have asked that. It wasn't any of her business. And Natasha would have told her so. Marina braced herself for Lila's rebuke.

But Lila only slurped up a noisy swallow through her straw, then shrugged. "Because I think I'll have enough to do figuring this place out. Plus, I didn't think it was fair. I just got here. I don't deserve to be an officer."

"To be fair, the nomination was to run for the position, not to actually get it."

Lila snorted. "Please. Even *I* could see how nominations go here."

"Yeah…" Marina stared into her lemonade.

"Are they always like that? The nominations?"

"Yeah, pretty much. Heidi and her crew run Blackwell…" Marina's voice trailed off. How much should she tell Valerie's best friend?

"And the school?" Lila guessed.

"Kinda. It's easiest if you stay out of their way." *Unless you can't because you're forced to room with one…or because one's your best friend from ages ago.* The second thought rose unbidden. It highlighted Marina's mistake. She hurried to correct it, "I mean, unless you're friends with them. Then, I mean, it's good."

The concern creasing Lila's brow deepened. "What do you —"

Clll-angg! Clll-angg! Clll-angg! Ms. Pershing shook a cow bell in front of the screen separating them from the rest of the cafeteria.

146

Marina expelled a sigh of relief. "That's the signal. Time to head to our table for dinner."

The senior and junior grade leads rolled the Eversfield-navy curtains to either side, revealing the front of the cafeteria. Like lit pearls, strings of yellow lights hung down from the lofty ceiling. Six burnished wood tables—one for each house—reflected the glow, as did the cream china emblazoned with a cursive Eversfield "E." A navy runner stretched down the center of each table. Collections of white and pink roses were gathered into crystal bowls distributed along each runner.

As the Eversfield student body flowed toward the tables, Marina glanced askance at Lila. Her green eyes had widened with awe. Surprising herself, Marina nudged a playful elbow into Lila's ribs. "You think this is something, just wait until the Masquerade Ball." She stepped over a carved bench near the end of Blackwell's table. Beside her, Lila followed suit.

"Can we join you?" Victoria hovered across from Marina, her forefinger twirling a chocolate lock. Sandy peeked behind her.

"Of course!" Marina replied—perhaps too enthusiastically—then shifted to her roommate. "Lila, have you met Victoria and Sandy? They're new just like you, only freshmen."

"N-nice to meet you, Victoria, Sandy." Lila gestured to each of them in turn as if memorizing their names. "So…how do you know Marina?"

An innocuous enough question, yet it sent Marina's heartbeat through the roof.

"Oh, um, our families are old friends." Sandy tossed a strawberry blond braid over her shoulder with an air of nonchalance. "You know how these old boarding schools are. Everyone knows everyone."

With a nod, Lila appeared to believe Sandy's lie, although her gaze pinned itself to her empty plate.

Marina searched for something for the four of them to talk about. She came up empty.

But only a few awkward moments passed before a hush spread throughout the cafeteria.

Headmaster Flynn strode along one side of the S-shaped counter facing the students. Upon reaching the wooden podium centered between the third and fourth house tables, he straightened a stack of papers waiting for him there. His sausage-like fingers adjusted his wire-rimmed glasses. Flipping the switch on the microphone, Headmaster Flynn surveyed the hundreds of upturned faces from left to right. "Welcome students, new and old, to Eversfield Preparatory Academy, your home away from home." Clapping echoed throughout the cafeteria, overwhelming even Headmaster Flynn's booming voice. He waited for it to die off, then continued, "First things first, I want to congratulate the Harriet Tubman house once again on winning Eversfield's house cup last year."

The entire Tubman table—located two over from Blackwell—erupted into cheers. At its head, president Evie Jones wrapped her fingers around the leaping trout that formed the handles of the golden trophy. She pumped it up and down with a grin that stretched from ear to ear. Her braids swung every which way.

The cowbell rang out. After two clangs, the Tubman members settled down and focused back on the headmaster.

A smile stretched Headmaster Flynn's thin lips to nothing more than rose-colored lines. "Good luck to all our houses this year. We anticipate a spirited battle in the weeks and months to come. To that end, I have a few reminders. First, if you need additional motivation — which I know you don't — the grades of each and every student count toward their house's score, as does their involvement in extracurricular activities, both in terms of quality and quantity. Of course, there are also the house trials."

"Woo!" A male voice cheered from the direction of Pasteur's table. They never won the house cup, but there were certain trials they took seriously, even if they ignored the rest.

"Yes, 'woo' indeed." Headmaster Flynn's gnarled finger pushed up his glasses. "As usual, the house trials will not begin until after midterms, but then we'll hit the ground running. For the midterm trials at the end of October, we'll have the academic competition, the flag football tournament, and the band and choral concert as usual. I'm pleased to announce that this year we've added an autumn art show to the mix. The esteemed professors of Juniper City College — which, as you all know, houses one of the best art schools in the country — have agreed to act as judges."

Polite applause reverberated off the brick walls of the cafeteria.

Headmaster Flynn stroked his white beard until it quieted down. "For the fall finale, we'll have our talent show followed by the Masquerade Ball, during which you are to make your own costumes as usual. This year, the top *ten* costumes will earn house points. How does that sound?"

Whoops and hurrahs abounded, although Marina barely clapped. If only she could focus on getting good grades and ignore the rest. At least her Cell duties counted as an extracurricular activity, thanks to the retired Diviners

149

and Warriors hidden in Eversfield's staff and school board. However, good grades and a single extracurricular activity weren't enough for Blackwell's officers, that she knew from last year. *Guess I'll have to start plotting out my talent show performance and costume now. Maybe Yuki can help me with something for that autumn art show.*

With the beginnings of a plan, Marina relaxed a bit, only to remember her assignment for the night. She glanced at Lila beside her.

Goosebumps prickled along Marina's forearms.

Lila's eyes were wide and unfocused. Her jaw was clenched.

Memories from last winter ambushed Marina. Her nails bored into the wooden bench beneath her. She was back in that car again. Gabe was the driver, she the passenger. They were heading home to visit their parents on a snowy afternoon, but the roads weren't too bad. Everything was going fine.

Then Gabe's face had become a mirror of Lila's, with that clenched jaw and unfocused gaze.

A red light loomed before them.

Gabe's foot stayed on the gas.

Marina yelled for them to stop.

Gabe didn't hear her.

They slid through the red light.

A truck barreled toward Marina.

She sucked in a breath. On instinct alone, she called — begged — for a gale to push them out of its way.

For the first time in her life, she summoned the Wind.

For the first time in her life, it answered. Her Wind saved her and maybe Gabe too. It had chosen the perfect moment to manifest.

Marina shook herself out of her memories. Now was not the time to relive that nightmare. Now was the time to focus on Lila. Could Portency be her Latent talent? And had it manifested just now?

With her gaze glued to the headmaster like nothing was amiss, Marina ran through her available Elementals one by one—Water, then Wind, then Mineral, then Floral.

And nothing *was* amiss, at least with the Elementals. Checking the Spirit-side required more effort—both in general and for Marina in particular—so she chose the easier option. Leaning toward Lila, Marina whispered below the din of excited students, "You okay, Lila?"

"H-how?" Lila's shocked stare inched toward Marina.

Marina's guts tied themselves into knots. What had Lila seen? "What do you mean?"

"H-how are we supposed to do all that?"

Marina smothered the sigh of relief. It was not Portency after all, but Eversfield-related stress, something that Marina was well-acquainted with. "Don't worry, Lila, there are close to a hundred girls in Blackwell. It's not like you have to do everything."

"Still…"

Marina opened her mouth to respond.

Clll-angg! Clll-angg! Clll-angg! Ms. Pershing's cowbell silenced all side conversations.

Behind his wooden podium, Headmaster Flynn raised both gnarled hands. "All right. I don't want to keep you away from your dinner and your houses any longer. Without further ado, the Eversfield Preparatory Academy Fall Semester has commenced!"

Waiters and waitresses in stark black and white uniforms approached the tables with loaded trays held high above their heads. Marina's sophomore year began.

CHAPTER 15

VAL

Drey and Elsie followed on Val's heels as she scurried back to Lizzie. Semester Start dinner had been ash in Val's mouth. Lila was supposed to be by her side, not sitting all the way at the end of Lizzie's table next to Marina and those *freshmen*. And it wasn't even Val's fault! She'd kept her end of the bargain. She'd had Lila's nomination—and election—as Lizzie's secretary locked up. But no, Lila went and ruined it, along with any path to an officer position next year. Now Elsie—boring, mousy Elsie— was secretary instead of the lovely Lila.

On either side, Val's fingers tightened into a fist of determination. She'd just have to make this work. There was no *requirement* that all their sophomore members also be house officers. Sara was the only one of their junior members to hold an officer position, so Val and Drey should be more than enough for the sophomores. Things would be a little harder, that was all. Perhaps a challenge. And if there was one thing Valerie Elizabeth Baker loved, it was a challenge.

Together, Val and Drey burst through the heavy front doors of Elizabeth Blackwell. Elsie trailed in their wake. In the middle of the cluttered lobby, Val assessed the destruction of the Semester Start meeting. When Elsie approached with cautious steps, Val waved at the navy armchairs set askew, then to the lone coffee tables speckling the wide hall. "Elsie, you put the chairs back while Drey and I prepare for the Writing Wall ceremony."

Like a well-trained dog, Elsie hurried past Lizzie's grand spiral staircase, wrapped her arms around a bulky chair, and hefted it up. She and the chair stumbled toward the nearest coffee table.

Drey's shoulder bumped against Val's. Her hazel eyes narrowed, bright with displeasure. "As nominated vice president, *Val*, I'll be giving the orders from now on."

Rage unfurled within her, but Val only shrugged. "Sorry, didn't mean to overstep there. Did you want Elsie to do something else?"

"No."

Of course not. Giving Elsie the heavy lifting made sense. In fact, maybe Lila's refusal was for the best. Having a minion within the ranks could benefit the rest of Lizzie's officers — soon to be herself, Sara, and Drey. "And should I do something other than prep the carts for the Writing Wall?"

"No."

Val wrapped an arm around Drey's waist. Her forearm brushed against Drey's tulle skirt. "Well there ya go, Drey. Everything's fine. And don't worry, I'll sit in the back just like I should from now on." *When you're paying attention.*

"Good." Drey wriggled out of Val's embrace, then led the way to Ms. van Straten's office. The door beneath the twisting glass staircase was cracked open, although old van Straten herself was nowhere to be found.

Probably indulging in all the dessert the eye can see, Val thought as she entered the office behind Drey. On the far side, two empty carts huddled beside a potted palm that reached for the floor-to-ceiling windows. A cardboard box nearly as long as Val was tall rested on the floor in front of the metal carts.

Careful of her tight skirt, Val lowered herself to sit on her heels in front of the box. She opened it. There, paper towel rolls cushioned rows of plastic spray bottles. Val wiggled a bottle out and held it to the light shining through the windows. A neon yellow liquid filled it to the brim.

With a quick count, Val verified that all Sara had requested was accounted for. While she transferred the spray bottles to the carts' top shelves and the paper towels to the bottom shelves, Drey dragged three ladders out of the coat closet. One by one, she leaned them against the gleaming wall outside Ms. van Straten's office door.

By the time Val and Drey rolled the carts out of the office — Val getting stuck with the one with squeaky wheels — the rest of Lizzie had gathered in the open area just past the Writing Wall. All but one of the armchairs had returned to the conversation nooks spaced along the hallway. Hardworking as a honeybee, Elsie zigzagged through the crowd to collect the lone remaining chair.

Perfect. Val had just enough time to retrieve Lila before the ceremony began. Excitement brewing within her, Val searched for Lila's curly head.

When she found it, she frowned. Tucked just inside the doors on the fringe of the crowd, Lila chatted with Marina and the same two freshmen from dinner, neither of which had any hope of becoming a Lizzard.

Looks like I have to save Lila from herself. Again. Val parked her cart in the middle of the hallway across from the Writing Wall. Acknowledging greetings from brownnosers with curt nods, Val cut through the crowd.

A stride or two behind Lila, she pulled her lips into a grin as large and grand as anything in Elizabeth Blackwell.

Val kept her tone cheerful, as if nothing had happened before dinner. "Hello, Lila dear!"

The conversation broke off.

Lila whipped around to face Val. "Oh, uh, hi Val."

Ignoring Lila's lack of enthusiasm, Val tilted her head back toward the cart stationed behind the mass of Lizzards and Blackwellians. "You mind helping me with something really quick?"

"Sure, I guess," trusty Lila agreed, then waved goodbye to the others. "See you later, Marina, Sandy, Victoria."

No you won't, Val vowed. *Except for Marina, but that can't be helped.* Val led Lila back to the cart, her lips clenched into a grim line of determination that Lila couldn't see. When they reached the cart, Val was as sunny as ever. Angling herself toward Lila, she gestured to the full cart. "See, Lila dear, our job tonight will be to pass these out."

Lila's brows furrowed. "For house bonding, we're...cleaning?"

"Not for all of it, Lila dear, but to start, yes." Val's hand fluttered toward the wall of scribbles, scratches, and sketches towering behind Lila. "You didn't think we could let that stay as it is, did you?"

Lila twisted around. Her jaw dropped. Before her stretched the Writing Wall, a bedazzling prism of colors, words, and designs that clashed with Lizzie's otherwise sophisticated decor. It spanned almost twenty feet in any direction.

How Lila hadn't noticed it earlier, Val would never know. "Pretty cool, huh?"

Her mouth still agape, Lila nodded.

156

Val checked over her shoulder. Heidi chatted with a few senior Lizzards. Based on the way her hands flew about, she wouldn't begin the ceremony for several minutes.

With a mischievous smile, Val grabbed Lila's hand and dragged her to the Writing Wall. In one section—an inch or two away from center and eye level with Val—swirling cerulean lines masked a cursive *shitastic*. The lines infected nearby designs, including a tangerine game of hangman, a neon portrait of the courtyard, a calligraphic *studying is for sissies*, and a dinosaur cartoon complete with spotted crest and sad, I'm-going-extinct eyes. After those, Val's lines tailed off, not quite reaching the scarlet *MG + LV*.

Her eyes shining, Val pointed toward the *shitastic*. "I put that up there this summer, when I found out you qualified for a scholarship, but there were no open spots."

Lila's face twisted with guilt. "I'm sorry about today, Val. For the record, I *am* happy to be here with you, even if I struggle to show it. It's just…the nomination was too much."

Val squeezed Lila's hand. "I know. Or at least I should have. I'm sorry I didn't share my plans with you beforehand. But we're hanging out tonight, right?"

"Of course, but I—"

"May I have your attention please?" Heidi's melodious voice rang out from the front of the assembly.

All chatting ceased with the obedience Heidi demanded. Val returned to the cart with Lila trailing behind her.

Standing beneath a chandelier that acted as a spotlight, Heidi spread her wine-red lips into a broad smile. Her white teeth shone. "Our last activity before we retire to house bonding tonight is our biannual Writing Wall cleanse. The Writing Wall exists for us to express our creativity, to vent our frustrations, to celebrate our victories, to document our hopes and dreams if only in a single image. It also exists as a reminder. *This* is a new semester. Time to make new friends and new sisters. Time to ace new classes. Time to win back our trophy!" Heidi raised her hand in a fist.

Whoops of support echoed through the hall.

When she lowered her hand, everyone quieted.

"Lastly, we move on from last semester. As of this moment, we forgive ourselves for last semester's mistakes. We forgive each other for last semester's arguments. And while we don't forget last semester's triumphs, we turn our attention to this semester's battles waiting to be won. We take this time to cleanse our Writing Wall and ourselves. To prepare for a better future. To get ready for a kick-ass semester!"

Cheers flooded the lobby of Elizabeth Blackwell. Val yelled as loudly as anyone, but Lila stared at the crowd with her mouth clamped shut.

Val elbowed her.

Lila jumped. Her green gaze shot to Val. Widening her eyes, Val gestured for Lila to join the uproar. Lila chewed on her lower lip with her brows furrowed, but after a moment of debate, she joined the rest of Lizzie.

When the hurrahs lessened in both number and volume, Val strode to Heidi's side. She wrapped her arm around Heidi's belted waist and leaned her head against Heidi's shoulder. "Thanks for that stirring speech, Heidi." After a final squeeze, Val placed her hands on her hips and faced her fellow Lizzards and Blackwellians. "Let's get to work. Everyone, get into groups of four or five. Each group gets a spray bottle and a roll of paper towel. Then find an area and start cleaning!" Val pointed at her cart with Lila standing sentry over it. "You can get supplies from Lila and me or from Sara and Drey *way* over there."

By the front doors, one of two antlike figures crossed her arms next to a full cart.

Val squashed a smirk. Drey had to be at least pouting — maybe even seething — at her "accidental" takeover of the Writing Wall ceremony. *Oops, so much for taking a back seat.* "And there are ladders outside Ms. van Straten's office for those who need them. Let's go!" Val flounced toward the cart and Lila, trusting the crowd to follow her.

They did.

An instant before the horde of students could demand cleaning supplies, Val whispered to Lila, "Make sure we get rid of all these. If we run out, we don't have to clean!"

And get rid of them they did. Not five minutes later, Val and Lila stood in front of an empty cart. All their spray bottles and paper towels were dispersed among the cleaning students.

Val directed the remaining groups to Sara and Drey's cart, then laced her arm through Lila's. "I'm so glad you're here, Lila dear." Val guided them to watch — er, *supervise* — the Writing Wall cleanse.

"Me too." Lila's hand waved toward the Writing Wall towering above them. Spots of stark white already appeared amid the rainbow of scribbles and doodles. "This is really cool, even for someone like me with no artistic talent whatsoever."

"That it is." Val elbowed Lila. "Maybe later tonight we'll sneak back down here and you can decorate it with the initials of that crush of yours."

Lila groaned.

Val's grin spread from ear to ear. "I hear it's good luck."

"Ugh, fine. Maybe in a week or two once things have calmed down. *And* the Writing Wall has more than a few designs to hide it in. *Maybe.*"

"'Maybe' it is." *For now.* Turning a maybe into a yes was one of Val's specialties.

Once the Writing Wall had returned to a solid white expanse, Val and Lila collected the spray bottles and half-used paper towel rolls while Elsie ran around with a garbage bag picking up the trash. By the time they wheeled the carts into Ms. van Straten's office, the crowd had moved on to the two common rooms at the opposite end of the hall.

Facing the mass of students, Heidi directed traffic with Sara and Drey stationed on either side of Louie's frosted glass door. Most members of Elizabeth Blackwell shuffled through the open, unguarded door of Beechy, where snacks, movies, and board games awaited them. A select few entered Louie. Sara and Drey closed the door behind each one.

Val puffed out her chest as she and Lila approached. Despite the disaster of Lila's failed nomination, none of them would object to Lila's admittance, not with Val by her side. Tonight would have to mend the fences snapped by Lila's mistake, though.

As expected, Heidi pointed them toward Louie. An obedient Sara opened the door for them, but her tomato-red lips curved downward. Her frown confirmed Val's suspicions.

But Val didn't allow it to distract her. Once Louie's door clicked shut, she spread her arms wide. Hiding her unease behind enthusiasm brighter than the summer sun, she announced, "All right, Lila dear, here we are. Time for house bonding!"

Lila's gaze swept over the room, at least half of which was taken up by three treadmills, two stationary bikes, and one elliptical machine. Her brows furrowed. "Shouldn't we move all the exercise stuff if we're gonna have a dance party or whatever?"

Her spirits higher than ever, Val hooked her arm through Lila's. She loved surprises, especially when she was the one in the know. "The dance party isn't *here*, silly."

"What?" What should have been an excited grin was a grimace.

"It's not here," Val repeated, then gestured toward the opposite wall of floor-to-ceiling windows.

There, a dozen or so Lizzards gathered. Current treasurer Sofia unlatched one panel of windows. Under her careful hands, it swung soundlessly up and open. Cat—Lizzie's secretary whom Elsie would replace—delivered a wooden chair to Sofia, then took a second one out the door. Elsie dragged a wide plank out of the closet and across the room. Its bottom edge scuffed the hardwood floor. *Guess that's a problem for the janitors later tonight.*

Lila saw it all, but still her frown didn't budge. "Where is it, if not here?"

At last, Val understood. Lila thought they were going *out* out. That explained her hesitation. Val squeezed Lila's upper arm. "Don't worry, we're just goin' to the gym. The Eversfield staff always transfers the leftovers there while a bunch of us sneak out."

"Why all the secrecy then?"

"It's more fun this way, that's all. Besides, this party isn't for simply *anyone*. And Pasteur always arranges it, so

I'm not sure how far up the knowledge goes." When Lila squirmed, Val rushed to amend, "I mean, Lila dear, it almost certainly goes up all the way up to Flynn! No one would risk their cushy job here at Eversfield for a bunch of students to go have a li'l innocent fun."

"Val, I—"

Before Lila could finish her sentence—and maybe bail on her—Val tugged her toward the wall of windows with a single open panel. "Oh, look, we're ready to go! The plank's through the window, over the hedge, and resting on a chair outside. Time to climb on through!"

Lila opened her mouth, gulping air like a fish out of water.

Val's index finger hovered in front of her glossy lips. "Remember, Lila dear, we are s-n-e-a-k, sneaking our way out. We hafta be quiet."

Grabbing Lila's hand, Val pulled her toward the front of the line, just in time to witness Heidi climb through the window on her hands and knees. Midway down the wooden board, a gust of wind pushed her skirt up over her thick thighs.

A pair of fuchsia undies flashed for all to see.

Val's idol, Heidi shot a grin over her bare shoulder and wiggled her hips at them. Then she flicked her flowery skirt back in place and continued her crawl.

As soon as Heidi stood on the ground outside Lizzie, Sara mounted the plank. When Sofia, Cat, and Drey each stepped forward, Val tucked herself and Lila into the open space, cutting in front of the rest of the line. No one dared to complain.

Sara, Sofia, and Cat all passed through the open window without incident. While Drey crawled along the wooden board, Val whispered in Lila's ear, "You ready? It's almost our turn."

Lila stared at her clenched fingers. "I dunno, Val. It's already kinda late, and I have those placement exams tomorrow."

"Lila, you promised." In Val's chest, a kernel of fury expanded in the heat of yet another refusal from Lila.

"And *you* said it was house bonding."

"It is!"

"You two goin' or not?" A freshman—Hayden if Val recalled correctly from Sara's list of "prospectives"—interrupted. The toe of her strappy sandal tapped in Val's direction.

"Yes, we're going, okay?" Val ushered Lila toward the plank.

Lila's feet stuck to the ground like it was quicksand. "Val, I really should—"

"I'm gonna go if you're not." Her dyed blond hair cascading down her back, Hayden moved to step in front of Val.

Not so fast. Val blocked her path and growled, "Hold on one hot second."

Glossed lips the color of raspberries flattened into a thin line, but Hayden backed off.

A wise decision, Hayden. Val turned back to Lila. Clasping both Lila's hands, Val widened her eyes, mimicking an innocent doe. "Lila, you *promised* we could hang out tonight."

"I know, but…" Lila tossed her head like a rebellious horse. "Fine, I guess it's not too late. But I can't stay out long."

We'll see about that. "Deal. And remember—"

"I know. Starting this Friday, you're gonna dress me up and make me stay out late. Got it."

Ignoring Hayden's tap-tap-tapping behind them, Val extended a hand toward the plank. "You first, Lila dear."

Lila climbed onto the chair. One careful knee, then the other pressed into the board. Lila crushed her marigold skirt against her thighs, then placed her palms on the plank.

Before Lila could crawl forward, one of Elsie's hands darted up from the wooden panel. "Hey, um, Lila? I just...I just want to thank you."

The board creaked as Lila twisted around to glance over her shoulder. "For what?"

"For declining your nomination. It would've been yours if you'd taken it."

Lila turned from Elsie to creep down the plank. "Yeah, well, I'm sure you'll be great. Um, I guess I'll see you there."

Elsie's pale eyes grew wide while she steadied the board beneath Lila's shifting weight. "Oh, no, I'm not going. I'm just supposed to help you guys, clean up, then go back to Beecher and play games and stuff."

A foot away from the open window, Lila hesitated.

Val's heart leapt into her throat. What would she do if Lila bailed on her here, in front of everyone?

But Lila crawled forward and passed through the open window.

The night's adventure began.

CHAPTER 16

G abe lowered the final crate of two-liter bottles to the gym floor, nestling it between the others tucked beneath the refreshment tables. When he rose, he surveyed the result of Pasteur's house bonding.

In the corner beside the main entrance was a dance floor outlined by speakers and Darius's DJ table. From there, the games took over: first corn hole, then air hockey, table tennis, and foosball. In the far corner, clusters of flat-screen monitors displayed video game options in front of a motley collection of bean bags and oversized pillows. Between those and the main entrance, folding tables overflowed with drinks, appetizers, and desserts — leftovers from Semester Start. While they'd spread their common room couches and armchairs throughout the gym, "borrowed" Snack Station cocktail tables and bar chairs formed a quarter-circle facing Gabe and the refreshments.

Only one thing was missing: the Pasteur stage. With hauling everything from their common room into the gym, they'd run out of time to dismantle it, let alone set it back up.

And that tied Gabe up into knots. In one of those visions that he couldn't forget, *she'd* sung on Pasteur's stage. Relief that a vision wouldn't come true tonight should course through his veins, yet disappointment hung like an anvil around his neck.

Gabe ignored it. Lila Lee was nothing to him, just a girl he had to monitor as a potential Latent, nothing more.

Gabe's rebellious eyes swept over the early arrivals scattered throughout the gym. As expected, they were all members of Mistral or Tecumseh. He joined a group of his Pasteur housemates, keeping the main entrance in his peripheral vision.

When curls the color of black coffee bounced through the double doors, his stomach flipped.

A moment later, it sunk. A short skirt and wine-red lips accompanied those curls. Heidi had arrived with three of her Blackwell cronies trailing behind her. An impulse to run away from it all — to lose himself in video games — itched at Gabe's fingers and toes. But as a member of Pasteur, he was obligated to greet those he knew. And Heidi qualified as that, even if it had been a while.

Gabe weaved between the empty cocktail tables to arrive at the main entrance. Not quite ready to play host, he shoved his hands into the pockets of his shorts, although his voice was warm and welcoming. "Hey, Heidi, nice of you to come, and with all your Blackwell buddies."

A fine eyebrow arching, Heidi looked him up and down. "You changed."

Gabe narrowed his eyes. Something was off with her. Not that she was wrong. After Semester Start, he'd dashed back to his room and changed into a T-shirt and shorts. But for the past year, Heidi had ignored his existence — something he hadn't minded in the least. "Yup."

Heidi lurched forward.

Gabe caught her in his arms based on instincts alone.

A flirtatious hazel gaze met his. "Sorry, tripped on something." Heidi straightened, but her hands remained clasped around his forearms. In her inches-high heels, she was tall enough to whisper in his ear, "You look good, Gabe. And I mean goooooood."

166

Gabe cleared his throat and stepped away, but Heidi didn't release him. "Um, thank you, Heidi."

"C'mon, let's chat. We haven't done that in ever so long." Heidi's fingers trailed down Gabe's forearm, then wriggled between his fingers.

Gabe's lips pressed into a thin line as Heidi half-dragged, half-led him to a couch at the far end of the video game area. It was a two-seater and more secluded than Gabe would like.

Heidi pulled him down with her. She folded toned legs beneath her, leaned forward, and glanced up at him through long lashes. It was an expression he remembered well.

"Heidi…" Gabe warned.

Holding it level with her chest, Heidi started massaging the hand she'd captured. "Gabe, we were so good together. Why'd you have to go and ruin it?"

Gabe ripped his hand away. Heidi pouted, but it meant nothing to him. This was just another game of hers. Back then, he'd looked forward to playing. Not anymore.

Gabe thought about reminding Heidi about the truth of their past. Reminding her that they weren't good together. Reminding her that to call them as ever having been "together" was a stretch. But on the off chance Heidi wasn't playing, he should be gentle. "Heidi, aren't you seeing someone right now?"

Heidi flopped backward, her back arching over the arm of the sofa. "No, not anymore. As of last night, he wants to see other people. Other *girls*."

Gabe hauled her back into a seated position. "Heidi, Heidi, not so loud. Unless you want everyone to know about you and Joe?"

Heidi crossed her arms around her chest, emphasizing the cleavage poking out of the low neckline of her dress. Her

167

eyes flashed up to see if Gabe had noticed. When his gaze didn't so much as flick downward, Heidi sighed. "There is no me and Joe. Not anymore." A finger topped with a teal nail traced the collar of Gabe's T-shirt. "There could be a you and me, though. For old time's sake?"

"Heidi, there was hardly an old time to begin with." Gabe stopped her wandering fingers and placed them in her lap.

Heidi returned to pouting. "What are you talking about? We dated for like six months."

"I wouldn't count what we were doing dating."

Heidi's lips spread into a mischievous smile. "But it was fun, wasn't it?"

"Yes, it was."

His admission — his mistake — emboldened her. A hand darted toward the back of Gabe's neck, reaching for him.

Gabe was too fast for her. He ducked out of Heidi's hold and used the movement to get off the couch and squat beside her. "Why don't I go get you a pop and maybe a cupcake or two?"

Heidi sighed as she stretched her legs out over the loveseat. "Okay, but get diet. And no cupcakes."

With a nod, Gabe turned on his heel, grateful for the escape. Three steps toward the drink table, his foot hovered in mid-air. Another set of dark curls waited in line, these ones less tamed and a shade or two lighter. Beneath them was a yellow knee-length dress.

Gabe's stomach somersaulted.

CHAPTER 17

LILA

Val chattered the entire way to the gym, but Lila didn't register one word. She was too busy dreading her future. The closer she got to the gym and its party, the more Lila wanted to hole up in her room. But Val would never let her.

Lila followed in Val's footsteps through the double doors into the gym, past the gaggle of boys who greeted them, straight for the group of four girls chatting on the outskirts of an empty dance floor. Two Lila identified as Sara and Drey from Lizzie's officer nominations, but she didn't recognize the other two.

"Everyone, pay attention!" Val wrapped an arm around Lila's shoulders and squeezed. "This is my dearest friend in the whole wide world, Miss Lila Lee. And Lila, this is simply everyone!"

If not for an attack of the killer butterflies, Lila might have rolled her eyes at the usefulness of Val's introduction. Instead, she mobilized her waning courage and flung her hand toward the lithe blonde front and center. With her brightest smile and most cheerful voice, Lila greeted the leader of the pack. "Hi, it's Sara, right?"

"Yes, nice to meet you." Sara's monotone implied the opposite. When they shook hands, Sara's hand was limp in Lila's. Her bored expression didn't budge an inch.

Next to Sara, a girl with flaming locks extended a hand toward Lila. A wide smile accentuated her heart-shaped face with its pointy chin. "And I'm Rudi."

At least one of them might like me. After shaking Rudi's hand, Lila shifted toward the brunettes lurking behind Sara and Rudi. Both inspected her from head to toe. From Val's earlier descriptions, Lila guessed the identity of the remaining stranger before her. "And you're Cheri?"

Cheri's gilded earrings swung back and forth as she nodded. She did not offer the traditional handshake.

Lila stilled her twitching fingers against her skirt. Her gaze switched to the girl beside Cheri, the one who would become Lizzie's vice president. "And you're Drey?"

Drey mimicked Sara's lifeless tone and expression. "Audrey, technically. But yes, I go by Drey." When she turned away from Lila and toward Sara, Drey's voice bounced with energy. "Anyway, Sara, you were saying? About the talent show?"

Lila's ears perked. The talent show was months away, but it didn't hurt to start planning early. Besides, the sooner she found a way out of it, the sooner she could ignore its existence.

Before Sara could respond, however, Val asked, "Where's Heidi?"

Sara rolled her eyes. Her chin jerked toward something behind Lila. "Backtracking."

Lila glanced over her shoulder. Near the far wall, Heidi cuddled on a secluded loveseat with none other than Gabe. A wave of disappointment crashed over Lila.

She forced herself to look away from the happy couple. Why did she care if Gabe and Heidi were getting back together? She'd never stood a chance with him anyway. No, Gabe was nothing more than her roommate's friendly older brother, that was all. Lila flushed all thoughts of him from her mind.

But it didn't work. No matter how she tried to listen to Val and her friends' discussion, images of what could be happening on that couch distracted her. When their conversation lulled, Lila gave up. "I'm gonna go get something to drink. Anyone need anything?"

A smirking Sara lifted her glass, half-full of a brown fizzy liquid. The others followed suit, all except Val...and Rudi.

"I'll take some Sprite, Lila dear. Perhaps with a li'l grenadine if they've got it?"

"Diet Coke with a squeeze of lime juice for me, please. Just tell Eli over there it's for Rudi—he knows my order." Rudi winked a heavily lined, heavily mascaraed eye. "And thanks for offerin', Lila."

"No problem." Lila turned on her heel. On her way to the refreshment area, she dodged a knee-high speaker, then a slouchy couch, and finally the blond cocktail tables with their clumps of happy, chattering, gesticulating students. The entire time, her gaze avoided that faraway loveseat like a starship avoiding a black hole. Since she wouldn't allow herself to think about *that*, Lila obsessed over the impossible task set before her. Based on her "welcome," befriending Val's clique would be an uphill battle, one for which she was ill-suited.

At the back of the line snaking away from the drinks table, Lila rubbed one flat against the toe of the other. Her fingers itched to poke at her phone, maybe google "how to make friends out of enemies" or something stupid like that. At the very least, she could look busy as the lone loser in this queue of couples, trios, and quartets.

A hand brushed against the small of Lila's back.

She jumped. When she flipped around, the butterflies nesting in her stomach rampaged.

A lock of inky hair fell into ice-blue eyes. Full lips formed a crooked smile. It lit up a too-handsome face. *Gabe.*

He gestured toward the table. "C'mon. Friends of mine don't wait in line."

The fingers of Gabe's opposite hand lingered against the small of her back, hot through her dress's thin material. They pressed her forward. With no small amount of guilt at cutting to the front, Lila stumbled toward the table, Gabe at her side. She wiped her clammy palms against her skirt. Her heart thundered in her chest.

Gabe moved behind the drinks table, one hand reaching for a plastic cup. "What can I get for you, Lila?"

The sound of her name exiting Gabe's lips muddied Lila's mind. She tugged at a curl, pulling it straight then releasing it to bounce upward while she hunted for Val's and Rudi's orders. "Oh, um…First, a Sprite. With some grenadine?"

Gabe nodded. With hardly a glance away from her, he combined the ice, Sprite, and grenadine into a transparent cup. "For Val, right?"

"Yeah, how did you know?"

"Just a hunch. Val always likes the sugary stuff."

Between that comment, Gabe's dating history, and yesterday's hint of drama between Marina and Val, Lila wondered how well he and Val knew each other. And whether that was a good thing.

As Gabe finished the pink-hued drink, Rudi's order popped into Lila's mind. "Oh, and, um…" Lila leaned over the table to whisper to Gabe. Her head tilted toward the guy next to him. "Is that Eli?"

Gabe's gaze narrowed. "Yeah, why?"

Ignoring his question, Lila straightened and summoned her bravery once again. Eli handed three full cups to the trio beside her. Before he could shift to the next in line, Lila called to him, "Hey, um, Eli?"

He raised chocolate brown eyes as gentle as a cow's. "Yeah?"

"Rudi said you'd know her order?"

"Oh, yeah, *Rudi*." Eli's straight white teeth shone in a wide smile. He selected a two liter of Diet Coke and a squeeze bottle in the shape and color of a lime.

Gabe slid Val's cup toward him, along with a can of pop. "Eli, when you're done, can you deliver Val's and Rudi's drinks? And get this Diet Coke to Heidi? And…try to keep her amused, okay? I can handle the table for a bit."

Grinning from ear to ear, Eli squeezed lime juice into Rudi's drink. The liquid popped and fizzled. "No problem."

Her mind tossing and turning over Eli's assignment from Gabe, Lila fumbled over her protest, "Oh, um, Eli, you don't have to do that. I can take Val's and Rudi's drinks."

Eli brandished the full cups. Val's pink drink kissed the rim but didn't spill. "Nonsense…and it's Lila, right?"

A confused Lila nodded.

"Well, Lila, you don't know this yet, but we at Pasteur live to serve." Eli bowed with a full cup grasped in either hand. From the bottom, his brown eyes flashed up at Lila, full of mirth.

For the first time in forever, Lila relaxed a smidge. A giggle or two even escaped her.

Gabe lightly cuffed the back of Eli's head. "Just deliver those drinks, Eli."

Eli straightened and saluted. Rudi's drink splashed near the edge of its cup. "Your wish is my command." After tucking Heidi's can of pop under an elbow, Eli strode away, leaving Lila alone with Gabe.

His hawklike gaze pinned her in place. Her breath stuck in her chest.

"So, Lila, what would you like this fine evening?"

Like a trapped animal, Lila sought to distract him. Her head tilted toward the line beside her. "Shouldn't you take care of them?"

"Nah." Gabe turned toward the queue. Waving toward the clusters of cups, cans, and two-liter bottles, he announced, "Help yourselves."

Without hesitation, the line broke up. Couples, trios, and quartets gathered around the opposite half of the table, their hands already reaching for supplies.

Lila grasped one last shred of hope. "Listen, if you need to get back to Heidi—"

"Why would I need to get back to her?"

A flush blossomed over the apples of Lila's cheeks. "Oh, um, I...it looked like...but I guess not. Anyway, um, I guess I'll take a root beer if that's okay?"

"'Course it's okay." Gabe's lips formed a wry smile. "Like Eli said, we at Pasteur live to serve. Can or over ice?"

"Just the can is fine."

With a single hand Gabe grasped two cans of root beer, then rounded the edge of the table to stand at her side. After handing Lila her drink, he gestured around the gym, from the dance floor to the cornhole platforms to the flat-screen monitors displaying live video games. "What do you think of your first Pasteur party?"

Lila examined the top of her pop can, avoiding that heart-stopping, mind-muddling stare of his. Her index finger traced the outline of the tab. "My first Pasteur party? You say it like there'll be others."

"Oh, there will be. Once you come to one, you can't stay away from the rest."

"Well, I guess…it's nice." Lila sipped her root beer.

Gabe's hand dashed to his chest in mock horror. "Nice? You think it's *nice*? No, no, no, that won't do."

"What do you mean?"

"You'll see." Gabe turned on his heel. Skirting the edge of the cocktail table maze, he headed toward the games spaced along the gym's opposite wall. When she didn't follow, he called over his shoulder, "You comin'?"

"Yeah, but…" Lila hurried to Gabe. "Don't you have to mind the drink table?"

"Believe me, it can take care of itself. That's one of the jobs we give to the freshmen to keep 'em busy." Gabe glanced down at her. "Now, what's your poison? Foosball? Air hockey?"

Dread at embarrassing herself smothered Lila's butterflies. "I'm terrible at both of those."

"Lucky for you, I'm an *excellent* teacher."

While Lila struggled to find a response, a girl in a worn T-shirt and ripped skinny jeans intercepted them. Ebony waves bounced around an oval face with almond eyes, a button nose, and pouty lips. A hand with neatly trimmed nails settled on Gabe's bare forearm. "Can we chat?" Her dark gaze surveyed Lila. "Unless you're *busy*…"

Something about the way she said "busy" made Lila want to flee. This time, she obeyed the urge. Before Gabe could reply, Lila answered for him, "No, he's not. See you later." Lila retreated, all but running away.

Whoever that was, whatever was going on, it didn't involve her. Gabe was dangerous. He was too nice, too handsome, with too many girls swirling around him. *He isn't for me*, Lila reminded herself for the umpteenth time.

When Lila arrived at the dance floor, her low spirits plummeted. Val and her friends had each paired off with a boy, leaving Lila utterly alone. Val didn't even notice her, nuzzling into some guy's chest while a slow song played over the speakers.

Gulping down the rest of her drink, Lila rushed toward the double doors she'd entered not even an hour ago. She threw the empty can in the recycling bin next to the exit, then left her first Eversfield party a total and complete failure.

Her stomach churned. Whether it was from too much pop too fast, Val's desertion for the second time in a single day, or…*him*, Lila had no idea. Only one thing was certain: it was time for bed.

CHAPTER 18

GABE

Gabe squashed his frown. Emilia and their Cell could wait this one time. After all, hadn't he called Emilia this morning and *she'd* been the one too busy? Not that it mattered. Lila had blown away like a dandelion fluff on a summer breeze.

But he didn't care. He'd only been checking on the potential Latent.

Emilia grabbed Gabe's elbow and tugged him into an empty corner behind the foosball, air hockey, and table tennis games. "Sorry 'bout bein' busy earlier. Turns out there's a lot more work bein' a Tubman officer than I thought. But don't worry. I know my priorities."

"It's okay, Emilia." Gabe offered her a weak smile, though he felt no joy. Emilia reminded him of the weight on his shoulders, something he'd buried in his subconscious for the party. Now he had to face it. Last night had been their first patrol of the year and already things had gone haywire. *Well, there's no use beating around the bush.*

"So…" Gabe licked his lips as he struggled to start this uncomfortable conversation. "Last night was weird, right? First, our Cull's activated without a whiff of Bloodlust, despite being alone in the state reserve."

"And before that, there was that weird restlessness I called you about. Almost like…I dunno, we knew the Cull was comin'."

"Okay, yeah…" Gabe's fingers pressed against his closed eyes. "You're right, first there was that weird restlessness, then activated Cull without Bloodlust, something that *should* only happen in a crowd and never in an empty forest. Then—and this is where I screwed up—I practically stepped on top of *one* without a hint of Bloodlust to warn me."

Emilia placed a calm hand on his forearm. "You didn't screw up, Gabe. Maybe you coulda been a li'l more careful, but we rely on our Bloodlust to tell us where *they* are. Without it…" Her gaze scrunched as she grew reflective. "Without it, any of us could be surprised. At least till we adapt."

"I guess." Despite Emilia's reassurances, Gabe wasn't convinced she, Simon, or any senior Warrior would make such a rookie mistake.

"And then what happened?" Emilia prompted.

"Well, like I said, there was no Bloodlust, so I assumed what we were hearing was an animal eating its kill. Then I saw the body. That was when the Bloodlust struck."

"Which was almost too late."

Shame and residual fear engulfed Gabe. The confession pressed against his clenched lips. His voice trembled over it. "It would have been, Emilia, if not for Teddi."

Emilia drew a deep breath, then squeezed his arm. "And that's why we patrol in pairs at the very least. What happened next?"

"After Teddi killed it, I thought I saw movement, I dunno, maybe fifty feet away. My Bloodlust agreed. At first, I thought it was left over from the fight and that the movement was Marius returning to us. But then—"

"Hold on a sec. Marius returning to us?"

The heels of Gabe's hands rubbed against his fatigued eyes. It had been a long night and longer day, something he'd only managed to forget in the face of a party. Now exhaustion hit him like a ton of bricks. "Yes. When it attacked, he ran away, leaving Teddi and me on our own."

Emilia's almond eyes widened. "That's gonna be a problem."

"Yes. Tomorrow I'll contact his Troupe, check on what kind of training he had with them. Ideally, he should have seen one killed before, even if from a safe distance."

"Either way, to just up and leave like that..."

"Emilia, believe me, I know. Maybe for now we can pair him with one of our seniors? Maybe with Simon?"

"Maybe...I mean, Simon's not the best teacher, but Simon can keep him safe and Marius should know that."

Emilia's words sliced through Gabe's battered heart. Yes, Simon was the better choice. Simon would not have almost gotten them all killed, whether Marius fled or not. In fact, Marius probably would have stayed to fight if he had the same confidence in Gabe's abilities as in Simon's. "Okay, so when I make this week's schedule, I'll include Simon in all of Marius's shifts. Fair warning: the change might mean you and I have to take on extra patrols."

Emilia shrugged. "That's fine. Now, do you wanna talk to Marius or should I?"

"No, it should come from me. I don't want Marius to think everyone's talking about him. While I'm at it, I'll find Simon tomorrow so he knows what's going on."

"Sounds good." Emilia leaned against the brick wall with her arms crossed. The dimmed light shone on biceps and triceps that were the product of their all-but-daily Warrior workouts. "Back to last night. You thought the movement in the forest was Marius returnin'?"

Gabe's fingers combed through his tousled hair. "Yeah, that's what I thought, but then Marius joined us from the opposite direction. It was weird, Emilia. My Bloodlust stayed active for nearly an *hour* after the fight. It seemed to pull me toward where I'd seen the movement, but that could've been my imagination."

"What about Teddi and Marius?"

"Their Bloodlust stayed active too, though I'm not sure for how long. Unfortunately, they're both too inexperienced to follow its pull, so we can't know whether what I felt was real."

"Okay, so…" Emilia laced her fingers behind her head. "The Marius thing aside, seems like our Bloodlust got messed up last night. First it was missin' from activated Cull in an empty forest, then it didn't warn you till it was almost too late. Then it stuck around way longer than usual."

"Yes."

"All right…" With her front teeth worrying her lower lip, Emilia stared past all their carefree classmates. "I guess the timing of your Bloodlust was just late, but that doesn't explain why the rest of us only got activated Cull."

"Maybe the body triggered it?"

"Yeah, I guess." Despite her words, Emilia's dark brows remained furrowed. "But why did your Bloodlust stick around after the fight?"

"I mean…maybe that pull I felt was right. Maybe there was another one out there. It's possible it didn't have enough time to attack the three of us before you and the others arrived."

"Your Bloodlust was *that* strong?"

Gabe's forehead wrinkled in thought. Encountering more than one member of the Indestructible was rare. When it happened, they were almost always in a group, not two unrelated individuals. "No, I...I wouldn't say it was that strong. If I didn't know better, I'd say it's like when we sense one in Juniper. You know, a sense of the general area, but not a distinct individual. Maybe that means there was one far away?"

Emilia nodded, her chocolate waves swinging with the movement. "Yeah, that could be. Your Bloodlust'd be extra sensitive after fightin' one."

"True." Gabe's spirits began to lift. Although he had no wish for multiple of *them* in his territory, Warriors relied on their Bloodlust. If it wasn't working properly, it would spell danger for them all—something that last night proved. Besides, the Indestructible never stayed in towns like Juniper for long. If there had indeed been another one last night, it was gone now.

Emilia peeled herself off the brick wall. "Okay, so we think a faraway second one caused the longer Bloodlust. But there's still the weirdness at the beginnin' of the night, up till you saw the body. Which, by the way, I checked in with the Juniper Troupe this mornin'—they got everythin' taken care of last night without a problem from civilians or otherwise."

"Thanks." An idea popped into Gabe's head. "Hey, Emilia, do you think a spell could affect our Bloodlust?"

Her lips pressed together. "I dunno, maybe...but what Diviner would cast that spell?"

"Yeah, you're right. That was...not my brightest idea." Indeed, none of their Diviners would dare tinker with the Warriors' Bloodlust—or their Cull for that matter. Gabe wasn't even sure it was possible. He'd ask Marina, but she was already stressed out about a certain new roommate. He wouldn't add to it unless strictly necessary. "Emilia, what do you think about assuming this was just a weird one-time phenomenon? Y' know, somethin' with the moon." Gabe flashed a sarcastic smile.

Emilia chuckled. "Somethin' with the moon, huh? Sounds good to me."

"Although…" Gabe's voice dropped a level, returning to its earlier grave tone. "We should probably be a bit more cautious than usual, at least for a few weeks."

"Like no paired patrols?"

"Exactly. The whole group can stay together. That way we're prepared for any surprises. And let's keep this whole thing between us. We lead the patrols, so we can remember it when we hunt. I'll warn Simon about it when I talk to him about Marius. I don't want the others to distrust their instincts, especially our freshmen who are learning to listen."

"Agreed. After all, it's pro'ly nothin'." Emilia hooked her arm through Gabe's. "Now, how 'bout I beat you at air hockey?"

Gabe swallowed the urge to search for a certain curly head. "Sounds good."

CHAPTER 19

KANE

*O**ne, two, turn. One, two, turn. One, two, turn.*
Kane's steps—normally so silent and careful—boomed as she paced across the tiny kitchen. The silver skirt of her favorite dress swirled around her toes. Her ebony waves tickled the gown's matching corset with every stride.

Ramrod and Brock were supposed to return from feeding before the sun rose this morning. They had not. Now it was well past sunset. Well past their scheduled start time. Already they'd ruined her plans.

Although, a tiny voice whispered in Kane's head, *we haven't fixed the Dampour yet, so maybe it's for the best.*

Kane squashed the thought. If Ramrod and Brock had bothered to show up, they could have followed the Clan's patrol from a safe distance without a Dampour. They could have started tonight like she'd planned.

"Where are they? We were supposed to begin stalking the Clan tonight. *Tonight*, not tomorrow." Kane's canines flashed. Her talons dug into her palms. Beads of blood oozed beneath them.

Fang sprawled over the battered sofa, his bare feet dangling over its arm. The sharp edge of a dagger glinted in the yellow lamplight. He pressed its point into a callused thumb. When no blood arose, he returned to sharpening the blade against a whetstone. "Relax. They'll be here."

"They were supposed to be here last night or early this morning at the latest." Kane rounded on Fang, seeking a victim for her frustration. "What are you doing with that thing anyway?"

"What's it look like? I'm sharpenin' it."

"Yes, but why?"

Fang waved the knife toward the decades-old TV in the corner of the living room. "Better than watchin' that crap. 'Sides, daggers make good cover. Hide what we are."

"If you do it right, there's no need to hide what we are."

Fang's cold black eyes met hers. "Not all of us can remake a human mind when it suits us."

"I'll have you know, I've never used my powers for that. I've never *needed* to."

Fang shrugged as if he didn't believe her.

Although it stoked the glowing coals of her fury, Kane let it go. With Ramrod and Brock already rebelling against her, she didn't need another enemy. After all, Fang *technically* predated her, not that anyone could tell by the way Duncan lifted Kane over Fang. Take this very mission for instance: Duncan had chosen Kane — not Fang — to lead it. "We're running out of time."

"It's just for tonight."

"What do you mean '*just*'?" Kane's fingertips clenched the edge of the laminate counter. She fought to contain her rage. *Together, we need to work together.*

His dark gaze glued to that blasted blade, Fang lifted his shoulders into yet another shrug. "'Snot like one night'll make a difference. Start tonight or start tomorrow. Doesn't matter."

Kane's wrath overflowed its levee.

She charged the sofa, leaping over its back and onto Fang. Her knees rammed into his soft abdomen. She

184

slammed her forearm against his windpipe. With her canines an inch away from his carotid artery, she whispered, "It. Matters."

Something plunged into Kane's stomach.

White-hot fire burned through her veins, spreading out from the wound. Invisible ropes coiled around her. They crawled up to her chest and down to her legs. Like a boa constrictor suffocating its prey, they tightened with each passing moment. Kane couldn't breathe, couldn't move, couldn't think.

"And *that's* why I keep a dagger on me." Fang ripped the knife out, slicing farther into Kane's insides in the process.

Her nerves screamed. Her blood torched everything in its path. Kane whimpered.

Fang tossed her limp body into the air.

Kane smashed into the merciless floor.

Wiping the blade off with the bottom of his charcoal T-shirt, Fang cast one final look at Kane.

She lay crumpled on the ground, broken. Blood stained a silver corset with severed strings.

Fang walked away.

CHAPTER 20

MONDAY

LILA

Mind-fracturing tests left Lila bruised and battered. She laid her temple against the polished wood of the cafeteria table, seeking to soothe its throbbing with slow inhales and slower exhales. Question-by-question replays danced before her closed eyes.

"Lila dear, what in the world are you doing?" Val's singsong voice reverberated off the brick walls of the empty cafeteria.

If Lila'd had the energy to startle, she would have. But she couldn't even lift her head.

Val tucked a few escaped curls back into Lila's messy ponytail. "Awww, that bad, huh? Don't worry, I'll take excellent care of you."

The caress gave Lila enough life to raise her chin onto her palm and open her eyes.

They widened with curiosity. A scrawny girl with a shock of unkempt orange hair stood behind Val, hardly her usual follower. She elbowed Val.

"Oh, Lila, this is…this is…"

"Margaret." The owner of the squeaky voice and too-bright hair thrust her hand toward Lila's chin.

Lila grasped it. Despite her fatigue, Lila's grip overpowered hers.

"She's my math tutor," Val answered Lila's unspoken question.

186

Although annoyance flashed over her face like lightning, Margaret said nothing.

Lila suppressed a frown. She needed to convince Val to do her own homework, but that was a conversation for a less exhausting day.

"The girls should be down soon, Lila dear." Val peeked over her shoulder at Margaret. When she didn't recede one inch, Val's glossy lips pressed into a thin line—one that Margaret couldn't *quite* see. A breath later, Val focused back on Lila, all sunny cheer again. "In the meantime, I'll get us dinner. Any requests?"

Lila's head drifted back toward her refreshing wooden pool. "No. Words. Left."

"Okay, sweetie. I'll go get us some absolutely scrumptious comfort food." Val patted Lila's back, then trotted toward the line. Carrying all three trays, Margaret followed her.

Lila wondered how Val was going to get rid of her. Then decided she'd solved enough problems for one day.

Waiting for Val to return with vital sustenance, Lila bent her arms into a makeshift pillow. Oh how she wished she could just collapse into bed right after dinner. But no, she had to meet with Headmaster Flynn to go over her exam results and class schedule. After that, she needed to figure out this whole "extracurricular" thing. Then determine what the exact requirements of the talent show were. And look up what she could do to help with Lizzie's house points. *Ugh, this school. It's ridiculous. And overwhelming. And stressful. And—*

A polite cough interrupted Lila's disgruntled daydream. "Hey, um, Lila? You okay there?"

Oh no, please no. Lila lifted her head an inch and peered at the intruder.

Her guess was correct. Lila sprang upright. "Oh, um, hi Gabe. What's up?" Lila's voice rippled with false energy as she tried to act livelier than a five-day-old corpse.

"Nothin'. Just comin' in for an early dinner and saw you there. You sure you're okay?"

"Yeah. Just tired. Really, *really* tired." At Gabe's furrowed brow, Lila explained, "Placement tests all day. My brain's totally fried."

"Oh, so that's why you left early last night." Gabe smiled down at Lila. "I don't blame you at all. Those entrance exams before freshman year were awful. I bet your placement exams were just as bad, if not worse."

"Yeah, apparently they customized them for me since I'm a sophomore and all."

"Oooph, that sucks…" Gabe's hand flew through his inky locks. His pale gaze cast about the Eversfield students trickling into the cafeteria around them. After several agonizing seconds — during which Lila searched her poor fatigued mind for something to say — Gabe tilted his head over his shoulder. "Well…I don't wanna bother you, and it looks like Val's got some good recovery food comin' your way. I'll see you later."

Lila sought the energy — and the courage — to explain that he wasn't bothering her, that he should stay and have dinner. *With her.*

Before Lila found the words, Gabe strode away, toward a round table with four empty chairs. In the fifth chair sat the perfectly toned, perfectly beautiful girl from last night. Her almond eyes crinkled as she beamed up at Gabe, her long fingers graceful when they gestured to the seat beside her.

Together, they laughed at a shared joke, the girl tossing lustrous ebony waves over her shoulder. Neither glanced back at Lila or even noticed she existed.

"Ah, I saw that good taste last night, Lila dear," Val whispered into Lila's ear, just loud enough for Lila to hear but too soft for the tray-depositing Margaret.

When Margaret moved to sit on the bench next to Lila, Val intervened, "Oh, can we get dinner another time? I simply must have some private gal time with my pal Lila."

"B-b-but you p-promised tha—"

Val cut Margaret off, "Thank you *so* much. You can't imagine what it means to me to have my dearest friend in the whole wide world here. I'll see you later?"

Margaret nodded, then stumbled to the closest empty table.

"I swear that girl would follow me off the edge of a cliff if I let her." Val ruffled her flawless pixie cut, then sat on the bench opposite Lila. "Anyway, tell me all about it. About *him*."

A flush blossomed over Lila's cheeks. "Um, about what? Gabe? He's Marina's brother. We're…kinda friends, I guess."

"Uh *huh*. And that's why you ditched me for him last night. Not that I mind of course."

"I did not—"

Val raised an elven hand. "Don't worry, Lila dear. Like I said, I don't mind, not in the least. And I won't tell anyone about the two of you until you're official. As long as you give me all the details, that is."

"Val, there aren't any details to give!"

"C'mon, Lila dear, I know better than that. S-p-i-double-l, spill! Look, I'll even give you a fry covered in disgusting mustard." Val waved a fry dripping with mustard in front of Lila.

Visions of stained uniforms flipped through Lila's mind. "Fine, fine, just put that thing down. You're endangering the safety of my shirt."

Val lowered the fry to rest between Lila's chili cheese dog and her heap of fries. Then Val tilted backward with one eyebrow cocked and her arms crossed over her chest. Her meaning was clear.

Lila sighed. "There's not anything to tell. Not really. I met him Saturday, you were there. Then we talked a little when he dropped by the room looking for Marina that night—"

"Hmmph, looking for Marina indeed."

"He was! A family thing or something."

Val's dark eyes sparkled. "Sounds like an excuse to get to know my Lila better. But I digress."

"Anyway, last night he offered to teach me how to play foosball, but we got, um, interrupted." Lila refused to peek at the happy couple a few tables away. "When I saw you were busy on the dance floor, I just went back to my room."

"Aw, Lila dear, you didn't hafta do that. I woulda been happy to ditch Tim to hang out with you!"

Lila's fingers rubbed at her bare biceps. "Yeah, well…I mean, I did have those placement exams today, so gettin' to bed early wasn't the worst idea."

"Next time just come and get me, okay?" Val reached across the table to squeeze Lila's hand.

"Sure." *Lie.* Interrupting Val with her various boy toys wasn't something Lila would do. Ever.

"And what about just now? I saw the two of you together. Which, by the way, he's an excellent choice. I mean, last year he was a bit of a recluse, but I personally think that only makes him more attractive. You know, tortured soul and all that."

Lila focused on Val's question and ignored the rest. The last thing Lila needed was to dwell on what an "excellent choice" Gabe was. "He came over to check on me since I was collapsed over the table, that's all. Then he left. The end." Lila bit into her chili cheese dog.

Her eyes glued to Lila, Val twisted a fry back and forth. "That's it, huh? And that's why you check in his direction every few minutes?"

"I do not!" Lila exclaimed around her mouthful. Despite her delicious chili cheese dog, her stomach sank. If she'd failed to fool Val, who else knew about her stupid, good-for-nothing crush? After gulping down a swig of pop, Lila murmured, "C'mon, Val, gimme a break. Yes, okay, I admit it: I think he's cute. But I don't have a chance with him. He's a senior, he's my roommate's brother, and he is definitely out of my league. Not to mention I struggle with complete sentences when I'm around him. So, you know, there's that."

"First, no one is out of your league, Lila dear," Val chided. "And, second, you—"

"And I suppose that girl over there is his girlfriend. They seem awfully close."

Val's chocolate gaze flicked to Gabe's table. "Who? Emilia? Nah. I mean, yeah, they're friends, but they're not an item or anything."

"How do you know?"

Val sent Lila a withering look. "Please. I—*we*—know everything that's going on in this school. There's no way they could have a clandestine relationship without me knowing."

"That's a lot of people to keep track of."

"True. But it's not like we know *everything* that's going on with *everyone* —"

"Didn't you just say that you did?"

"No, we know everything that's going on with the important people. You know, the populars, the jocks, the pretties." Val waggled her eyebrows at Lila.

But she missed it, for the implication behind Val's words stung. "So you're saying that if you're not popular, into sports, and/or 'pretty,' then you're not important?"

"No, I'm not saying that at all! They're just not worth gossiping about." Val returned Lila's frown for a moment, then sighed. Her fingers brushed against Lila's. "Let's not argue. It's just the way high school is. Besides," Val waved toward the perfect girls from last night cutting to the front of the line for food, "it's about time."

"Time for what?"

"Time for you to try again. As I'm sure you know, last night wasn't your best performance, but of course we *all* understand the draw of a cute boy. So today is your second chance. But you've got to make a good impression this time."

Lila almost rolled her eyes. Val's friends were a whole lot of work, something she didn't need after eight hours of exams.

Val squeezed Lila's hand. "Don't worry, Lila dear, I'll take care of most of it. You just be your lovely self. But don't talk too very much. And remember: Sara — the blonde in the front of pack — is in charge. Come November, she'll run this school, so we hafta stay on her good side."

Based on last night, Lila wondered how much room remained on Sara's good side.

"And watch out for Drey. She's a snake in the grass. *Technically*, she lost to me last year, but she won't give up till the fat lady sings in a year from now. Cheri and Rudi aren't too much to worry about, since they're both in Tubby and juniors. Although, Rudi's got a temper to match that hair. Or rather, she dyed her hair fire-engine red to match that temper. Anyway…" Val surveyed Lila. "You getting this?"

"Yeah, um, I think so. Only what do you mean Drey lost to you? And what happens in a year?"

"Oh, Lila, Lila, Lila, sometimes I forget how naive and inexperienced you are. Our group, it's kinda like a secret society. All these old college prep schools have them. For ours, we collect the three most popular girls from each class. Seniors typically bow out this time of year because they have to focus on the whole college thing. So right now it's only sophomores and juniors while we scout the freshmen, with the seniors coming and going as they please. And because Tasha up and left us this year, we have an additional slot for a sophomore." Val's catlike eyes narrowed in appraisal. Canting her head, she muttered, "We will have to do something about that hair. Or maybe just go with the whole wild thing? That's pretty in right now. Perhaps both, switching it up depending on the day?"

"Val…" Lila warned in a low tone.

Wide-eyed innocence met her. "What?"

"You are not making me over. I'm fine the way I am. My get-ready routine is simple, easy, fast. Perfect for me."

Val nodded.

Stress coiled around Lila's stomach. It was never that easy to convince Val of anything.

Val swirled a fry in ketchup, then held it up between her and Lila. "Isn't the food here just so good? I love it. Not that either of my parents cook at home, but I love this cafeteria food. Lots of people complain about it, but I think it's simply de-lish. And we have all-you-can-eat soft serve right over there." Val gestured toward the far corner behind Lila.

Although the stress strangled her stomach, Lila twisted around. A line already snaked past a bulky silver machine. Apparently, some students went straight to ice cream for dinner. *I should've done that.*

"If you're not up for soft serve after dinner, Lila dear, I *may* have some premium ice cream squirrelled away that I *might* be willing to share with you."

Lila's attention snapped back to Val. That was a bribe if she'd ever heard one. Val did not share ice cream— especially not the good stuff—without wanting something in return. "Uh *huh*. That sounds good and all, but what's the catch?"

"Why, Lila dear, I'm appalled. Agog! Aghast! Why would there be a catch? I just wanna share my favorite ice cream with my poor distressed best friend."

"Mmhmm. And when did you start sharing ice cream so altruistically? Because that's not the Val I remember from middle school."

"I mean...I'll have to bring the ice cream to you anyway... So we might as well try on those dresses I borrowed for you!" Val rushed through the last part as if Lila wouldn't notice the chore if she said it quickly enough. "And you did promise, Lila dear."

"I know, I know. You're right, I did promise. But I won't have a lot of time. I have to meet with Headmaster Flynn—"

"Just call him Flynn, we talked about this. But, y' know, not to his face."

"Fine, whatever, Flynn."

Val smiled with approval.

"I have to meet him at six. I don't know how long it'll take, and I want to get to bed early—"

"I understand, Lila dear. I suppose it can wait for another day."

Relief soothed the pit of vipers that was Lila's stomach. Val had backed down, and it hadn't even required much pleading and cajoling from Lila. Although…why *did* Val give in so easily?

Val peered over Lila's shoulder. Her lips spread into a wide welcoming smile. Her arms followed suit. "Hello, ladies."

All concern about Val's unexpected compromise disappeared when Lila twisted around. The four girls from last night had arrived. *Sara, Drey, Cheri, and Rudi*, Lila reminded herself.

Greetings of "Hey, Val" echoed through the group. At least one muddled "Hi, Lila" crept in. Cheri and Rudi climbed over the carved wooden bench to sit next to Lila.

As Sara and Drey crossed to the opposite side of the table, a realization hit Lila. Drey's imitation of Sara didn't stop with her bored expression and snooty attitude. No, Sara and Drey matched from their meticulously messy braids through their tight Eversfield V-necks. Even their plaid skirts were hemmed to the same "pushing Eversfield limits" length. The only differences were in color scheme, with Sara in navy and Drey in cream.

Lila's gaze flowed over Rudi, Cheri, and Val, analyzing them for the same mimicry. While their similarities weren't as obvious as those between Sara and Drey, none of them wore the loose blouse or slouchy pants Lila did. She didn't fit in with them, that much was clear.

"So, Sara has some news." Drey's narrow shoulder bumped into Sara's bony one.

Like a pet hamster with its favorite treat, Sara nibbled on a ranch-less baby carrot. She drew out the suspense while she swallowed the miniscule bite. "Yes. I think we have our opening."

Val's eyebrow cocked. She leaned over Drey to reach Sara. "Really? You think Jen's vulnerable?"

Her blond braid bobbing up and down, Sara nodded. "Yes, for sure. I was talking to Meg, Juana, and Fattie this morning. None of them think we can win a decent competition with Jen as our captain."

From there, the conversation departed without Lila. After a day of stressful exams, her brain couldn't piece together the puzzle of what and who they talked about as names of people, places, and things were tossed about without explanation. She did catch that Sara, Drey, Val, and Cheri were all members of the school's dance team and that Sara wanted to overthrow the current captain. Other than that — and the resulting debate over strategies — Lila had no idea what they discussed. At least Val had recommended that she not "talk too very much."

Then the words "talent show" registered. With the distraction of Gabe, Lila had forgotten to ask Val about it earlier. Her hands twitched over a plate of bread crumbs and smears of mustard-tinged chili. Lila had to know all the details. *Right. Now.* She listened for a break in their chatter.

"Seriously, our dance number is going to be ah-mazing! Drey and I were texting about it all summer. We're definitely winning first place this year," Sara trumpeted.

The others agreed around their mouthfuls of salad leaves.

Lila lurched into the opening, "Ummm, so what's the deal with the talent show again?"

Val's perpetual smile stretched into a grin. "Oh, that's right, I completely forgot! You know how we all live in separate houses, right? Well, each house competes for the Eversfield house cup every year, and—"

"Good Lord, Val, you never told her about the house competitions?" Rudi's dark brows climbed up her short forehead.

Val mouthed, "Oops."

Rudi shook her head. Her flaming locks—stick-straight today—swung from side to side. "You may as well get on with it."

Collecting the others in her cornflower blue gaze, Sara gestured to the opposite end of the bench. The *empty* opposite end. If not for Val's lips bending into the briefest of frowns, Lila wouldn't have minded their departure one bit.

Lila tugged at a wild curl. "No, um, it's okay, I think I got the gist of it last night from Head—I mean, Flynn's announcement."

But Sara slithered down the russet bench anyway. Drey, Cheri, and Rudi followed, although Rudi's shoulders rose into a shrug of apology first.

When Val returned to Lila, her voice was as cheery as ever. "Anyway, Lila dear…like you heard last night we compete for the Eversfield house cup every year. As you probably guessed, the house with the most points at the end of the year wins. You get points through grades, extracurriculars, and the house trials. And that's where things get interesting if you ask me. For instance, at the end of this semester we have a talent show in the afternoon and a school-sanctioned Masquerade Ball in the evening, only it's more like a Halloween party since fall break almost always coincides with actual Halloween. Oh and you have to make your own costume for the Masquerade Ball, where the best costumes win bonus house points. And there's another set of house trials after midterms in October, but that one's way less fun than the one at the end of this semester."

"Wait, so…what?" Lila failed to absorb Val's rapid-fire explanation even after last night. She concentrated on the last portion. "We have to *make* our own costumes? Why can't we just buy a costume like normal people?"

Val's chocolate gaze flashed with pride. "Because we're *not* normal. But don't you worry your curly li'l head about it. I've got some friends I'll introduce you to. They'll take *real* good care of you." Val winked.

"But…wouldn't that be, y' know, cheating?"

"I dunno. All's fair in love and war, right?"

So this was war, then? Lila's stress returned tenfold. Her chest ached from it.

Lila took a deep breath. *Calm down. Val's got this whole costume thing figured out. Time to move on.* "Okay, then for the talent show, do we nominate people? Or is it volunteers?"

"In the sense that we're all volunteers, yes."

Lila's chili dog roiled in her stomach. Despite Gabe's earlier implications, she'd hoped to avoid the talent show altogether.

Val rubbed the back of Lila's clammy hand. "Oh, c'mon, don't look so terrified. It'll be fun! I already know what I'm doing: an interpretation of 'The Lady of Shalott.' You know, like how we used to do back in middle school. Only this will be *much* more dramatic."

Slowing her ragged breaths, Lila concentrated on Val's talent show appearance instead of her own. "I thought you were doing a dance number or something. With them." Lila's head tilted toward Sara's gang, chittering nonstop a foot and a half away.

"A dance number?" Val's forehead wrinkled with confusion. After a moment, it smoothed. "Oh, *that*. No, we were talkin' 'bout the big group number at the end. In addition to everyone doing a solo-ish act, each house has to put together a group performance. So me, Sara, and Drey will be dancing. We will have to find something for you though. If I recall correctly, you're not a fan of dancing, at least not yet." Val's index finger pulled at her lower lip. Her brow furrowed in thought.

Lila's brain popped and fizzled with anxiety, too overloaded to address Val's ominous "not yet."

"Wait, you don't still sing, do you? Of course you do, you've always loved to sing. That's simply perfection! We don't have nearly enough singers!"

Dread strangled Lila's voice. "Val, please…"

"What?"

Lila's fingers pressed into the shiny tabletop. Between her clenched teeth, she muttered, "I don't really sing in front of people, remember?"

Val waved away Lila's concerns like they were nothing more than pesky fruit flies. "Oh pish posh. It's time for you to grow out of that anyway. You have a wonderful voice, I've heard it!"

"No offense, Val, but you don't count. You're pretty much tone deaf."

Val's face scrunched in confusion. "What do you mean? Why does that matter? Besides, I'm working on it. I'm in Choir and everything!"

Lila didn't say anything. Knowing Val and her endless charm, she'd get an A anyway. In Choir. In spite of being tone deaf.

Lila also knew she was beaten. Val wouldn't let her escape, and it sounded like Eversfield wouldn't either. Maybe Lila could be one of the many singing the chorus? "So…if I do this—and I'm not saying I will—what exactly will I have to sing?"

"I dunno. Sara's taking care of everything." Val picked up the neon leather bag beside her tray and got out her phone.

Lila frowned. Sara—who obviously didn't like her in spite of barely knowing her—was in charge.

A light bulb flashed in Lila's mind.

Sara—who obviously didn't like her in spite of barely knowing her—would never cast her in an important role for the group performance. Reassured about that portion of the talent show, Lila summoned a shard of bravery. "And I have to do a solo? For the individual portion?"

Her fingers tap-tap-tapping at her phone, Val answered without looking up, "A solo-ish. You know, a solo, a duet, et cetera. Up to a small group. No official ruling on what actually constitutes a small group, but I would guess no more than four people. You know it's after six, right?"

Panic shot through Lila like a poisoned arrow. "Really? Oh no, I've gotta go!" Her heart sprinting away from her, Lila grabbed her empty backpack and piled the dirty dishes onto her tray. She checked the clock hanging over the busy serving area to see how late she was.

And did a double take.

It wasn't after six at all. No, she still had ten entire minutes before her appointment with Headmaster Flynn. "What...Val!"

"Just messin' with ya, Lila dear. Although, if I know you, you pro'ly wanna leave now so you can sit outside Flynn's office all early."

A chuckle escaped Lila. With it went most of her stress. After all, the talent show and Masquerade Ball were *months* away. They were nothing to worry about now.

On her way past Val, Lila playfully thwacked the back of Val's head. "That's for freakin' me out unnecessarily. And yes, I'm gonna make sure I'm on time, if not a bit early. Unlike *some* chronically late people."

Val shrugged, already sliding down the wooden bench toward Sara and company. "Good luck, Lila dear."

As Lila strode to the side doors closest to Admin, a hint of a smile played over her lips. Yes, this school was impossible with its crazy placement exams and its talent shows and its make-your-own-costume Masquerade Balls. But with Val laughing by her side, she could survive it. She could survive anything.

VAL

TUGGING HER LONG-EMPTY TRAY ALONG THE POLISHED tabletop, Val scooched down the bench until she arrived at

Drey's side. *Technically,* it should be her — not Drey — sitting next to Sara, but she'd let it go this one time.

While Val caught up to the others' conversation, a relaxed smile masked her inner thoughts. Lila could have done a whole lot better tonight if she'd bothered to try. But she'd done well enough. At least Lila didn't get into an argument with Sara, unlike what brewed between Sara and Rudi at the moment.

"No, you absolutely should *not* go darker." Sara's low tone neared a growl.

"But I thought it'd be fun. Y' know, kinda vintage-y, pin-up-girl-esque. Maybe even get some bangs." A tremor of defiance hid beneath Rudi's words.

Sara rolled her eyes. "Hmmph, next you'll be saying you wanna get a tattoo."

"What's wrong with tattoos?"

"What's wrong with…what's wrong with tattoos? Are you kidding me? Sure, I mean, a discreet *small* tattoo in certain areas, that would be fine, but in general? C'mon, Rudi, you know better than that."

Rudi crossed her arms and scowled at Sara.

Leaning forward, Val caught Sara's gaze around the silent Drey. When Sara's chin tipped downward, Val took over. "Rudi, tattoos are all fine and good, but tell me, what would your parents do if you came home with one?"

Rudi snorted. "Disown me, pro'ly. At least take away my car."

"And none of us want that. That li'l Benz and you should be together forever. Or at least for a few years until you get a newer model."

"I suppose…" Rudi chewed on her lower lip, a lovely shade of plum today.

"As for the hair, I think bangs would look far cuter with your current color. Besides, if you went darker, who would be our lone redhead?"

"Y' think?" Rudi tossed her head so that a flaming lock slipped over her shoulder. She gave Val a flirtatious smile.

Val's hands flew to her phone and snapped the photo. She passed her phone to Rudi. "See? Look how cute you are today. I mean, bangs *might* be a fun change, but I think you're gorgeous just the way you are. Of course, it's up to you." Val watched Rudi, waiting to see if her seed of doubt took root.

"Hmmm, I'll hafta think about it." Rudi flipped a lock over to examine its ends. "Doesn't look like I'm ready for a trim anyway."

Val shot a look of triumph at Sara. Allowing Rudi to decide on her own was far superior to Sara's bullying, whether Sara realized it or not. If Rudi did choose poorly in the future, Val would try the doubt route again. Only if that failed would she resort to the methods Sara and Drey preferred.

"Well, now that *that's* settled…"

Val bit back a frown at Sara's jab at Rudi.

But Rudi was too busy zooming in and out of her photo to notice. "Hey, Val, you mind if I use this for a new profile pic?"

"'Course not. It is *such* a cute picture of you."

"Thanks, Va—"

"Val, are you absolutely positive about Lila?" Sara interrupted.

The table hushed. All eyes fell on Val. Rudi handed her phone back.

Val tucked it into her neon yellow pouch and zipped it shut. As she did so, she chased away all hints of her own misgivings. "Yes, of course. I wouldn't have suggested she be our late addition if I wasn't."

"But those pants! And her shirt! Did you see them?" Drey leaned over the table toward Rudi and Cheri. The corners of her mouth quirked up and down with barely contained laughter.

Val resisted the urge to yank Drey away from them, her potential allies. "She didn't have much choice, *Drey*. Not with the late notice from Eversfield. But don't worry, I'm taking care of it."

Drey twisted in her seat to face Val. "What about her hair then? Certainly she could have done *something* with it. And she didn't wear any makeup today. What's your excuse for that, Val?"

"That I'm taking care of it, *Drey*." Val collected the gazes of Rudi and Cheri, seeking to get them on her — and Lila's — side. "Look, Lila had placement exams today. I'm sure we all remember how stressful those were when we were freshmen."

Drey flipped her coffee-brown braid over her shoulder. "*I* still managed to do my hair and makeup. As did y — "

Sara's hands slapped against the wooden table. "Enough. Drey, it's only been a couple of days and she did just get here."

Val lifted her chin and smiled at Drey.

Drey glared back.

"And Val, Drey's not wrong. There's quite a bit to fix with Lila…"

Drey vaulted into Sara's opening. "And she straight up disappeared last night — "

"Because she was hanging out with Gabe Lazare! Who, if you remember, dated Heidi. Even you can't say that's an unfortunate choice, Drey."

Drey's tone turned haughty. "Except that she shouldn't go after Heidi's cast-offs, particularly the reclusive ones."

Val rolled her eyes. "Please. Like we all haven't dated each other's exes at one point or another. Besides, from what I've heard, Heidi and Gabe were never serious."

"It's still early to go aft—"

Sara's fists pounded into the tabletop. "I said *enough* you two." She bent over to peer around Drey, her blue eyes meeting Val's brown ones. "Val, you say you're fixing it? Well then *fix* it." She ticked Val's chores off manicured fingers. "The clothes, the hair, the makeup, it all needs work. And I don't mean next week, I mean *now*. In addition, she hardly even talked during dinner, aside from quizzing us about the talent show." Sara's forehead tilted toward Cheri across from her. "We've already got one member who wouldn't have gotten in except for who she knows. Or in Cheri's case, who she's related to."

Cheri's ample cheeks flushed, but she said nothing to defend herself. Not that there was much she could say. They never would have considered Cheri were she not Heidi's little sister, that Val had heard from Heidi herself.

Sara leaned over the tabletop around Drey. "Look, Val, I'll be nice. I'll overlook today. I'll even give her some time to warm up to us. Hell, I'll let her off the hook for the October house trials so she can focus on getting top-notch grades for Lizzie—something that you promised us when we agreed about Lila. But come December, she better be ready for the talent show, both for her individual performance and for Lizzie's group performance."

205

"She will be," Val promised.

Sara's rose-tinted lips flattened into a shiny line. "She better be. Or you're out too, Val."

CHAPTER 21

Hovering before the glass door of the Administration office, Lila sucked in a breath. She could do this. And if not…well, what was Val always saying? Fake it till you make it?

Lila straightened to her full height and lifted her chin. She repeated, *fake it till you make it*. Then Lila swept through the door and headed straight for the front of Ms. Pershing's U-shaped desk. "Ms. Pershing?" This time her tongue didn't fumble.

From behind the gleaming counter, a charcoal eyebrow cocked upward. "Hello, Miss Lee. Is there something you need?"

Lila took a moment to arrange her words before speaking. "Yes, I received a note that Headmaster Flynn would like to meet with me."

"Yes, I remember, Miss Lee. I will inform Headmaster Flynn that you're here. You may take a seat." Ms. Pershing gestured to the waiting area behind Lila.

"Thank you, Ms. Pershing."

While Ms. Pershing alerted Flynn to her arrival, Lila placed her empty backpack beneath a bowl-shaped chair, then sat on its edge. She folded her hands in her lap and crossed her legs at the ankle, just like Val had taught her. She held her spine rigid and straight. Her gaze roamed the waiting area, seeking something to distract her from the impatience tinged with dread.

Said something ended up being an untidy reflection in the window opposite Lila. Wrinkles covered both navy pants and ivory blouse. Three drops of mustard speckled the shirt's hem. Flyaway hairs stuck out every which way.

After a glance over her shoulder at Ms. Pershing's still-empty desk, Lila scurried to the window. Her fingers tucked her blouse into her pants, hiding the mustard stains. Then she pressed and pulled at the wrinkles. Each time they sprang back.

Lila frowned at her reflection. How had she not known that she was a mess? And why hadn't Val suggested she change before her meeting?

At least I can do something about my stupid hair. Lila ripped the tie out. She flipped upside down and combed her fingers through her curls. After tying her mane into what she hoped was a tidier ponytail, Lila snapped back upright. A few rebellious strands remained, but far less than before.

A throat cleared behind her. "Miss Lee, I hate to remind you, but an Eversfield woman does not fidget, even in the most pressing of situations."

Heat spread over Lila's cheeks as she returned to her chair. "S-sorry."

"Headmaster Flynn will be with you shortly, Miss Lee. I presume you brought your backpack?"

Lila's stomach tensed. Then she remembered the limp bag lying beneath her chair. "Y-yes, Ms. Pershing."

Without another word, Ms. Pershing returned to her computer. Lila sat there, her fingers clenched around the cool metal frame of her chair and her feet pressed into the marble floor. Once again, she counted the leaves of that potted palm, trying not to fidget.

At the sound of a door gliding open, Lila twisted around. Flynn emerged from the opening, his bald head shining in the overhead lighting. His stubby fingers stroked a white beard while he examined a clipboard resting on his belly. Between his beard, slight paunch, and tweed suit, he looked like a preppy, more fit Santa Claus examining his list of naughty and nice.

"Miss Lee?" Flynn's hazel gaze shifted from the clipboard to the waiting area, empty except for Lila.

Her butterflies awoke with a vengeance. "Yes, that's me." Lila bit her lower lip at her high tone. After collecting her backpack off the ground, she approached Flynn. Her hands skidded over her blouse in a final attempt to smooth the stubborn wrinkles. It was no use.

Flynn extended an arm toward the opening behind him. "After you, Miss Lee."

An obedient Lila entered his office. Not three steps in, she stood next to a gleaming mahogany desk. On its surface was nothing but a computer monitor and a carved wooden container of pens and mechanical pencils. But there were no chairs facing the desk. Lila shifted her weight between her feet.

Behind her, Flynn rolled the glass door shut. In a clear—but stiff—voice, he began, "Miss Lee, it's nice to see you again. I hope you're enjoying Eversfield." Flynn gestured to a set of four over-stuffed armchairs assembled around a low coffee table on the opposite side of the office. A steaming mug of tea and a laptop rested in front of one. "Please take a seat. We have a few things to discuss."

Lila selected the chair farthest from the tea and laptop. Lest it swallow her whole, she perched on the edge of a cushion fluffier than a marshmallow.

Flynn had no such fear. He collected his mug, then sank into the depths of his chair, leaning into its padded back. After a swallow of tea with closed eyes, he returned to Lila. "Once again, welcome to Eversfield Preparatory Academy. If you apply yourself, I am positive you will achieve your goals, whatever they may be." He glanced at her through the tea's steam as if to secure her full attention.

"As you've heard several times now, the path ahead may be rocky. We do not lightly admit students after freshman year. This is for good reason: every student here was at the top of their respective middle schools. Every student desires—nay, *expects*—to attend an ivy league college. With this kind of competition, we find it best to start all students off on the same footing. Regardless, we have made an exception for you. Why, you may ask?" With his gaze trained on Lila, Flynn sipped his tea.

The familiar flush crept up Lila's neck. While she'd had the grades, the standardized test scores, and the teacher recommendations, Val's assistance—and that of Val's parents, colossal Eversfield donors—had likely tipped the scales in her favor.

"Not for the reasons you may think, Miss Lee. We did not admit you because of your, *ahem*, connections, although I did field many a beseeching phone call on your behalf. No, we admitted you because you showed great potential during the scholarship application process. That said, potential does not guarantee success, especially not here. No, to succeed you must combine that potential with unparalleled industry. You must never quit, never become complacent. We at Eversfield Preparatory Academy challenge our students, body and soul. I believe you have greatness within you, and it is our job—nay, our duty—to uncover it. To cultivate it."

During his speech, the headmaster had bent forward toward Lila. His broad forehead glistened with sweat born of his fervor.

Lila's nails dug into the cushion beneath her thighs. She stared at the cursive *E* adorning Flynn's mug. "Um, thank you, sir. I-I won't disappoint you."

"It's not me you should worry about disappointing."

Lila's gaze snapped up to Flynn's. All her life she'd tried to please various authority figures, whether it be teachers, principals, or babysitters, not to mention her parents.

"No, Miss Lee, you must not disappoint yourself. It is the more difficult task, but a worthier one. Do you understand?"

Lila squirmed beneath his stare. "Y-Yes, sir, I understand."

"All right, very good. Now, what you've been waiting for." Flynn lifted his laptop to reveal a manila envelope beneath it, which he handed to Lila.

With trembling hands, Lila pulled out the crisp piece of paper inside. Her jaw dropped.

"Yes, Miss Lee, you did quite well on your placement exams. Congratulations. Although, I must say I was a bit disappointed by your history results." When Lila blushed, Flynn's hazel eyes twinkled behind wire-rimmed glasses. "Yes, I thought so. Not a big fan of history then?"

Lila shrugged. "It was the last exam, and…" Her voice trailed off before she could admit the weakness to her principal.

Flynn wagged a finger at her. "Remember, Miss Lee, those who do not learn history are doomed to repeat it."

"Yes, I'll remember," Lila replied without looking up from the list of honors classes swimming before her eyes.

"Well, that's all I have for you at the moment. Ms. Pershing has collected the relevant textbooks for you, so you may be on your way."

Lila nodded, still ogling her class schedule.

"You're dismissed." Flynn's voice sounded softer than before. *Farther away than before.*

Lila glanced up. Flynn stood beside the door, waiting for her to leave his office.

"Oh, yes. Of course." Lila folded up the class schedule and shoved it into her pocket. The manila envelope somehow ended up in her limp backpack. At the door, she remembered her manners. "Thank you. Sir."

Chapter 22

Air heavy with humidity drifted in through the open window, comforting Marina while she connected miniscule dots on graph paper. When she finished, Marina compared her creation with the example displayed on her laptop screen. After only two tweaks, the graphs matched.

Six down, thirteen to go. Marina stretched her achy fingers, wishing she could switch to Chemistry — or even World History. But no, this was due tomorrow afternoon, so she had to finish it tonight.

Indulging in a quick break, Marina closed her eyes and reached for the Wind outside her open window.

It caught her fingertips. When she flexed a finger, a breeze blew forward like an invisible string connected them. Marina could stop there and consider it enough practice for a weeknight.

But working on her Diviner skills was almost as important as finishing her Eversfield homework. That was doubly true when she was alone. Like all Diviners, Marina couldn't practice her magic in front of civilians, but she had an added wrinkle. No one — not even her fellow Eversfield Cell members — could know about her developing Wind and Earth talents. If anyone let it slip that she could work with Wind and Earth in addition to her Water, Weaving, and Healing, the Bureau Diviners would cart her off to headquarters in an instant. Then they'd never let her have a normal life. They might not even let her leave headquarters.

Marina's fingertips pulsed with power. Her Wind grew impatient.

Holding her breath, Marina chose control over strength. She curled one finger.

A tendril of air flowed through the open window. It weaved through her fingers, starting slow, then spinning faster and faster. It climbed up and down her bare forearm, tickling her skin. Marina smiled.

Her door burst open.

Marina's breeze died. So did her high spirits. With a frown, Marina swiveled around to face the door.

Lila crossed their room in four rushed strides, her arms and backpack overflowing with textbooks. A foot in front of her empty bookcase, they spilled out. Rather than pick them up, Lila dropped her bag and collapsed onto the ground next to them. She didn't even bother crawling into the empty desk chair that waited inches away. No, Lila hunkered down, hugging her knees to her chest with her chin resting on top of them. She stared at the wooden floor.

Marina's inner coward pleaded with her. She should ignore Lila's obvious distress and return to her math homework. Natasha would rebuke her for daring to speak. Lila could do the same.

And yet...hadn't Lila already proven to be different from Natasha and Sara and Audrey and Valerie? Lila's nose was in a book half the time, she seemed to have no interest in fashion, and she'd been...*nice*, both during their tour and during the Semester Start dinner.

But what if all that was a trick to convince Marina to trust her?

What if it wasn't?

Marina licked her lips, filled with indecision.

But maybe that was the answer. Until Marina knew Lila was as bad as the rest of them, she should try, at least a little. Besides, if she and Lila were friendly, monitoring Lila as a potential Latent would be easier. "Hey, um, Lila? Are you okay?"

Without looking up, Lila tugged a crumpled sheet of paper out of her pocket. She passed it to Marina.

Using her ruler and the empty area of her desk, Marina smoothed it out. Then she read it. Then she understood.

"Um, wow. That's quite the list." Marina kept her voice upbeat for Lila's sake, even though she would be trapped in full nuclear reactor-level meltdown if this was her class schedule. When Lila didn't respond, Marina studied it again, this time analyzing it. "Do you want to…talk about it? Or maybe you want to wait for Valerie."

Lila's green gaze shot to Marina. "No! No way would Val understand. No, Val would be like 'Oh, Lila, you'll be fine, you're my little genius!'" Lila's singsong imitation of Valerie was dead-on. "Not that I think I'm a genius of course. Val just likes to call me that to justify her own bad grades. She doesn't get the whole studying thing."

"Well, if it helps, I don't think your schedule's that bad after all."

Lila's eyes widened with hope. "Really?"

"Really. Let's break it down." Marina's index finger trailed down Lila's class schedule. "The worst looks like Honors Pre-Calc. I can't really comment on that since I won't take it until next year. But I've heard it's pretty tough."

"I'm…actually not too worried about that one." Lila pinched a wrinkle in her pants. "Math isn't that hard for me. What's next?"

Hmm, that's interesting. If Lila proved to be…not horrible, maybe she could help Marina with Algebra II. "Honors American Lit, which I have too, although I'm in a different class. Lots of reading there, but not too many papers according to the syllabus. We are graded partially on discussion though, which is not my favorite."

Lila scrunched her nose with displeasure. "Yuck."

Despite Marina's reservations, her mouth twitched toward a smile. "Yeah, agreed. Let's see, you've also got regular World History, so that should be fine."

"Yeah, that was my last placement test. I *may* not have tried so hard on it, which I think Flynn guessed. But I mean, I'm not really into history anyway…" In spite of the excuse, guilt colored Lila's voice.

Marina bit back the reminder about the hazards of not learning history and returned to Lila's schedule. Her clipped nail skimmed down the page to the afternoon classes. "Oh, here we go. Looks like we have Honors Inorganic Chemistry and Genetics together. I can't say how good I am at Genetics yet, but I do like Chemistry. So I could help you with that…if, you know, you need it."

"Yes! That would be great! I mean, I think I'm okay with Chem, but I'm definitely not great at it. Especially the lab stuff." Lila grimaced.

"Yeah, we take the labs pretty seriously here, especially for the honors and AP classes. For Chem, the schedule is to have at least one four-hour lab per month. Plus some labs will be stretched through multiple days."

"Yikes."

Heat crawled up Marina's neck. "Um, I like it actually. That's…that's kind of what I want to do. You know, when I grow up." Marina flushed even more at her admission to

Lila, her possible nemesis. "Um, what about you? Do you want to do something with math since it comes so easily?"

"Oh, I dunno. I mean, yeah, it comes easily enough, and I enjoy that part. But I don't know how much I actually like the math part. My mom…" Lila watched her fidgeting fingers. Her front teeth chewed on her lower lip. "My mom always says not to pick a path just because it's the easiest or the safest. I'm pretty sure that's what I would be doing if I became a mathematician or something. Other than that, I don't really know."

Marina's phone buzzed on her desk. It was a text from Lex.

> Ice cream before we check on the border?

With a grin, Marina texted back.

> Sounds good. Meet you @ Snack Station in 5.

Standing up, Marina tucked her phone into the pocket of her loose shorts, then closed her laptop. On top of it, she stacked her math textbook, binder, and notebook — the latter two maize-colored for math. She swept the entire pile into her waiting backpack. She and Lex would check on the border protecting Eversfield throughout the night, but there would be breaks for homework — or naps in Lex's case. "Hey, Lila, I gotta go, but we can talk more about your schedule later."

Marina shifted to the bottom drawer of her dresser, but her hand hovered over the handle. Maybe she could trust Lila with this one thing. And if not, it was a half-decent test that would allow Marina to sleep in her bed for one night. "I've got Astronomy Club tonight, so I might be in and out of the room late. It's all approved by Administration, but let me know if it bothers you."

Lila waved Marina's concerns away. "I'm sure it won't. I sleep like a rock." A whisper of a frown darted across Lila's face. "Um, I guess I'll see you later."

Guilt bubbled within Marina. She remembered her first lonely weeks at Eversfield all too well.

As she zipped her backpack shut and hurried to the door, Marina gulped down the guilt. Keeping Lila company wasn't her responsibility. "Yeah, see you later."

CHAPTER 23

Lila's stomach rumbled as she rushed into the classroom; she'd been far too nervous this morning to eat more than a couple bites of cereal. And it appeared Lila had every reason to be nervous. Not only was she getting piles of homework, but she'd had to do that stupid "stand in the front and say something interesting" thing in each of her past three classes. You'd think that after the first one, Lila would have it down pat, but no, she blanked on every single one. *And I'm probably not finished yet.*

Avoiding eye contact with the students who'd already taken their seats, Lila stumbled to the metal podium front and center. Behind it, a teacher with a snowy beehive shuffled through a stack of papers. Lila assembled what might be the last of her courage.

"Hi, Ms…" Lila stared at her worn class schedule, deliberating between various pronunciations of her math teacher's name. "Ms. Petoskanov?"

Only when her index finger reached the bottom of the top sheet did Ms. Petoskanov look up. "Yes?" Her voice creaked over her single word.

"I'm new, I'm supposed to give this to you?" Lila offered a note the color of Pepto-Bismol, identical to the ones she'd handed the previous three teachers.

Ms. Petoskanov collected the quarter-sheet of paper and examined it through bespectacled eyes. She gestured to where Lila stood. "Stay here until class starts." Spry steps at odds with her raspy voice and wrinkled-as-a-raisin face delivered Ms. Petoskanov to a coffee mug on the corner of a cluttered desk.

With a frown, Lila set her bursting backpack between her feet. Instead of racking her brain for the non-existent interesting fact, she studied her fingernails, the pattern of her plaid skirt, the brand-new scuff marks laced throughout her brand-new flats, anything to avoid that sea of chattering students in front of her.

Brrringhh! B-b-brrringhh! Brrringhh! Eversfield's old-fashioned bells chimed, announcing the beginning of class.

Lila drew a deep breath, a futile attempt to prepare for her big introduction. An empty desk waited in either back corner of Ms. Petoskanov's tidy grid. Which was supposed to be hers? Maybe she could pick? In which case, she would choose the one closest to the door and the escape route.

From behind her desk, Ms. Petoskanov clapped her hands together to quiet Lila's classmates. "All right, class. We will begin in a moment. First, we need to welcome our newest student, Miss Delilah Lee."

Lila winced. While she appreciated Ms. Petoskanov's peppy "teaching" voice, she wished she'd gotten Val's memo. Lila hated correcting people about her name, something she'd had to do her whole entire life. "Oh, um, actually it's—"

"Oh, that's right. I'm sorry, Miss Lee prefers to be called Lila. Okay, Miss Lee, why don't you introduce—"

A blur of inky hair dashed through the open door. It stopped Ms. Petoskanov in her tracks.

"I'm sorry, I'm sorry, Ms. Petoskanov, I had to run an errand during study hall that went a bit late. But it won't happen again, I promise." Gabe lowered his voice to a whisper, "I did get this for you though, as an apology." Using his hand to shield it from the vision of the other students — all except Lila — Gabe placed a four pack of chocolate truffles behind a stack of textbooks on Ms. Petoskanov's desk.

"Mr. Lazare, you know I do not tolerate tardiness. But I suppose..." Ms. Petoskanov completed a quick — but thorough — investigation of the chocolate, obvious only from Lila's standing perspective. "In this case, you have not missed anything. *Yet.* Take your seat while Miss Lee introduces herself. Miss Lee, go ahead."

"Yes, um..." Lila dared a peek at Gabe. She'd expected to see nothing but his muscular back as he retreated to his desk.

Instead, Gabe walked backwards along the wall of windows. He flashed a crooked smile and winked at her.

Lila's legs turned to mush. Her brain did the same. Her fingers flew to pick at her hair only to find this morning's tight braid.

Everyone's eyes were on Lila and here she was, losing her mind over some boy. Lila's breath hitched, but she forced herself forward. Her voice shook. "Uh, hi everyone. Um, like Ms...like she said, my name is Lila Lee. I'm a sophomore, and I just started at Eversfield this year." Lila glanced at Ms. Petoskanov for help, but she was too busy drooling over her truffles. "Um, I'm in Lizzie, I mean, Elizabeth Blackwell...house. Um..." Biting her bottom lip, Lila searched for something else to say. Should she just give up and ask Ms. Petoskanov whether she could be done?

Ms. Petoskanov dropped her chocolates into a drawer and closed it. A lock clicked into place. "Yes, very good, dear. You may take your seat." Ms. Petoskanov pointed at the final open seat, the one in the back corner near the exit. The one all the way across the classroom from *him*.

"Okay, class, let's go over last night's homework. Switch papers with your assigned partners. Oh, and Miss Lee, please see me after class. We'll have to get you caught up with the summer's work as soon as possible."

Lila sighed. Her homework pile was about to become a mountain.

SHIFTING FROM ONE FOOT TO THE OTHER, LILA stretched her frozen claw of a hand. How did a little old lady like Ms. Petoskanov generate pages and pages of notes during a single hour-long class? And how many questions could this too-zealous classmate ask? At the close of class, he'd headed straight for Ms. Petoskanov. Since Lila still had to collect her things at that point, it hadn't worried her. Now she'd spent the last five minutes standing a respectful distance away, watching the clock and waiting. All for the glory of adding more homework to her endless heap.

It wasn't all terrible, though. Lila had lunch next, so he wasn't making her late for her next class. And being late for her first lunch at Eversfield might be good. With everyone settled by the time she got there, maybe she could find a friendly face or two. At the very least, she could tuck her invisible self into an invisible corner.

"Okay, Mr. Frazer? I need to speak with Miss Lee now if there's nothing else." Despite Mr. Frazer's working lips, Ms. Petoskanov ushered him to the open door. "Remember, Mr. Frazer, you can bring any other questions to my weekly office hours."

With Mr. Frazer out the door, Ms. Petoskanov walked past Lila to her cluttered desk. She sank into her chair, crossed one leg over the other, then waved Lila over. "All right, Miss Lee, I apologize for the wait. I've taken the liberty of compiling the homework we completed over the summer."

Lila suppressed a frown. She should be used to it by now. After all, this was her fourth class of the day and the fourth class to assign her overdue homework from the summer. And Ms. Petoskanov had mentioned it earlier.

"As you've likely guessed, the entire class completed a bundle of assignments over the summer and turned them in yesterday. Obviously, you could not do this." Ms. Petoskanov handed Lila a hefty pile of papers fastened together with an extra-large binder clip. "On top you'll see the list of assignments. I expect you to finish them in a timely manner, say by next Monday?" Not waiting for Lila to accept the deadline, Ms. Petoskanov pointed at the heavy packet clutched to Lila's chest. "Below the top sheet are copies of the relevant lecture notes from our Algebra II class. They may help you with the assignments, should you need it. Our textbook also contains review chapters. I assume you have the textbook?"

Lila nodded, her eyes now flowing over the top sheet of the packet from Ms. Petoskanov. It listed eight assignments, each consisting of twenty problems. One hundred and sixty problems to complete in less than a week. In addition to the homework Ms. Petoskanov had given them today. In addition to the homework—both current and overdue—from the rest of her classes. Lila wiggled the packet into a space between two textbooks in her backpack. Only with great effort did her backpack zip shut.

Ms. Petoskanov smiled, displaying a dull snaggletooth to the right of her front teeth. "Wonderful. The textbook is an excellent resource. Now, my weekly office hours are posted outside the door, as well as the meeting times of a few study groups. I suggest you use at least one method to catch up." Ms. Petoskanov assessed Lila through lenses that magnified her amber eyes. "I know, Miss Lee, this must be quite different from your old school. Should you need help, please come to my office hours or join one of the study groups. Remember, we would not have admitted you if we did not think you up to the challenge. Yes, you have a good deal of work ahead of you, both now and over the next three years. But I assure you it will be well worth it."

Her motivational speech complete, Ms. Petoskanov stood and guided the staggering Lila toward the exit. In the two minutes it had taken for Lila to "chat" with Ms. Petoskanov, gravity had quadrupled its force. Lila's feet dragged toward the door.

"I'll see you tomorrow, Miss Lee."

"Yes. Thank you." The door closed behind Lila. She untucked her navy polo, then tugged at the hem. Had she just thanked her teacher for assigning her months' worth of homework to complete in less than a week? Shaking her head at her stupidity, Lila glanced up to get her bearings. She'd already gotten lost twice today. She didn't want to make it a third time.

Icy blue eyes collided with hers.

Lila's heart hiccuped. Her breath stuttered. Her thoughts slammed to a halt. Gabe — *Gabe* — leaned against the opposite wall. A lock of wavy hair dipped past his inky brows. His mouth was cocked in that crooked half-smile.

Gabe slid his phone into his pocket. "Hey. Thought I'd walk you to the caf for lunch."

CHAPTER 24

GABE

Gabe wasn't sure why he'd done it, but done it he had. Now Lila was here in front of him with shock painted over her face like she couldn't believe that he would wait for her. Gabe peeled himself off the brick wall and started down the hallway.

Lila's shoes slapped against the tile as she caught up to him. "What…I mean, how…I mean, how did you know?"

"Marina told me you have Chem together." Gabe's stomach twisted at the admission that he'd checked up on her. "So when I saw you in my math class, I just put two and two together." He elbowed Lila, desperate to make her smile, though he had no idea why. "Get it? Math, two and two?"

Lila shook her head at his terrible joke, but a giggle or two escaped her. "Did you really just make a math pun?"

"Yup, and I'm darn proud of it." Gabe led Lila down the stairs and into the covered walkway between the math and science building and the cafeteria. Her fingers fiddled with a backpack strap. Trained as he was to notice any movement out of the ordinary, it caught his eye.

Gabe leaned back onto his heels, then whistled. "Geez, Lila, what did you fill your backpack with? Books for your entire course load? That thing looks like it's about ready to explode."

"Um…" Lila bit her lip and shoved her hands into the pockets of her plaid skirt. She avoided his gaze like a naughty dog.

It was better than a confession. "Really? You're carrying *all* of the books for *all* of your classes?"

Lila shrugged. The straps of her overloaded backpack dug into her shoulders. "I didn't know what I would need. And the teachers *have* been adding to it."

The fingers of Gabe's free hand twitched at his side. He could carry that stuffed backpack without an ounce of pain, thanks to his supernatural nature. But it wasn't a line he was willing to cross. "Okay, that's fair. I'm guessing they've given you enough homework to last a month or so?"

"If not longer," Lila grumbled.

"Well, here's a tip, courtesy of one Gabriel Lazare. It's okay to go back to your room between classes. In fact, I encourage it."

Lila's bright green eyes darted up to his. "I didn't think I would have enough time. This campus is so big, how do people do it?"

"Now that depends on who you are. Take Marina, for example. She plots out each and every stop in her day based on proximity to her—*your*—room. Me, on the other hand, you saw my strategy today."

Lila snorted. "What? Bribe the teachers?"

"No, I wouldn't say bribe. I just keep…little gifts in my room. Just in case."

"Mmhmm." One of Lila's dark eyebrows arched upward. "Does this mean your room is always stocked with chocolate?"

Gabe grinned. Energy that had nothing to do with fighting *them* pulsed along his limbs. "Maybe…you're welcome to find out."

"Hmmm." Lila tugged at the end of her braid. "No, I think you'll have to prove it to me first. Should be easy since we have math together and all."

"All right, I'll see what I can do. No promises, though. My stash is for bribing teachers, not sophomore girls." Gabe held the cafeteria's back door open for Lila.

Walking through it backward, she pointed at his chest. "Aha! You admit it! You *do* bribe the teachers!" Lila turned around. Her brows rose and her mouth fell agape.

Even this rear portion of the cafeteria swam with students. Although Gabe had expected nothing less, it was brand new for Lila. She stopped just inside the door, her face slack while her eyes crawled over the crowd. Along the wall of windows, two cafeteria workers swiped card after card while the other three handed out boxed lunches from neat piles on the tables spread in front of them.

Ignoring the tickle of butterfly wings, Gabe grabbed Lila's hand and squeezed them through the mass of students. Only once they had both entered the dim hallway in the opposite corner did Gabe release her.

His shaky fingers swept through his hair.

Gabe's jaw clenched. *She's just a potential Latent I have to keep an eye on. That's all.* His heart beat in time to the two pairs of feet hitting the tile floor.

When they emerged from the narrow hallway, Gabe gulped away whatever-that-was and spread his arms wide. He squinted against the blazing light streaming through the floor-to-ceiling windows. "Here we are."

The front of the cafeteria was even more packed than the back. Most waited in a line extending from the serving stations next to him and Lila, down the wall of windows, and past the side doors. It stopped a few feet shy of the back corner. Scattered along the reddish-brown benches and chairs were the few students who'd already made it through that line and those who'd chosen a boxed lunch instead of a hot meal. In the far corner, teachers climbed up a stairway to the overhanging staff lounge, including a tray-laden Ms. Pershing.

Emilia waved to Gabe from his usual table near the middle of the maze. He sent her a smile, but his nails bit into his notebook. She was a reminder that he could not stay with Lila. He had responsibilities that were too important to ignore, even for a half hour. He'd done his part. He'd walked her here. He'd watched for manifesting talents. His work was done. Now it was time to leave her.

But what harm could it cause to stay? It was Lila's first day, and here she was, all alone again, just like at Semester Start. He could stay with her.

His gaze collided with Emilia's. No, he couldn't. "Well, this is my stop."

"Oh, okay." Lila covered her frown with a half-hearted smile.

Compassion surged within Gabe.

He ground his teeth against it. A breath later, he grinned and pointed a teasing finger at Lila. "Now, don't forget, Lila…"

Her emerald stare dashed up to his.

Gabe's stomach flipped, but he got the words out. "Stop by your room before your next class and unload that thing. You look like a giant tortoise." Gabe turned away from her, retreating to Emilia and the Clan.

Until he remembered. Then he spun on his heel and walked toward Emilia backward. He called, "Oh and Lila! You don't have to bring every textbook to every class. In fact, you probably don't need to bring them at all. That was tip number two." He winked—the perfect disguise—then jogged the few remaining feet to Emilia.

With a cocked eyebrow, Emilia handed him his usual plate of pizza. "What was all that about?"

"All what?" Gabe dug into his pizza, grateful for the excuse to compose his thoughts.

"Back there. With the girl from Sunday night."

Gabe swallowed a bite. When he spoke, nonchalance dripped from his voice. "Marina's new roommate. I'm s'posed to keep an eye on her, you know, because of last year." Gabe had long forgotten about those worries from only a few days ago, but they'd popped up again just in time. "We're in the same math class right before this, so I walked her back."

Emilia nodded, accepting his half-truth as complete. "You gonna keep doin' that?"

Gabe hadn't thought about it. Yet his decision was made in an instant. "Think so. At least till we know she's no threat."

The lies piled up around Gabe. To Emilia, his relationship with Lila was all about protecting Marina, something from which it had started. To Marina, it was about discovering whether Lila was a Latent, something that still concerned him. To him…well, he didn't know what it was about. And maybe he liked that. A touch of uncertainty when his future was certain. Plus, when he was around her, all the…*complications* of life as a Clan Warrior faded away like they were someone else's memories. Like he had a normal, human future.

"So, about patrol tonight…"

Gabe squashed his grimace. For that short while, he was almost normal, almost a regular person, not a supernatural freak. That time had passed.

CHAPTER 25

Joining the tail end of the lunch line, Lila swallowed her swelling dejection. She'd expected Gabe to ditch her as soon as they arrived at the cafeteria. Yet a tiny, stubborn, *stupid* part of her had refused to believe it. It had insisted that she could sit with him, that she could get to know him, that she could avoid stereotypical newbie lunchtime drama. It was wrong.

Now Gabe sat next to that girl from Sunday night's party and from last night's dinner. She handed him a plate of pizza from her own tray.

Emilia. First Heidi, now her. All the girls buzzed around Gabe. Girls much prettier and more confident than Lila. She would never catch his eye.

Not that Lila cared. Based on Flynn's speech last night and this morning's classes, she should focus on school, not on some guy who wouldn't know she existed if she wasn't his little sister's roommate.

Someone tapped Lila's shoulder.

Lila flinched. Careful to avoid smacking her fellow students with her turtle shell of a backpack, she turned around.

Marina greeted her with a tentative smile. "Hey, um, hi, Lila. Sorry, I didn't mean to startle you."

"No, it's okay." Lila rubbed at her tired eyes. "So, how's your day going?"

"Good. How about you?"

Lila bit her lower lip. A rant about all the stresses of Eversfield and Marina's too-cute, too-friendly brother threatened to tumble out. But there was no way Marina wanted to hear about all that. "Fine."

"So…" Marina's navy eyes skimmed over the heads of the students around them. "Have you had a proper lunch here yet?"

Lila clamped onto the question like a drowning swimmer onto a life preserver. Small talk was not her specialty. "No! They brought in a sandwich and chips during my exams yesterday."

"Ah, the infamous Eversfield boxed lunch." Marina gestured to the S-shaped counter that they inched toward. "Not sure if you know, but the boxed lunches are available for students out back, behind the serving area. Come midterm time, they regularly sell out. There's also a dinner version, in case you want something quick before studying."

"Oh, okay. That's good to know."

"Yeah. I mean, technically we're not allowed to bring food into the main part of the library or the computer labs…"

"But everyone does anyway?"

Marina flashed a rare grin. "Exactly. If you do, just, you know, be careful. And clean up afterward."

Lila winced. A vision of her unmade bed, her cluttered desk, her scattered books, and Val's leaning tower of dresses popped up. At least she'd kept the mess to her side? "Yeah. And don't worry, I'll clean up the room tonight."

Marina shoved her hands into the pockets of her loose khakis. "Oh, um, it's okay."

"Really, Marina. I don't have a ton of work thus far." *Lie.* "And Val has dance team practice all night." *Truth.*

"Oh, yeah, that's right. The football team scrimmage is this Saturday. That's usually the dance team's first performance."

"Are you going?" Within the pockets of her plaid skirt, Lila crossed her fingers. Val had made it clear that Lila would be going.

"To what?"

"The football scrimmage."

Marina's inky braid slapped either shoulder as she shook her head. "Oh, no, definitely not. I mean, I'm sure that's fun for some people and all…"

"Yeah." Her lips pressed into a thin line, Lila cast for a new topic. "So…what do you recommend for lunch?"

Marina scanned a pair of monitors hanging above the stainless steel counters. "Well…the grilled cheese and fries are pretty popular, but I find that a bit heavy for lunch. Of course, there's pizza, but that's pretty much in the same boat. I usually go with either the chicken Caesar salad or the soup and sandwich combo. If I have junk food, I get sleepy." Marina glanced askance at Lila. "But I mean, yeah, people seem to really like the grilled cheese. And you can get it with tomato or avocado."

"Yeah, I'm not gonna lie, grilled cheese sounds way better than your salad." Lila smirked. "Maybe I'll get it with tomato to make it healthy."

Rolling her eyes, Marina grabbed an energy drink from one of the fridges ahead of the serving counters. "Yes, *that* makes it healthy. And for the record, I'd get it if I could, but every time I did, I ended up snoozing through my classes."

"Maybe if you didn't stay up super late with Astronomy Club…"

Marina's cheeks flushed. "I didn't have a choice. That's just…what you get when you're part of that club."

"Hmmph. Sounds like I shouldn't join Astronomy Club then. Hey, Marina, is there by any chance a Sleep Club?"

"No, there is not a Sleep Club, Lila." Despite the exasperation edging her tone, Marina smiled. "Besides, I would've been up almost as late with that math homework anyway. It took *forever*, even with me cheating and looking it up on the internet."

"Next time let me help." Lila watched Marina swipe her keycard through the machine. The last thing she wanted was to be forever labeled as the stupid new girl who couldn't figure out how to pay for lunch.

Marina stepped to the side, making room for Lila in front of the register. "Oh, um, okay. I mean, if you really want to." Marina's fingers wrapped around the edges of her plastic tray.

"I do." Lila mimicked Marina's movements: swipe the card, wait for a nod from the attendant, then clear out for the next person.

To her relief, it went without a hitch. Lila then followed Marina through the maze of wooden tables, chairs, and benches, refusing to notice that Gabe chatted with Emilia and three other students a couple tables away. "So, we have Chem after this, right?"

Marina stopped short of a rectangular table next to a floor-to-ceiling window. A single empty space remained on one of its copper-colored benches. Three pairs of eyes stared at Lila.

Lila's guts plunged past her toes. *Guess I'm the stupid new girl after all.*

CHAPTER 26

Marina pressed her lips together. Lila gazed at the single empty space on the bench, the one reserved for Marina.

"Oh, um, well, I guess I'll see you later." Lila's voice trembled despite its upbeat tone. She turned to leave.

Marina's insides knotted with guilt. She sucked in a breath. "No, Lila, it's okay. I'm sure we can...we can find a chair or something. Or maybe squeeze together?"

"'Course we can!" Yuki, the sun glinting off her spiky hair, slid over. Her muscular shoulder brushed against the window displaying the carpet of grass between the cafeteria and the brick façade of Blackwell. The familiar forest peeked out from behind the dorms. Its leaves fluttered in the light breeze.

Marina's fingers dug into her laden tray. If only they were outside, she could summon a hint of that power to comfort her, to strengthen her. But to bring the wind into the cafeteria would require a display that would leave no doubt as to what she was.

Marina swallowed a sigh. After a quick inspection of the floor—this was the second of three lunch periods after all—she tucked her backpack beneath the carved wooden bench. Then she stepped over it and sat next to Yuki. Patting the narrow spot beside her, Marina offered a weak smile to Lila.

When Lila sank onto the bench, Marina's smile faded away. Foreboding darkened her heart. Maybe this was Lila's master plan. She'd find Marina's hard-won friends, then steal them away. And Marina, like an idiot, had led Lila right to them.

Yuki leaned over the tabletop, bypassing Marina to get to Lila. "You're Lila, right?"

Her grilled cheese hovering in the air, Lila nodded.

Yuki's rosebud of a mouth stretched wider. "Don't worry, I haven't been stalking you or anything. We have AmLit together, so technically I've already met you."

Lila rolled her eyes. "Oh, yeah, *that*."

"Yeah, that. Which, by the way, I think is totally ridiculous. I mean, it's not like we have to do that when we're freshmen. So why do you have to do that now? It's stupid." Yuki bit into her ham and cheese sandwich.

Lila twirled a crinkled fry, then dipped it in mustard. "I couldn't agree more. But at least I won't have to do it again. You know, until this afternoon."

A wave of nausea hit Marina. Two classes, she had *two* classes with Lila this afternoon. During which Marina would probably believe Lila was an archnemesis of the utmost skill one moment and a potential friend the next. It was far more drama than Marina liked in her regular, non-Clan life.

Yuki shook her head. Her spikes quivered with the movement. "Ugh, like I said, it's so stupid and unnecessary. Like some dull introduction at the front of class is going to make everyone friends."

"I know! And yet every single teacher seems to think it's the best idea ever." Lila swallowed a sip of pop.

"Lila," Angelo interrupted from across the table, his hand sweeping black locks behind an ear, "don't get Yuki started. Believe me. In other news, I'll be seein' you at eight

236

a.m. every weekday. Or should I say 'ocho?'" Angelo clicked finger guns at Lila.

Only when Yuki slapped them down did Marina remember her manners. "Sorry, Lila, I forgot to introduce you to everyone." Businesslike, she pointed to Yuki next to her. "This is Yuki, with whom you apparently have AmLit."

Yuki waved, all smiles and altogether friendlier than Marina would have liked.

"Across from her is Angelo. Apparently you have Spanish together?"

"*Sí, señorita.*" Angelo pushed frameless glasses up his hooked nose.

"And Mickey's next to him."

Mickey extended a hand the size of a frying pan across the table toward Lila. "Nice to meet you, Lila."

"You too. Though…" Lila's voice trailed off. Her green eyes narrowed. "Don't we have math together? Honors Pre-Calc, right before this?"

Mickey's lips spread into a grin, revealing the gap between his front teeth. "We sure do! I didn't think you would remember. You know, with all the other students I'm sure you've been meeting today."

"Yeah, I'm not gonna lie, it's been a lot. But I'm trying to remember everyone." Lila bit into her grilled cheese.

With the introductions complete, silence hung over the table. Marina crunched through her lettuce leaves dripping with Caesar dressing, hunting for something the five of them could talk about.

Yuki saved her, "So Lila, do you know what extracurriculars you'll be doing?"

"No, not really. Are there any you recommend?"

"Well…there's Engaging Eversfield, the school newspaper. I do photography for it and the yearbook. Angelo and Marina are on double-E too." Yuki glanced toward Angelo, whose mouth burst with beef and bean burrito. "Angelo, who obviously lacks any semblance of etiquette, reports on international news, and Marina covers science."

Angelo's hand floated to his chest like a horrified southern belle. Then he opened his mouth, displaying its contents for all to see.

Everyone at the table groaned—except for Yuki, who reached across the table to cuff Angelo's ear.

Picking up a fry from the heap on her plate, Yuki shifted back to Lila. "Anyway…Mickey, nerd that he is, is on the math competition team."

Mickey's callused hands rose in protest. "Hey, hey, hey! Gimme some credit. I'm also on the basketball team."

"And when was the last time you saw the court during a game?" When Mickey began to respond, Yuki cut him off, "When Eversfield wasn't losing by a ton?"

Mickey's mouth snapped shut with an audible click.

"That's what I thought. As you can see, Lila, there are plenty of options. I'm sure you'll find something. Hey, you don't by any chance play volleyball, do you?" Yuki stared at Lila, her almond eyes greedy.

Stress congealed into a sticky lump that filled Marina's stomach. If Lila played on the volleyball team, she'd have no trouble stealing Yuki away.

Lila shook her head.

Marina fought the sigh of relief pressing against her lips.

Snapping her fingers, Yuki replied, "Darn. I'm also on the volleyball team. We're not exactly good, so we're always searching for new talent."

Lila wiped up a spot of mustard on her tray with a paper napkin. "I'm afraid I'm not very coordinated, so sports aren't really my thing."

"What *is* your thing, Lila?" Mickey leaned over the table toward her.

"Oh, um…" Lila tugged on the end of her braid and chewed her lower lip.

Pity trickled through Marina's veins. Eversfield asked a lot of its students. It couldn't be an easy adjustment for a transfer. And her friends might be making it worse right now. "Don't worry about it, Lila. I'm sure you'll find something. If you want…if you want, we can chat about it later. You know, if—"

"If she wants?" Angelo's thick lips twitched toward a smirk.

Marina grabbed a fry off Yuki's plate and tossed it at him. It hit Angelo square in the middle of his oily forehead.

"Hey! I was going to eat that!" Yuki protested.

"Here, you can have one of mine." Mickey threw a fry toward Yuki.

It hit the back of Marina's hand.

One of Yuki's fine eyebrows quirked upward. "You sure you're on the basketball team with that kind of expert passing?"

"If any of you came to a game, you could find out," Mickey retorted.

With her gaze trained on Mickey, Marina bumped her shoulder into Yuki's. "If you guys actually won games, maybe we'd come."

Rolling his hazel eyes, Mickey began stuffing fries into his grilled cheese. "No, you wouldn't."

"You're right. We wouldn't." Yuki stuck her tongue out at Mickey.

"What're you doing?" Lila stared at Mickey's plate.

Marina—along with Angelo and Yuki—shook her head, but she allowed Mickey to explain his abominable creation to the newcomer.

"Making grilled freese obviously." Mickey stuck one final fry into the gooey cheese. Then he smushed the sandwich together. Potato burst from the inside of the fries.

"Grilled freese?"

Mickey waved his modified sandwich at Lila. "Grilled freese. Grilled cheese with fries in it. Wanna try?"

Yuki leaned over Marina toward Lila. "Do not, I repeat, *do not* try it, Lila. It is possibly the most disgusting thing in the world."

"It is not!"

"It is so!"

As Mickey and Yuki argued, Lila cast a questioning look at Marina.

Marina shrugged. "It's…not great. But I guess it's not altogether terrible either." On a strange impulse, she whispered in Lila's ear, "Yuki just likes to argue."

"Okay, okay," Lila interrupted Mickey and Yuki. "I'll try it."

With a triumphant grin, Mickey extended the sandwich across the table.

Lila took a delicate bite, then swallowed. "It's not terrible—"

"See, I told you!" Mickey trumpeted.

240

Lila held up a hand with her fingers outstretched. "But it's not good either. Would not recommend."

"See, *I* told *you*!" Yuki turned toward Lila, bending around Marina once again. "Lila, I think this is the beginning of a beautiful friendship."

Lila's brows dropped and her lips pursed. "*Casablanca*, right?"

Yuki beamed. "Right."

Lila flashed a grin at Marina, who struggled to return even a shadow of a smile. *Already Lila fits in better with my friends than I do.*

CHAPTER 27

With stuffed shopping bags bumping against her hip, Val swiped the illicit keycard through the lock on Lila's door. She held her breath.

Green pinpricks of lights flashed. The lock clanged as it unlatched.

Grinning at Rudi behind her, Val opened the door. "See, I told you, Margaret *always* comes through in a pinch." Val tossed her bags onto Marina's battered loveseat.

Rudi followed suit. "Seems like. And you're good until the appointment?"

"Of course. And thank you, Rudi. I know how you like to use study hall for, you know, actual studying." Rolling her eyes like that was the least common use ever in the history of Eversfield Preparatory Academy, Val strode to Lila's closet.

"I do, but it's early in the year. 'Sides I like skippin' outta here, you know that." In the doorway, Rudi flipped a fiery lock over her shoulder. "I'll pick you and Lila up over at Admin in a couple hours?"

"Yup, see you then. And close that door most of the way, please." Val straightened a tuft of rebellious hair in the mirror on the back of the closet door. In the reflection, she watched Rudi exit. Per Val's request, Rudi left the heavy wooden door of Lila's room ajar. Yellow light from the hallway formed a line along its side and top no wider than Val's thumb.

Twisting the knob next to the mirror, Val opened Lila's closet. Without hesitation, she wrapped her arms around the pants, blouses, and sweaters — all of Lila's uniforms. The clothes dropped onto the floor in a heap to be dealt with later. Next, Val hauled the shopping bags from the couch into the shadow of the open closet door. Three of the bags matched, all a lilac color with two intertwined roses in the middle. The last was plain brown and creased. That was where Val started.

From the wrinkled bag, Val removed a smaller paper bag and placed it in the freezer section of the mini-fridge between Marina's lofted bed and Lila's closet. Then Val took out the four freshly altered plaid skirts, along with the empty garbage bag for Lila's old clothes. After removing the hangers from Lila's too-long, too-loose plaid skirts, Val dropped them into the garbage bag. She hung up the new ones in their place with a satisfied smile.

Val repeated the process with the contents of the three lilac bags, replacing Lila's old ill-fitting shirts, sweaters, and pants with the new stylish ones. She'd even gotten Lila a few dresses — perfect for JCC house parties — two pairs of tighter jeans, and several shirts that were more appropriate for Lila and her status. By the time Val finished, the garbage bag stood up on its own.

The door creaked behind Val.

From her spot kneeling in front of Lila's open dresser drawer, Val turned around with her biggest smile.

A scowl met her. The dour Marina rumbled, "What are you doing in here?"

Val returned to tucking in the last of Lila's new clothes. Marina didn't deserve her attention.

"I said…" Marina dared to approach Val. Her hand grasped Val's shoulder. "What are you doing?"

Val peeled Marina's hand off like it was covered with slime. "None of your business."

"Excuse me. You're in *my* room doing something, and it's none of my business?"

"Correct." Val caressed Lila's lovely new clothes, then shut the now-full dresser drawer.

Marina walked to the garbage bag sitting in front of the mini-fridge. Her big toe bumped in and out of it. "What's this?"

Enough. Val whirled on Marina. "I said…" Val dragged the bag away from Marina. "None of your business."

"Does Lila know you're doing this?"

"Why do you care?"

"She's my…" Marina's voice trailed off. She bit her lower lip.

Pressing her advantage, Val crossed the remaining distance between them in a single stride. When Val glared up at Marina, her forehead was an inch away from Marina's pointy chin. "Listen, *Marina*," Val spat out her name. "Let's get one thing straight here. Despite *this*," Val's hand waved around the room, "Lila is my friend, not yours."

Marina gulped.

A burst of pleasure exploded in Val's gut. This was the Marina she remembered from last year, the one who was easy to back into a corner. The one who always yielded.

Marina's stance widened. Her hands dug into her narrow hips. "That may be, but Lila ought to know what's going on. From the way you snuck in here, I'm guessing she does not." From the pocket of her baggy khakis, Marina whipped out her phone.

Val fought the urge to bat it away. Now was not the time for violence. Now was the time for smug certainty. "Go ahead. I guarantee Lila will be happy with my actions, not upset."

Marina's fingers hovered over her phone.

Gotcha.

They picked up their typing again.

Val sucked in an angry breath.

"There, text sent. We'll see how happy Lila is." Marina retreated to the cavern beneath her lofted bed.

Val scowled. *Might as well clean up while I wait, I guess.* With a grumble, Val dragged the stuffed garbage bag to rest next to stupid Marina's stupid closet, then folded the empty shopping bags and tucked them between the garbage bag and the wall. The room once again spick and span, Val leaned against Lila's closed closet door. She pulled out her phone and stared at the screen. Should she text Rudi now? They could start an offensive against Marina.

No, not just yet.

The open door cracked wider. A frowning Lila stepped over the threshold. Her fingers wound around her backpack straps. "Val, what's going on?"

Val suppressed hurling a glare toward the hidden Marina. *Nothing but bright optimism, Val.*

With an excited smile, Val collected Lila's hands and squeezed. "Just the most wonderful thing, Lila dear."

Lila's emerald gaze narrowed. "What do you mean?"

"I mean…" Val beamed at Lila, then flicked open the closet door behind her. "I got you new uniforms. Nothing but the best for my Lila!"

"I don't need new uniforms, Val." Fatigue laced Lila's voice. She didn't so much as peek inside the closet.

"It's not about 'need,' silly, it's about want. And what you, as my best friend in the whole wide world, deserve."

"Val…"

Marina approached Lila, shouldering a loaded backpack. She tilted her head toward the open door. "Hey, I'm gonna go. It sounds like you two have a bit to discuss."

Lila's eyes widened with alarm. "No, Marina, it's fine. You have the room. I'll go to Val's. She's got a single. We can talk there. I don't wanna kick you out of your own room."

"It's okay, Lila. Really. I was gonna go to the library and work on some math homework anyway."

Lila's brow furrowed. "Okay, if you're sure…but if the math's not due tomorrow, at least let me help you with it later. You know, to make up for hogging the room."

Marina grinned at Lila. "Sounds good. I'll get the first draft down tonight, then you can help me tweak it tomorrow."

"Deal." Lila followed Marina to the doorway, then whispered, "And I *am* sorry, Marina. Next time, I'll meet Val in her room."

Val crossed her arms over her chest. *That* was not appropriate behavior for a Lizzard to a lowly Blackwellian.

"Sounds good. See you later, Lila." Marina's heavy steps echoed down the hallway.

When Lila turned away from the door, she glared at Val. "What did you think you were doing?"

Squashing her irritation, Val mimicked surprise, "What do you mean? I thought your uniforms could use a nice li'l upgrade, so I used my allowance to do so." Val gestured to the haphazard pile of dresses stacked on Lila's dresser. By now, they were probably as wrinkly as Lila's shirt. "I even

246

got you a few more dresses, so you won't hafta borrow any of those."

"That's not what I mean, Val. And I think you know it." Lila's gaze flashed toward Val's, all accusation. "You practically threw Marina out of here."

"I did not! She could have stayed. Her wardrobe could certainly use some updating."

"That, Val, *that's* what I'm talking about! That's mean. What does it matter what she wears? Or what I wear? Or what you wear? We wear uniforms ninety percent of the time anyway."

"Lila, Lila, Lila, let's not fight. You just got here!" Val rushed to the fridge and removed the paper bag. "I even brought you some super yummy ice cream for while we play dress up." Val wiggled the pint of banana walnut ice cream — Lila's favorite — in front of her.

Lila's brow smoothed, but her full lips remained pursed. "Okay, fine. But next time we meet at your place." She reached for the ice cream.

Val whipped it away. "Not quite yet, Lila dear. You only get ice cream after you try on an outfit. Let's say…three spoonfuls per outfit?" Val got out the other pint — chocolate raspberry fudge — and placed both on top of the mini-fridge. Her chin jerked toward the open closet next to them. "You forgot to look inside, Lila dear."

An instant after she obeyed, Lila poked her head around the open closet door. "Did you keep *any* of my old uniforms?"

Val snuck an arm around Lila's waist, then leaned her head against Lila's round shoulder. "Why would I? These are *so* much better."

"But Val, I already had perfectly good uniforms."

Val rolled her eyes. "Puh-lease. Ms. Pershing's cast-offs aren't fit for anyone, let alone you."

"What do you mean 'let alone me?'" Lila wriggled out of Val's hold.

Val's thoughts raced. Lila clearly didn't approve of the natural distinctions of Lizzard and Blackwellian. "Just as a friend of mine, you deserve the very best. That's all."

"No, Val, I can't take these. The uniforms I have are fine." Lila strode toward the full garbage bag in the corner.

"They are not."

Lila scowled at Val, then upended the garbage bag. All Lila's old, wrinkly, ill-fitting uniforms tumbled out.

Val frowned for only a moment. Then she switched to her most persuasive voice. "C'mon, Lila dear. I only meant it as a lovely li'l surprise to show you how happy I am that you're here. It's the *least* I can do."

Lila's hands hovered over the pile of clothes.

Val pressed onward. "And don't worry, no one blames you. We all know that you didn't have time to shop for your uniforms, let alone get the right sizes. Lucky for you, you have me! I've already arranged to drop off all your old stuff at Ms. Pershing's, so it's not like anything will be wasted. See, Lila dear, I remembered how much you hate waste."

Lila chewed on her lower lip but didn't say anything.

That was a win in Val's book. Stepping around the spilt clothes, Val took Lila's hand and dragged her back to the closet. She pulled out a pair of khakis, identical to the ones Val wore, if a couple of sizes larger. "See, first, we've got the pants, in both the allowed khaki and navy. I made sure to get the ones that don't wrinkle, so they always look good, no ironing required. When you don't feel like wearing pants, you've got new plaid skirts, all altered to your specifications – "

"Wait, how did you..." The light dawned in Lila's green eyes. "When you insisted on being cc'd on the email about uniform sizes?"

"Yes, Lila dear. I had a feeling that you might...*struggle* finding the right wardrobe. But like I said, you have me for that!" Val continued pulling hangers out of the closet, displaying all of Lila's lovely new clothes. "Then we've got tanks for you to wear under these sweaters or these Henleys, all of which are emblazoned with the Eversfield logo, so they're perfectly legal to wear to class."

Lila's brows furrowed as she touched one of her new sweaters. "Didn't I already own some of these?"

"Certainly, Lila dear." *Two sizes too big and in last year's style.* "These are just li'l upgrades."

"I...I guess..."

Val guided Lila to the back of the closet where Val's favorite new things hung: the sparkly dresses. "I also took the liberty of getting you a few dresses. Before you complain, Lila dear," for Lila had indeed opened her mouth, "if you look closely, the straps are a bit wider than usual, and I did opt for either sparkles *or* bright colors, see?" Val held out a black sequined dress and compared it to the red and white polka-dotted one.

Lila's fingers caressed the silk skirt of the vintage dress.

Val beamed. Even Lila could be tamed by the right clothes. "See, it's not so bad, right?"

Lila pursed her lips. "I guess...but Val, this must've cost you a fortune."

The thrill of victory radiated through Val's limbs, pulsating through her fingertips. If they had made it to the financial portion of the discussion, Lila was ready to accept her fate. "Only a small one."

"Val, you shouldn't have. My clothes were fine as they were…actually, no, wait, I'll pay you back. How much was all this?" Lila waved at the closet.

"No, Lila dear, don't worry about it. Like you said, your clothes were fine as they were." Val struggled to keep a straight face through the lie. "This is my gift to you, no strings attached." *Well, there are strings, but they can wait a beat.*

"Still, I feel like I should pa—"

"Don't worry about it. Seriously, Lila." Val squeezed Lila's waist.

"Okay, just…thank you, Val."

"You're *very* welcome!" With her arm slung about Lila's waist, Val led them back toward the sofa. "Now that your clothes are taken care of—"

Lila stopped in her tracks. Panic twisted her round face. "Wait, you didn't do anything with my regular clothes, did you?"

"No, of course not, Lila dear. All I did was add a few more options."

Val reached the couch, but Lila stayed where she was, stranded in the middle of the room.

Sinking onto a cushion, Val patted the seat beside her. "But we'll look at those another day. I promise I didn't touch one item of your non-uniform clothes."

"Okay." Lila's front teeth worried her lower lip, but she crossed the rest of the distance to sit next to Val.

After turning to face Lila, Val folded her bare legs beneath her. "Anyway, I have a few more gifts for you, but we hafta go pick them up. You don't have plans tonight, do you?"

Lila's brows dropped. "No, but I thought you had dance team practice."

"Nah, I'm blowin' it off. *I* have more important things to do."

"Like?"

Val tugged on the end of Lila's braid. "Like gettin' you a haircut that'll tame these curls of yours." *And supervising a makeup lesson after.* "According to Heidi — who, you have to admit, has the *loveliest* curls — the key for curly hair is the right maintained haircut. She even pulled some strings at her salon so we could get you in tonight. And don't worry, we're only gonna do a trim, nothin' crazy."

Lila fingered her braid. "And it will…keep my hair in check?"

"Of course, Lila dear. We're going to Heidi's stylist, who specializes in curly hair." Val wagged a finger at Lila's parting lips. "And don't even think about complaining about the price. Like I said, these are gifts. You don't hafta repay me one penny. Being my friend is enough."

LILA

IF LILA HAD WAVERED BETWEEN INDIGNATION AT VAL'S unasked-for changes and guilt at Val having spent so much money on her, that last sentence pushed her over the edge. Guilt it was, with a side of nerves.

Staring at her clenched hands, Lila mumbled, "All right, well, thank you."

Val's arm wrapped around Lila's tight shoulders and squeezed. "That's my brave girl."

"Is that it then?" Lila raised her eyes to Val's, almost afraid to hear the answer.

"Almost, Lila dear, but let's have a li'l chat first."

Lila scrunched her nose. "A li'l chat" was code for lecture. "About what?"

"About…" Val pressed her lips into a bright, shiny line. "About certain compromises we both must make."

"Like?"

"Well, as the smartest person I know, I'm sure you've noticed that there are certain…*expectations* that come with being part of my group. And I know," Val's hand rose with her fingers outspread, halting Lila's objections before they could begin, "you never asked for them. Nor would you even try to satisfy them if I wasn't in the middle. But here's the thing, Lila: I *am* in the middle. Not all the pretty clothes in the world can change that. I need you to try a bit harder with my friends."

Lila frowned. *Haven't I been trying hard?* "Can't…can't the two of us just be friends? You know, without all the others?"

"That's not the way it works, not in my world."

Lila bit back a sigh. In her few days at Eversfield, she'd begun to doubt whether Val would choose her over popularity if it came down to it. "So?"

Val flashed a reassuring smile.

It sent Lila into a deeper depression.

"So just a few tweaks, Lila dear, and you'll be fine. I mean Cheri's part of our group. Surely you can do better than her!"

"Okay…but what does that mean exactly?"

"First: appearance. That one we've got nearly solved. You have your nice new uniforms, several dresses, and a few appropriate non-uniform choices, which we can expand over time. For the next week or two, I'll swing by before classes to help you pick out what to wear." Val rolled her eyes when Lila opened her mouth. "Before you ask: yes, I'll arrive early enough for you to get a quick breakfast and be on time to your first class." Val pinched Lila's upper arm. "You're so predictable, Lila dear. Anyway, before I arrive, you'll shower, and then I'll help you get ready."

Lila grimaced. If she knew Val—and she did—Val wouldn't stop at her clothes. No, it would be the whole shebang: hair, makeup, shoes, accessories, everything.

"Oh, don't gimme that look. I swear it won't take more than five minutes."

Lila arched a skeptical eyebrow.

"Okay, maybe ten, but that's it, I swear! And I'll prove it to you tomorrow."

Smothering the urge to cross her arms over her chest, Lila folded her hands in her lap. "And I suppose you'll also be doing my hair and makeup tomorrow?"

"Almost. I'm gonna *teach* you to do your hair and makeup tomorrow. I mean, yes, for the remainder of this week and perhaps next, I imagine it will be mostly me. But after that, you'll take over and eventually gain your full independence."

"You've got this all planned out, huh?"

A storm cloud descended over Val's usual cheer. Her tone dropped a level. "Well, after you disappeared from the Pasteur party Sunday night, I had plenty of time to think."

Lila winced. Based on their conversation yesterday, she'd thought Val hadn't noticed her early departure.

Val's voice returned to sunny and bright. "Which brings us to the second part of my plan."

"Wait, can you hold up a sec? Instead of you coming down here each morning, why don't I come to you?"

Val's brows furrowed. "But how will I decide what you're wearing?"

"The night before?"

Val continued to frown.

"Or we can take a picture of my closet now and you can text me your decision in the morning?"

Val arched an eyebrow. "You're that desperate to leave her alone?"

"It's polite, Val. I shouldn't have someone over before classes start. I mean, yes, Marina seems like she typically gets up super early to study, but that doesn't mean she won't sometimes be in the room when you want to make me over. I don't wanna wake her up or get in her way. She *is* my roommate after all."

"All right, fine, Lila. I'll text you with my decision in the morning until you can pick it out for yourself. Then you'll come up to me with all your hair and makeup stuff, and we'll do that in my room."

"Thank you."

"No problem. You ready to move on to part two?"

Lila nodded.

"Okay, so, your behavior. As you know, Sunday night was not a success."

"Val…"

"I know. It's my fault entirely. I saw you there with Gabe and I thought that was it. I think, though, we should put the whole 'boys' thing on hold for you at the moment. At least until you get used to everything here at Eversfield."

From Val's tender tone, the boy hiatus was meant to be a punishment, but Lila didn't mind. Her one and only crush was most likely taken—or soon to be, whether he chose Heidi or Emilia. Even if he was single, she was nothing more than his little sister's roommate. *Which is perfectly fine*, Lila reminded herself.

"In the meantime, you'll eat dinners with us, then hang out most nights. On Fridays, you'll wear one of your lovely new dresses. Unfortunately, you're on your own for lunch since none of us have the middle lunch period. But that should change when we select our freshman members at the end of October. And of course, you'll come out with us on weekends."

Lila sucked her lower lip between her teeth. She had an idea of where Val and her friends went on weekends. It was not her cup of tea. "Val, I don't want—"

"Relax, Lila dear. I've got it all under control. First, right now there are six of us. Rudi's li'l Benz only seats five. Since you're the newest member, you don't get a ride, which means you don't have to go. Of course, if anyone bails, you're the next one up. But this, Lila dear," Val squeezed Lila's kneecap, "*this* is where my compromise comes in. When you do go, we—both of us—will stay until Sara and Drey are sufficiently distracted. Then we'll leave and go do our own thing. How does that sound?"

Lila chewed on her lower lip. That might be…okay. Besides, she doubted any of Val's friends would skip a party. In that case, she'd never have to go in the first place. "Okay."

Val beamed. "And I'll start working on Sara and Drey to do more movie nights, bowling, that sort of thing. You know, *tame*, just how my Lila likes it."

"Thanks."

"No problem. See Lila, if we both compromise, just a hair, we can make this work! Of course, once we select our new freshmen, you'll have to go out a bit more since we'll take two cars, but even then, like I said, we'll stay for a bit, then leave."

"Sounds good…" Lila wiped her clammy palms against her plaid skirt. "Is that all?"

"Not quite, Lila dear. There's just one more thing…"

Lila held her breath.

"You need to make the dance team."

Lila groaned. It was worse than she expected. She slid down her seat on the couch, wishing its cushions would eat her alive. "Val, I can't dance, you know that."

"Nonsense, Lila dear. Of course you can, especially if we begin practicing tomorrow. Tryouts aren't till the end of October."

"Val!"

"Listen, Lila, I'll teach you the basics now. Once we get closer to tryouts, I'll teach you the exact routine we use. Sara will've ousted Jen by then, so she'll be captain. That means she'll design the routine, which means I'll know the routine."

"Isn't that unfair to the others?"

Val's breath exploded in a *whoosh*. "No. What's unfair is that they have years of training that you don't. We'll only be making up for that."

"There must be something else I can —"

"You need an extracurricular by the end of October and this is it. Easy peasy." Val dusted her hands off as if Lila had already made the dance team.

Maybe it wouldn't be so bad. And Val was right. Lila needed an extracurricular. Plus, it would be a little exercise, which was more than she was getting now. "Okay, deal."

Val hugged Lila with the enthusiasm of a dog reunited with its long-lost owner. "Oh, Lila dear, everything is gonna be perfect. You'll see!"

CHAPTER 28

Kane's breath hitched. Her fingers poked at the pink puckered skin that slashed across her abdomen. After the…*incident*, Kane had dragged herself on her hands and knees to her room. A trail of blood had followed her. For two days, she'd hidden there, unwilling to face them. They probably laughed at her behind her back.

::Stop that.::

Kane opened her silver eyes.

Her unwelcome companion loomed over her. Today, Grace's shimmering waves were tied into a loose ponytail. She wore inky leggings and a matching tank top, the same as Kane.

Kane tugged her shirt down over her stomach, then shifted to lie on her side. Pins pricked down the length of her wound. Most likely, it wouldn't fully heal until after her next meal, a side effect of her sparse feeding schedule.

Kane injected a grumble into her mental voice. *::Stop what?::*

::Feeling sorry for yourself.::

With her forearm draped over her eyes, Kane blocked Grace from her sight. *::Why should I? Seems like plenty has gone wrong.::*

::Because you're being stupid. If Fang wanted to kill you, he would have.::

Kane peered at Grace around her forearm. *::But where did he get that bespelled dagger?::*

Grace waved a translucent hand. *::That doesn't matter. And by the way, you could not have known to check it for spells beforehand. After all, he pressed that dagger into his own thumb. I've never heard of vampires subjecting themselves to the Clan's spells. Of course, Fang didn't draw blood, so the spells wouldn't have gotten far. Still, his thumb must've burned like –::*

::Enough, Grace. I get it. I couldn't have known to check. But you can bet I'll check every weapon I see around here in the future.::

::As you should. Now back to what matters. Why didn't Fang kill you?::

Kane pushed herself into a seated position. Her scar burned as if the skin had been stretched too tight. *::I don't know. Maybe because he's an evil vampire who sometimes does evil things without remorse? Ugh, I knew I should've kept that spell going to make them docile like the ones back at Duncan's.::*

Grace shook her head, her ponytail swinging from side to side. *::No. We talked about that. If a Clan Diviner stumbled across it, we'd be found in an instant.::*

Kane crossed her arms but couldn't disagree.

::Back to our actual problem, Kane. Fang is one of Duncan's lieutenants, as you know. And as you know, he predates you. He wouldn't have lasted this long if he lashed out without finishing off his enemy. So, why didn't he kill you?::

::I told you. I don't know.:: Kane slicked back her hair into a tight ponytail with a sigh. *::Fine. Yes, okay, I attacked Fang. Obviously, I shouldn't have –::*

::At least not without being prepared to end him, magically or otherwise.::

::So Fang…I don't know, just wanted me out of the way?::

Grace's index finger pulled at her lower lip. *::No, I don't think so. And I don't think it was pure self-defense. I think he was sending you a message.::*

Kane rolled her eyes. ::*And what message would that be, Grace?*::

::*I think…that you need him.*::

::*And why would I need Fang?*::

Grace snickered. ::*Really? Have you been paying attention at all or just complaining this whole time?*::

A growl—a real one, not her mental approximation—pressed against Kane's clenched lips.

::*Oh, please, you don't scare me. We both know you can't get rid of me, no matter how you've tried in the past.*:: Grace smirked, then switched to a condescending tone. ::*Now answer the question, Kane. Why do you need Fang?*::

Kane sighed. She knew the answer. ::*Because the others don't respect me since I'm not a pure vampire.*::

Grace's head tilted to the side. Her mouth pursed. ::*I don't know if that's one hundred percent true. I would say they don't* trust *you since you're not a pure vampire. And that it could have something to do with your threats to scramble their brains every other night.*::

Kane dismissed Grace's last statement. She enjoyed her threats and would not abandon them any time soon. ::*So I need Fang to get the others on my side, is that it?*::

Grace's index finger touched the tip of her snub nose. The opposite one pointed at Kane. ::*Bingo.*::

::*And you think Fang was trying to send me that message by stabbing me?*::

::*No, I think Fang was trying to send you that message by* not *killing you when he had every right to.*::

Indignation rose within Kane like a tidal wave. ::*What do you want me to do, Grace? Apologize?*::

::*No, I don't think that's necessary.*:: Grace's chin jerked toward Kane's scarred stomach. ::*I think* that's *good enough for*

Fang. When you go out there, just look for an opening to enlist Fang's help. I think he'll be waiting for it.::

Kane scowled at Grace, but kept her mental mouth shut. These first few days at Eversfield had proven that she had limited—if any—control of her vampires. If Fang was willing to help, perhaps she should take it.

Grace dusted her translucent hands off. *::Now that that's settled, how's your Dampour? When we chatted yesterday, you said you were gonna work on it while you healed.::*

Kane's frown deepened. She hated when Grace acted like her boss, which was often. *::It's fine. I mean, it isn't, but I have some thoughts on how to tweak it.::*

::Like?::

::Really? You want to get into the nitty-gritty, Grace?::

::Perhaps not the nitty-gritty, but I'd appreciate the broad brush strokes.::

Kane pulled her ponytail so tight it hurt her scalp. *::Okay, fine. Best I can tell, my initial attempt affected the Warriors' Cull and Bloodlust directly, instead of altering them around me. Further, the Dampour might not work at all if their Bloodlust is triggered. The latter problem, I'm not sure if I can fix. But the former I have some ideas about. Namely, making something akin to a flexible bubble around myself, instead of the skin-tight armor I used before. Does that make sense?::*

Grace shrugged. *::Makes enough sense. How sure are you that this'll work?::*

::Not at all. It's going to require extensive testing. First in the crowds in Florence with just me, then whittling down to Juniper, and then to patrols. Then start the whole process over again with multiple vampires shrouded.::

::So you're no longer planning to stalk their patrols right away?:: Grace asked.

::I don't think so. At first I thought we could stay far enough away. But now I'm thinking it would be better to wait until I can guarantee everyone's safety.::

::Sounds like a patient plan that prioritizes stealth and safety, one that Duncan would approve of.::

Kane swelled with pride.

::There's just one thing. May I make a suggestion?::

Kane deflated like a pierced balloon. Of course Grace wouldn't let Kane enjoy success for long. ::Don't you always?::

::Fair enough.:: Grace's sly smile crinkled her wide-set eyes, but her tone remained businesslike. ::I suggest you send two of the others away to harass the nearby Cells while you perfect your Dampour. You know, keep those Cells too busy to work with the Eversfield Cell. The other two can focus on ridding this area of strays. Based on Saturday night, the last thing we need is a random vampire triggering the Warriors' Bloodlust. Oh, and you should switch the shifts regularly since they'll be able to feed more freely when they're farther away.::

::But they shouldn't feed freely.::

Grace shrugged. ::It's their funeral. If they come back feral, Duncan'll put them down in an instant, which they should know.::

::True.::

Grace cocked her head. In the living room, the couch creaked. ::Sounds like it's time to get up. I think Fang's waiting for you out there.::

Kane's canines poked at her lower lip. She wasn't ready.

Rolling her eyes, Grace dug her hands into her hips. ::Stop that right now. You – we – are not this weak. Go.:: With that final rebuke, Grace vanished.

Kane pressed her palms into the lumpy mattress and shoved herself into a standing position. Grace wasn't wrong.

It was past time Kane faced him. At least she now had a plan and a peace offering.

While she reapplied her coral lip gloss in a broken mirror, Kane gathered her confidence. She could and she would do this.

With her chin held high and her chest puffed out, Kane opened her bedroom door. She stepped onto the kitchen's tile floor.

Around the back of the couch, a pair of coal-black eyes met her. *Fang.*

His wormlike lips spread into a wrinkled smile. He shifted out of his customary sprawl and into a seated position. "Hi there." Fang patted the now-empty seat beside him.

Kane strode past the kitchen and into the living room, oozing the confidence she wished she felt. Sunday's trail of blood had disappeared. So had Fang's dagger.

She perched on the edge of a slouchy cushion with her back held rigid and straight. Her hands lay folded in her lap. Her legs crossed at the ankle. Kane stared at the dark TV, watching Fang out of the corner of her eye.

Fang looked her up and down. "You good?"

"Of course." Kane's voice came out high and tight, not the relaxed, "I don't remember you stabbing me" tone she'd aimed for.

Fang smirked. "Good."

Rage surged within Kane.

She swallowed it down. In her current state, she doubted whether she could access enough magic to punish Fang. And like Grace said, she needed him to bring the others on board. Kane slid back on the couch and angled herself toward him. Her spine pressed into the corner of the backrest. She leaned against the sofa's arm. *Calm, cool, and collected.*

Polite curiosity dripped from Kane's voice. "Where are the others?"

"Out. I gave 'em the night off."

Kane bristled at the audacity of Fang giving *her* vampires the night off, but her tone and body remained casual. "Oh?"

"Don't worry, I told 'em not to feed. They're checkin' out the lay of the land over in Florence."

"Isn't that dangerous?"

"What? Without you to shield us?" Fang sneered.

"Well, I mean…"

"I've got news for you, *Kane*." Disdain colored Fang's gravelly voice. "We survived long before you existed, and we'll continue to survive long after you don't."

"Excuse me?" Was that a blatant threat? Kane ought to cast caution aside and drive Fang mad. Right here. Right now.

Fang's index finger wagged, the tip an inch away from Kane's snub nose. "That. *That* is the problem."

"I'm sorry?" While Kane feigned politeness, her nails bit into the armrest.

Fang shook his head. His greasy tendrils mirrored the movement, if half a second later. "You're haughty. You think you're better than the rest of us."

"That's because…"

Fang's dark eyebrow arched.

Kane trod in dangerous territory. Her mouth snapped shut.

"Because?" Fang prompted.

"Well…" Kane summoned all five of her Spirit Diviner affinities. They tickled her fingertips, a far cry from the almost painful pulse they usually created. It would have to be enough. If Kane was going down, it wouldn't be without a fight. "Because I am, if you must know. Fang, I can do things you've never dreamt of. In addition to all the usual vampire stuff." She waved the last portion off like it was nothing.

"And yet the 'usual vampire stuff' can kill you just as well. I proved that a few nights ago."

Kane's silver eyes flashed, molten steel. Her fingers twitched. This time she was ready. Between clenched teeth, Kane growled, "Try it again. I dare you."

A bark of a laugh erupted from Fang. "I'm not here to fight you, Kane, although it certainly would be interesting. We—both of us—are here to destroy the Clan. We should not fight amongst ourselves."

"I agree, though I'm not sure why you're telling me this."

"I'm telling you, my dear Kane, because you're the one instigating this…conflict."

Kane's jaw dropped. "Excuse me?"

"You heard me perfectly well."

"You and the others don't listen to a single word I say!"

"That's because you seem to be under the mistaken impression that you're in charge."

"Perhaps *you're* under the mistaken impression that I'm *not* in charge. Duncan made *me* the leader of this expedition, not any of you." Kane crossed her arms and scowled.

"And you think that after one word from Duncan, we'll mindlessly follow you? Back at the base, it might appear that way, thanks to the mind juju you and your kind use to keep us in line." Fang raised a hand, halting Kane's rising objection. "Yes, Kane, I get it. I was there, remember? Back before you existed, when Duncan was trying to build his army. Without you and your powers, we can't amass the numbers we need to take on the Clan, I know. But you haven't been using your powers here, so you can't expect the same dumb obedience as before."

Kane glared at Fang. When she spoke, she forced her voice to be low and calm. "May I ask one thing? What exactly of my plan do you object to?"

"It's more contingent on your magic than I would like, but otherwise nothing."

Fighting her exasperation, Kane smashed her fingertips into her bare biceps. "Then what's the problem?"

"The problem is that you act like you have all the answers, that our experience out in the real world—out *here*—is nothing compared to your magic. We know how to do things too. We're not just killing machines."

Kane pressed her lips together, considering Fang's words. Maybe it didn't have to be all her, all the time. Maybe she could allow the others to provide input, even if she chose to ignore it. Besides, didn't this fit in with Grace's proposal? The others would focus on their goals—harassing the Clan and cleaning out strays—while she perfected her Dampour. And Fang sending Brock, Toulouse, and Ramrod out into Florence tonight could help her. Knowing the safest areas to test her Dampour—not to mention several escape routes—would be useful.

Releasing her biceps, Kane folded her hands back in her lap. "What if…" Her voice trailed off as a final plan formed. "What if you and I work more closely together? You as a representative for my, I mean, for *Duncan's* fighters, me as the lead for this project."

Fang tilted his head. His obsidian eyes gleamed. "Yes, that could work."

"In that case, I have some modifications to the original plan that I'd like to discuss."

"Sounds good. You wanna do it over a drink?" Fang cocked a bushy brow.

Kane's throat burned at the thought. Healing from a bespelled stab wound required more energy than she'd budgeted for. She might not be able to make it to her next scheduled feeding. Plus, sharing a drink could be a bonding experience, one that she and Fang needed. "Sure."

Fang's canines shone in the fluorescent lighting. He rose to his feet, then extended a hand to Kane. "Good. Let's go get one."

CHAPTER 29

A line of sleigh bells attached to a leather thong tinkled as Kane and Fang entered downtown Juniper's lone coffee shop. Stocking up on caffeine before an all-nighter was a habit from Kane's human days, one of the few remaining. Despite the late hour — well past dinner — three people preceded them in the line. Twenty or so others hunkered down in the booths lining the brick walls and around the mishmash of high cocktail tables and chipped dining room tables scattered throughout the café. The humans chattered away, none of them suspecting the monsters in their midst. If Kane had brought any of her other vampires, she'd worry about their control around so many tasty morsels.

Beside her, Fang's hands remained relaxed at his sides and his canines hidden. Only his unnatural black-as-night gaze hinted at the truth. But anyone who noticed it would think Fang wore colored contacts — which they'd also assume of Kane and her liquid silver eyes.

"So, um, what's the difference between a mocha, a latte, and a cappuccino?" A girl who looked about twelve years old asked the barista.

When the barista launched into a far-too-detailed explanation, Kane crossed her arms over her chest. *Isn't this what phones are for?* The girl could have pulled herself out of the line and asked the wondrous internet for answers instead of the busy barista. Then the rest of them — including the two middle-aged men in suits in front of her and Fang — could order their drinks and move on with their lives. After all, Kane and Fang had things to do tonight. They'd drive the required one hundred miles. They'd find a good place to hunt. Together, they'd select a target. Together, they'd feed. Together, they'd kill.

Kane's fangs pulsed. Her throat burned. Her stomach rumbled.

The scent of all that hot blood enveloped her. Like a heavy fog, it caressed her face, her neck, her bare arms. It curled up her nostrils. Kane's mouth salivated.

She clenched her jaw. With a shaky breath, Kane buried the urges.

In the next useless breath, she summoned her Cyphering. *Might as well check for Latents.* While Kane didn't want Adara here, looking for Latents would amuse her while she waited for this indecisive girl to decide — and keep her mind off certain other things. Plus, Duncan liked Latents, even ones who couldn't be turned. Who could blame him? Kane herself had once been a Latent. And maybe if she found one and turned it, Kane could train it instead of Adara.

Scanning the groups sprinkled throughout the café, Kane searched for that shimmering halo marking a Latent.

Nothing but dark figures in a darker room met her. No one was the least bit sparkly or shimmery.

::*Look harder.*:: Grace's voice rang in her ears.

Kane narrowed her eyes but obeyed. Her pale gaze crawled over the people. Still nothing.

Something tickled her brain, though. It came from the corner booth hosting three girls, one a brunette with a pixie cut, another a redhead, and the last fingering dark curls.

That last one had caused the tickle. There was something off with her, but Kane couldn't figure out what. She yanked on her Cyphering.

The world swam before her eyes. Feathers filled her skull, making her head feel light and full at the same time.

Despite the warnings, Kane held fast to the thick rope of her Cyphering. She stared at the girl.

A sheer glaze came to life. It coated the girl's body, clinging to her curves. It was nothing like the diffuse halo branding a Latent.

Whatever was going on with this girl, it was more than unusual. Even at full strength, Kane would have missed it if she hadn't been looking for something — *anything* — out of the ordinary.

Kane stepped toward her prize.

"Kane," Fang hissed from multiple feet of empty space ahead. Only one person remained between him and the cash register.

While the girl had distracted Kane, the line had moved forward without her. Kane and Fang were next.

Her trance broken, Kane sucked in a breath. They shouldn't be so close to this girl. On the off-chance the girl was a Latent, either one of them could trigger her abilities. And that would prevent even Kane from turning her into a vampire.

With haste, Kane Weaved a billowing shield, a crisscross of the lavender cords of Cyphering and the mauve threads of Portency. The Weave's gray frame showed through here and there. The spell should be enough to hide her and Fang from the girl's Latent abilities, if they existed. But it was sloppy. Almost any Spirit Diviner in the area — Weaver, Cypher, or Portent — would notice it.

No one cast Kane a second glance.

Good, no other Spirit Diviners are here.

"Kane, what do you want?" From the cash register, Fang twisted around to face Kane with a frown.

Kane struggled to peel her eyes off the people sitting at their booths and tables. Although she'd stopped staring at the girl, she'd kept her in her peripheral vision. Swallowing a sigh, Kane turned away from the girl and approached the cash register. Her supernatural ears listened for the chime of sleigh bells announcing the comings and goings of the coffee shop's patrons. The girl would not leave until Kane let her. "I'll have a plain coffee. Black."

Fang returned to the barista. "Make that two."

At least Fang had never accompanied Kane to a coffee shop before. Otherwise, he'd know something was up. Kane *never* drank black coffee. But she made an exception in this case. Kane wanted no distractions—not even that of a delicious sugary beverage. After Fang paid with one of the credit cards from Four Eyes, he and Kane flowed down the counter to wait.

Kane angled herself toward the trio. They still giggled and chatted with exaggerated gestures. Well, the other two did. Kane's target watched the talkative, showy girls from across the table and offered a slight smile now and again.

Using the moment of calm before the storm, Kane checked her spell-shield. While it seemed to work all right for now, she doubted that it would hold if they were closer—say, across the table from this mystery girl. If that shiny glaze marked the girl as a Latent whose powers were far from manifestation—she did look a year or two younger than Kane had been when Duncan found her—she or Fang could cause the girl's abilities to manifest early.

Kane chewed on the inside of her cheek. She would have to ask Fang to go. Then she could use her old Dampour—the body armor one—to hide the truth from this girl's abilities. It wasn't ideal, but it should be good enough. There was no way Kane was going to sit back and let her escape. If she triggered the girl's Latent powers despite her Dampour, so be it.

Leaning toward Fang, Kane muttered, "Fang, I need you to go wait in the car once you get your coffee."

Fang arched a bushy brow.

::*Beg.*:: Grace's voice whispered.

Bile climbed up Kane's throat. She hated begging. But it might be the only way to investigate her treasure. "Please?"

Fang's ebony eyes narrowed. "Why?"

Placing a slender hand on Fang's bare forearm, Kane adopted a soft, gentle, uncharacteristic tone. "I know we're not up to trusting each other yet, but this one time, can you try? I only need five minutes, maybe ten." *Provided those other two girls get out of my way.*

"Two black coffees. Hot," a scruffy guy called out, sliding matching Styrofoam cups over the counter. The coffee inside sloshed toward the rims. A bit escaped one of the cups and streamed down its side.

Kane's upper lip curled. *He should take his job more seriously. Though, I shouldn't be surprised. He didn't even bother to put a hairnet over that ugly mini-beard.*

Fang grabbed the cups from the counter and handed the clean one to Kane. "Fine. Ten minutes. Then I'm coming back in here."

"Deal." On instinct, Kane added, "Thank you."

With a smile close to a wince, Fang dipped his chin into a brisk nod, then exited the coffee shop through the side door. Sipping her bitter coffee, Kane Weaved her original Dampour beneath the rippling folds of her spell-shield. Only after checking every inch of her new spell did Kane ease the old one off. It disintegrated around her feet.

Her Dampour coating her body, Kane wormed her way through the clutter of tables and chairs set askew. She slid onto a bar stool at the empty cocktail table closest to that corner booth. After wiggling her phone out of her pocket, Kane pretended to peruse its contents while drinking her less-than-delicious coffee. She listened to the girls.

"So, Lila…" The girl with the pixie cut eyed Kane's target. "Rudi and I were thinking. Now that you're done up all pretty, why don't we go check out what's goin' on over at JCC?"

Kane's target — Lila apparently — choked on her coffee. "Wh-what?"

"Just a li'l harmless fun. Get you used to everything over there." The girl — not-Rudi and not-Lila — flashed a brilliant smile.

"B-but curfew's in like an hour, Val."

The redhead — *Rudi* — joined the other one — *Val* — at grinning at Lila. "And I can get you back in time. Cross my heart, hope to die." Rudi's mint green nail traced an "X" into her bare chest, skirting the edge of her cleavage.

Kane almost shook her head. These teenagers, they were so naive, so unaware of the demons stalking in the shadows — or in this case, in plain sight. Then again, hadn't she been too?

"But didn't you say we have to dress up or something?" Lila gestured to her worn T-shirt and jeans.

Val waved away her concerns. "Don't worry about it this one time, Lila dear. After all, it's a Tuesday. Things can be pretty low-key during the week."

"Oh, well, um, thanks..." Lila played with a curl, extending it straight, then letting it bounce back up. "But I don't think so. I got a *ton* of homework today that I should really get started on." Her toe jammed into an indigo backpack that slouched against the table's center post.

After glancing at Rudi, Val leaned over the scratched tabletop. "Please? This is what Rudi and me wanna do tonight. And we'd like you to come with us."

"Val..." Lila's front teeth worried her lower lip. "Just...please let me out of this tonight? We've updated my wardrobe. We've gotten my hair cut. I learned how to do my makeup. Can I please have the rest of the night to myself? We're hanging out back at Eversfield tomorrow night and then going out this weekend, which somehow includes Thursday. I could really use tonight to work on school stuff. Like I said, I've got a bunch of stuff to catch up on from summer."

Val pushed herself away from Lila. Her arms crossed over her meager chest. "Fine, but Rudi and I *are* going."

"And that's fine with me. I understand. But I'm going to stay here and get some work done, if that's all right. When I'm done, I'll just call an Uber or a Lyft or something. We have those here, right?"

"Of course we have those here, Lila." Gulping down the rest of her coffee, Val nudged Rudi out of the booth. "Have fun with your homework, I guess." She stomped toward the front door with Rudi trailing in her wake. As a single unit, they threw out their empty cups and left the coffee shop.

Kane's supernatural hearing picked up their whispered conversation as they hurried down the busy Juniper street.

"Rudi, you absolutely can*not* tell anyone about this, okay? As far as anyone knows, we didn't invite Lila out with us tonight."

"For sure, Val. And don't be too hard on her. Today was her first real day. She needs some time to adjust."

"If I thought Sara and Drey would give her that time, I'd be fine with that. But you heard Sara last night."

"I know, Val. But you did what you could tonight. The rest'll be up to Lila."

"I know. I just hope she doesn't come up short."

"She won't. Not with us helpin' her."

With the two girls' voices fading into the noise of an early autumn night, Kane focused back on her target.

At the booth, Lila sat alone. Vulnerable.

CHAPTER 30

LILA

With her eyes closed, Lila savored one final sip of chocolate fudge mocha. Then she dragged out her math textbook and Ms. Petoskanov's thick packet. *Might as well get started.* As Lila bent down to dig out her pencil pouch, an air current brushed against her round cheek. Lila glanced up.

A girl in a plain black tank top had slipped onto the bench opposite her. She sat in its exact center, her dark hair slicked back into a tight ponytail. With her light makeup, she didn't look too much older than Lila—maybe a senior in high school or a freshman in college. Her slender fingers clutched a half-empty Styrofoam cup. Her coral lips pursed. The girl's strange silver eyes bored into Lila.

Shivers crawled up Lila's spine—and not the good kind. She sat up straight and forced her hands to rest on the scarred table. "Um, can I help you?"

Breaking off her stare, the girl picked at a crimson nail. "I hope so."

"Okay…um, what do you want help with?" Lila's gaze roamed the shop. There was something creepy about this girl, but plenty of people lingered in the café. *Plenty of witnesses.*

Those strange silver eyes collided with Lila's.

A cold sweat seeped out of Lila's pores.

"Oh, don't be so afraid. Although it does smell delicious." The girl's index finger traced a pattern along the back of Lila's hand.

276

Lila tried to yank it away but couldn't. Somehow, she couldn't move, not even an inch. Her breath stuck in her chest. Her thoughts oozed forward, slow as molasses. A lump clogged her throat.

"Relax. I'm not going to hurt you. Not yet anyway." The girl scrutinized Lila, then returned to doodling that pattern on the back of Lila's hand. "Not until I know what you are. And even then, perhaps not. Now, I have a few tasks for you. See, I overheard—pardon me for eavesdropping, but it's quite difficult when you've got such sensitive hearing—that you go to Eversfield. Is that correct?"

On autopilot, Lila nodded.

"Excellent. Then I'll *definitely* need your help. You can call me Kane, by the way. Hello, Lila. Nice to meet you." Releasing Lila's hand at last, Kane sipped from her Styrofoam cup.

Her mouth bone-dry, Lila croaked, "Hello, Kane. Nice to meet you."

"Not too bad, but we will have to work on that. But don't worry, we've got plenty of time ahead of us." Kane smiled. Her incisors shone in the dim lighting.

The binds around Lila's chest tightened. She gulped for air like a fish out of water.

"Well, Lila—what's your last name?"

"Lee."

"Well, Lila Lee, we have some fun times ahead of us. But first, I'm going to need you to keep track of a few of your fellow Eversfield students. Nothing big, just note their daily comings and goings. Specifically: Gabe Lazare, Emilia Rivers, Teddi—you might know her as Theodora—Brown, and Marius Klein. I believe the first two are seniors and the latter two are freshmen. And actually, let's go ahead and throw in sophomore Marina Lazare too. Does that sound like something you can do?"

Inside, Lila screamed "no." Her traitorous tongue answered, "Y-yes."

"Wonderful. Give me your phone."

With a mind of its own, Lila's hand shot into her backpack's front pocket. There, it sifted through a tangle of headphones, tissues, bandages, and lip balm until it found her phone. Without Lila's permission, her hand slid her phone across the scratched surface to Kane.

Kane poked and swiped at Lila's phone. After a few minutes, she flipped it around to face Lila. "Do you see this email app right here?" Kane pointed to an app with a bright yellow star over a violet background.

Lila nodded.

"All you're going to do is log into this app each day and compose an email with your notes. You don't need to send it to anyone. Just write it up and save. I'll take it from there."

Again, Lila nodded. Again, she tried not to. Again, she failed.

"Wonderful. That's all I have for you at the moment. Thank you for being so…well, so human. I'll be in touch." Kane rose, but she wavered on her feet. With a grimace, she dropped back down to Lila's level. The heels of her hands dug into the wooden tabletop. Kane's silver eyes pierced Lila's dull green ones. "And Lila, you're not going to tell anyone about our little meeting here tonight, are you?"

"No, I won't tell anyone."

"Or about your assignment?"

Lila saw nothing but Kane. "No, I won't tell anyone."

"In fact, Lila…" Kane's index finger toyed with Lila's. "You're not going to remember this at all, save for when it's time to write down your notes each night before bed, right?"

"Right. I won't remember except for when I write down my notes each night before bed."

"Excellent. I'll be seeing you around, Lila." Kane tossed back the last of her coffee, then spun on her heel and strode out the coffee shop's front door.

Lila's head sank onto her palms. It swirled and throbbed and throbbed and swirled.

After several minutes, she rubbed at her eyes. Where had she been? About to work on her math homework, right?

Across from Lila was an empty Styrofoam cup with a coral lipstick stain.

A feeling of foreboding crept up Lila's spine. Guilt trailed it.

Lila shook both off. Val must have left that cup. The guilt was from not having started her homework earlier. And the foreboding was from having all this homework to do in the first place. What else could it be?

TWO HOURS LATER, LILA CLIMBED INTO HER LOFTED bed with her phone in hand. On the opposite side of the room, Marina typed away at her laptop, the click-clack almost a soothing rhythm.

Almost. From the moment she'd decided it was time for bed, a sense of unease had brewed in Lila. Faint at first, she'd written it off as getting used to her new bed in her new room at her new school. But as Lila fiddled with her phone's crinkly charging cord, a restless energy beat at her fingertips. Her heart banged against her ribs. She couldn't plug in her phone yet. She needed it for something.

279

Hunched in her bed with a rebellious curl or two reaching for the ceiling, Lila rubbed at her wrinkled forehead. What was it? Her Spanish homework was done. So were tomorrow's readings for AmLit and World History. She'd finished her Pre-Calc and Chem homework, and there was nothing due tomorrow for Choir or Genetics.

A hammer swung back and forth in her skull like the world's most painful pendulum. What was she missing?

Knock knock

Despite its throbbing, Lila's head snapped up. Blood pulsed in her fingers and toes. It was at least an hour past curfew. Who would knock on their door this late?

Waving off Lila's attention, Marina shuffled to the door. "It's for me, Lila. Don't worry about it." She eased it open, lest their creaky door alert their hall monitor.

The heel of her hand pressing into the mattress, Lila leaned over the edge of her bed to see who it was.

Her brows furrowed. She didn't recognize Marina's visitor, a tall and curvy girl with gleaming black curls tickling her waist. Hazel eyes as big as boulders fastened to Marina. The girl whispered, her plump ruby lips moving a mile a minute beneath a Greek nose.

No matter how she tried, Lila couldn't make out one word of their conversation.

After a couple nods, Marina peeked over her shoulder at Lila. She frowned. "Um, Lila, I gotta go with Diana here for a bit. Astronomy Club stuff. I shouldn't be gone long."

"Okay. See you later," Lila replied. *Diana's her name. But Diana what?* An inexplicable urge to figure out Diana's last name burned within Lila.

Marina tugged the door shut behind her.

The moment it clicked closed, Lila knew what she had to do. She got out her phone and swiped until she found that purple app with the yellow star. She opened it and began typing an email without an address or a subject.

> Tonight, Marina left after curfew with Diana (last name TBD) to work on something for Astronomy Club. Seemed unexpected and/or last minute.

Lila chewed on her lower lip, sticky with the lip balm that was now part of her nightly routine thanks to Val. At least it tasted like vanilla ice cream.

> Gabe sat with Emilia at lunch. Later, three others joined them. No names yet. Also, Gabe used to date Heidi Malik.

Lila's guts knotted, but she ignored them. There were two others she was supposed to report on: Teddi and Marius.

> Haven't seen Teddi or Marius around yet. Will keep an eye out for them.

Should she add anything else? Like a grainy black-and-white movie, memories from the past few days played in Lila's mind.

> Lex Wilmer is almost always at Marina's side. Marina's other friends include Yuki Mori, Mickey Laufner, and Angelo Alfonsi. And Sandy Sala and Victoria Serrano. Sandy knows Marina because their families are old friends. Maybe the same goes for Victoria? Unclear.

With a relieved sigh, Lila tapped "Save" and closed the app. Her headache vanished. Her fingers relaxed. *She* relaxed.

After plugging in her phone and tucking it beneath a fluffy pillow, Lila nestled into her bed beneath covers as light as air. The memory of that purple app with the yellow star — and its contents — faded away like a wispy fog in the bright light of morning.

Miles away, a vampire with strange silver eyes bent over a phone. She cackled with delight.

Thanks for reading!

If you enjoyed this book, don't forget to post a review wherever you go looking for books. Your review helps other readers find this book!

If you need help posting a review, go to betsyflak.com/review_instructions.

You can also let me know what you think by emailing me at betsy@betsyflak.com or finding me on Facebook (@betsyflakwritesfantasy) or Twitter (@Betsy_Flak).

WANT MORE?

**A Brush with Betrayal
The Clan-Vampire Clash:
Book Two**

She doesn't know her own power. He's trying to still his beating heart. Will a vampire's deadly plan push them further apart?

With a popular best friend and a handsome crush, Lila's sophomore year seems destined for success. But when Gabe gives her the cold shoulder, she has no idea that darkness lies right around the corner.

While Gabe knows he and his fellow vampire hunters keep his classmates alive, he wonders if it's all worth it if it means shunning Lila. As the latent magic builds within the girl of his dreams, an attack at the local carnival leaves the senior unprepared and Lila missing...

As Gabe searches for Lila, he has no clue that the greatest threat is yet to come. And the powerful sophomore he craves may be the one who lets the undead evil inside.

Read *A Brush with Betrayal* to take a vampire thrill ride today!

Find out more at betsyflak.com/a_brush_with_betrayal.

THE CLAN-VAMPIRE CLASH

Episode Two: A Brush with Betrayal

(Sneak Peek Edition)

Lila's Sophomore Year, First Semester

October

CHAPTER 1

Lila twisted and turned. A pair of silver eyes followed her wherever she went. Coral lips whispered words she couldn't hear. Snakes grew from crooked fingers and circled around and around her ribs.

They trapped her.

They strangled her.

They became a black mist that blew away in the breeze.

Lila opened her eyes. She stood on a path of woodchips. Trees surrounded her, their leafy limbs stretching toward the night's stars. Beneath them, a tangle of thorny shrubs guarded the trail. They barred Lila from straying to the left or to the right.

Around her, not a cricket chirped. Nor did an owl hoot or a coyote howl in the distance. Not even the fallen leaves rustled. The silence beat against Lila's eardrums. They throbbed beneath it.

Something tugged on a curl.

Lila whipped around.

"This waaaaay," a voice sang in the dark. Unnatural moonlight streamed down Lila's path.

She chewed on her lower lip. The toe of one sneaker rubbed against the other.

Something grabbed Lila's pant leg and yanked.

Lila stumbled forward, down that lit trail.

Guess I don't have a choice. Her heart thumping away, Lila strode down the path. Her steps—usually heavy or clumsy if not both—were light and nimble over the woodchips, leaving the eerie silence unbroken.

The trail led to a decrepit cabin. Like a spotlight, the full moon hung over it. White paint peeled away from wooden siding cracked and split in more places than Lila could count. Shingles from the roof lay amid weeds that crawled up and over the bowed porch. The glass of three windows had broken, two in a spiderweb pattern, the last in a zigzag with the upper half missing.

Smoke puffed out of its lopsided chimney.

The front door spilled open. Its creak echoed through the mute forest.

Lila stopped where she was. Something wasn't right.

Tiny fists crashed into the small of Lila's back.

She lurched forward. After regaining her balance, Lila shot a scowl over her shoulder, at whoever had pushed her.

Nothing but an empty path met her.

Lila sucked her lower lip in and out. This had all the makings of a horror movie. Middle of the night: check. Creepy abandoned-but-not-abandoned house: check. Stupid teenage girl going in all alone: check. All she needed was the psycho serial killer waiting for her behind that open door.

And here she was, about to walk through it like an idiot.

Something rammed into her rear end.

"Ow!" Lila rubbed her right butt cheek where twin pins had pricked her. "I'm going, okay?" Lila rolled her eyes at herself. Who was she talking to?

Her bottom still smarting, Lila dragged her feet down that path, then up and onto the failing porch. It shuddered beneath her steps.

She slipped through the open door.

And gasped.

290

In the middle of the living room lay Valerie Elizabeth Baker — also known as Lila's best friend. Val stared at the ceiling, her dark gaze unblinking, dim, dead. Her limbs bent at awkward angles no one living could bare. The scent of blood mixed with that of burning wood from a fire in a stone fireplace. Its flickering was the only source of light in the cabin.

A figure entered the room opposite Lila. Fresh blood covered his pointy chin and dripped down his neck. The ends of his greasy hair stuck together in clumps. Eyes like black holes sucked in every speck of light and life and hope. They targeted Lila.

She gulped.

His face split into a sinister smile, his teeth stained red with blood. "Hello there, li'l dear. Come to visit your friend?" He pointed at Val's broken body.

Terror seized Lila. She tried to swallow it away, but her tongue stuck to the roof of her mouth. "No, um…" Lila's voice trembled. Tears filled her eyes.

The creature — for no human could kill like this — cocked its head. "Then why are you here?"

A rough hand grabbed Lila's elbow and flung her backward. She tripped over something and started to fall.

He caught her. Setting her upright, Gabe met Lila's shocked stare for a heartbeat. Then he shifted back toward the beast, positioning his muscled body in front of hers. His icy gaze glued to the creature that had killed Val, Gabe ordered in a low tone, "Stay behind me, Lila. No matter what happens."

Lila's heart thundered in her chest. Her best friend was dead at the hands of a monster and here was her crush, risking himself because of her. "Gabe, you shouldn't be here. It's dangerous."

"This is exactly where I should be." Keeping one eye on the beast, Gabe tucked an escaped curl behind Lila's ear. His fingers were gentle, at odds with the ferocity radiating off him. "You're the one who shouldn't be here."

Lila's brows furrowed. What was he talking about?

Gabe turned back to the creature. It tilted its head at him like a curious, bloodthirsty puppy. A smile unfolded over lips painted scarlet with Val's blood.

Slashing his arm across Lila's body, Gabe backed them both up, out the door, over the dilapidated porch, and into the front lawn—if something that was more dying weeds than green grass could be called a lawn. The beast drifted after them, taking its sweet time.

His eyes on the monster, Gabe tugged something out from beneath his belt. He pressed it into Lila's open palm. "Just in case. You know what to do."

Lila wound her fingers around the stake, its wood smooth and polished, without a single splinter to prick her.

There was just one problem. She didn't know what to do.

She could, however, put two and two together. *Blood plus wooden stake equals vampire.*

Except that didn't make any sense. Vampires didn't exist.

His hands hovering around the scabbards dangling from his hips, Gabe murmured, "Lila, promise me you'll run if things go bad. You've got my spare stake, but—"

"If things go bad? What do you mean?"

"I have to kill it, you know that."

"No, I…" Lila licked her chapped lips. "You have to kill it? Gabe, we should get out of here. *Both* of us should get out of here."

"Lila, that's not an option for me. You know this." Impatience, irritation, maybe even anger streamed out of Gabe.

"I don't understand. What—"

Gabe's head snapped around. The beast barreled toward them on all fours.

Spreading his arms wide, Gabe dropped into a crouch. Moonlight glittered off the wicked blade in one hand. Lila hadn't seen him draw it from its scabbard, but there it was.

The beast leapt.

Gabe sprang to meet it. In the air, they collided. Gabe drove his hand into its jaw, keeping the creature's razor-sharp fangs at bay. In his opposite hand, the sword slashed at the demon.

Their tangled form crashed into the ground. The impact split them back into two. Pebbles and dirt spewed out around them as they hurtled to their feet.

With little more than a body's length separating them, Gabe and the beast glared at each other. Gabe twisted the short sword back and forth. The fingers of his empty hand twitched.

The creature's obsidian eyes flicked to Lila, standing behind the pair.

"No," Gabe growled. "You're not getting her."

A maniacal grin pasted itself over the beast's ragged face. "We'll see about that." It surged toward Gabe again.

Gabe dipped down once more. At the last moment, he lunged to the side, so quick that he seemed to appear in his new position. His sword darted into the space where he'd been a breath before.

The demon wasn't there. No, the creature had mirrored Gabe, as fast as he was, maybe faster. Its shoulder plunged into Gabe's stomach, driving them both into the ground.

Fallen twigs snapped beneath them, each one a crack of thunder.

The monster pinned Gabe's arms to his sides. Its canines swollen to half the length of Lila's pinky, it lunged for Gabe's throat.

Lila clasped her stake even harder, so hard that her nails clawed at the wood. In the heart, right? She was supposed to stab it in the heart?

But her feet wouldn't budge.

Gabe's knee blasted into the creature's groin. In one fluid movement, he flipped them over and slammed his forearm into the beast's chest. One arm grinding it into the dirt and dying weeds, Gabe's free hand flew to his back. It jerked out a wooden stake that gleamed in the light of the stars.

Fingertips bored into Lila's shoulder.

Lila winced. *That's gonna leave a bruise.*

The foreign fingers spun Lila around. Malevolent silver eyes devoured her world. "What are you doing here, Lila Lee?"

"I dunno, I—"

The woman shook her head, her raven waves swinging over her shoulders. "Never mind, it doesn't matter. One thing is certain: you don't *belong* here." Like twin hammers, the woman's fists smashed into Lila's skull.

The stake fell out of her limp hand. Lila crumpled to the ground.

"LILA? LILA, ARE YOU OKAY?"

Why does Gabe sound so worried? Like cotton stuffing, a dense fog filled Lila's mind. Her thoughts moved slower than a snail on a Sunday stroll.

Callused fingertips grazed Lila's forehead and temples. They caressed her neck and collarbone, then her arms. Skipping her chest, they continued down her torso to her legs. Everywhere they went, electric tingles chased them. Lila shuddered.

The fingers stopped where they were and hovered over her body. Heat radiated from them. "Lila?"

Lila opened her eyes.

Gabe knelt over her, his too-handsome face scrunched with concern. After an instant, relief flowed through it. He smoothed her hair off her forehead, his fingers light against her skin. "How do you feel?"

"Okay, I guess." With a grimace, Lila shifted to her side and dug out the stone lodged against her back. She tossed it away, sending it swishing through the dying weeds.

Around her, crickets sang a pulsing hymn. Owls hooted, calling to each other. Leaves rustled in every breeze. The music of the night had returned to the forest.

Lila lifted herself onto her elbows. "I mean, I've been better."

"Yeah, I bet. Here, let's get you up and moving." Gabe wiggled his arm beneath her shoulders.

Lila grasped his opposite forearm, its muscles like cords of steel. Together, they hauled her to her feet.

The moment she stood without wobbling, Gabe's arm darted away, leaving a cold, empty space across Lila's shoulders.

Peeking up at Gabe, Lila trailed her fingers down his bare forearm. Her heart pounded, a fist-sized lump in her throat.

Gabe stood still and rigid, like a stray dog tolerating his first human contact.

"Gabe, I—"

Faster than she could breathe, Gabe crushed the distance between them. His hands pressed against her cheeks, bringing her face to his. His thumbs skimmed over her cheekbones. Soft lips met hers.

Shivers raced through Lila's body. Heat lingered behind them, melting her bones. She wrapped her arms around Gabe's waist and pulled him even closer.

Mip. Mip. Mip-mip. Mip. Miiiiiiiip. Lila's alarm shattered the dream.

After shutting it off, Lila slammed her head back into her pillow. Her fists rubbed at her bleary eyes. Over and over again, the dream played in her mind. Gabe's hands trailing along her body. His lips against hers.

Bzzzzt bzzzzt

Sighing, Lila rolled over to check her phone. Sure enough, it was a text from Val.

> Rise and shine, sleepyhead! Today's outfit is the black capris and a tank top of your choice. See you for practice in a few!

Lila groaned. Val was eating up every spare minute to teach Lila the routine for the dance team tryouts on Friday — also known as two days from now. Also known as two midterm exams, a history paper, and a Choir performance from now. Not that Val cared about any of that.

First the dance lessons, then the studying. Lila swallowed the stress away. Half-awake, she climbed down the ladder from her lofted bed. She stumbled past her roommate Marina's area — a pristine desk and dresser beneath a neat bed, all of which matched Lila's except for the spick-and-span part. Her hand on the knob of her closet door, Lila caught her reflection in the mirror.

She frowned. Beneath her spaghetti strap, four bruises dotted her left shoulder. Four bruises that she didn't remember having last night.

With a gulp, Lila placed her opposite hand over them. They fit, like the bruises were from fingers gripping her shoulder. *Must've done it in my sleep.*

A tiny voice whispered in Lila's head, *But how?*

Chasing it away, Lila opened her closet door.

Something flashed a dazzling shade of white from across the room.

Lila froze, her breath caught in her chest. The...*thing* from her dream had had fangs that bright.

Her jaw clenched, Lila poked her head around the closet door. On her desk, the antique comb that Val had bought her shone in the dim light. The jewels adorning its handle winked at her.

Lila's fingers raked through her hair, catching on the tangles. *Great, now I'm imagining things. It was just a dream, Lila. That comb did not wink at you. Monsters like that don't exist. Val's alive and well. And Gabe's never going to kiss you. It was just a dream.*

Her shower caddy hooked over one arm, Lila left the room. *Time to wash that dream away.*

Want more?

Find out where you can get your copy of *A Brush with Betrayal (The Clan-Vampire Clash: Book Two)* at betsyflak.com/a_brush_with_betrayal.

SEE HOW IT ALL BEGAN

The Unleashed Creation
The Clan-Vampire Clash: A Stand-Alone Prequel

Vampire Duncan lives in a world where it's kill or be killed, whether that's by his allies or by vampire hunters. But he wants freedom.

When he stumbles across a rogue fire witch, it's his chance. Can Duncan convince the witch to switch sides before she kills him?

Find out more at betsyflak.com/the_unleashed_creation.

The Impossible Creation
The Clan-Vampire Clash: A Stand-Alone Prequel

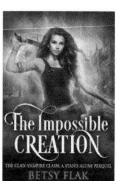

A nightmarish Halloween threat. A vampire hunter on red alert. Will a high school starlet end up the death of the party?

If you like feisty heroines, fierce vampire action, and supernatural suspense, then you'll love Betsy Flak's thrilling novel.

Find out more at betsyflak.com/the_impossible_creation.

GET ALL YOUR QUESTIONS ANSWERED

Lex Explains It All
The Clan-Vampire Clash: Insider's Guide

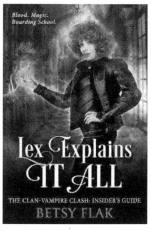

Find out all you ever wanted to know about vampires, vampire hunters, their history, Warriors and their superhuman abilities, Diviners and their magic, and more.

All your questions about the world of The Clan-Vampire Clash are answered by Lex Wilmer, a character introduced in *A Brush with Vampires (The Clan-Vampire Clash: Book One)*.

Find out more at betsyflak.com/lex_explains_it_all.

CHARACTER LIST

Adara
> One of Duncan's lieutenants; used to be an extremely strong Fire Diviner that killed vampires left and right until her flames consumed her and her entire Cell; now it's unclear what she is, but she still has her magic

Adela Lazare
> Retired Cypher living in the Juniper Troupe; Gabe and Marina's mom

Alex Wong
> Freshman Warrior in the Eversfield Cell; Eli's roommate in Pasteur

Angelo Alfonsi
> Civilian; one of Marina's friends, along with Mickey, Yuki, and Kylie; Mickey's roommate in Douglass; member of Engaging Eversfield, Eversfield's newspaper; sophomore at Eversfield

Brock
> Vampire; one of Duncan's best fighters; sent to Eversfield along with Kane, Fang, Toulouse, and Ramrod

Cat Calderon
> Civilian; Lizzard but not part of Heidi's clique; Blackwell's secretary; senior at Eversfield

Cheri Malik
> Civilian; popular and part of Heidi's clique which includes Sara, Val, Drey, and Rudi; Heidi's little sister; lives in Mistral; on Eversfield's dance team; junior at Eversfield

Clara Wilmer
> Lead Augur and Lex's mom

Cosmina Harris
> Senior Warrior in the Eversfield Cell; Emilia's roommate in Tubman

Darius Hernandez
> Senior Warrior in the Eversfield Cell; one of Gabe's closest friends and his roommate in Pasteur

David Lazare
> Retired Healer living in the Juniper Troupe; Gabe and Marina's dad

Diana Ruglere
> Spirit Diviner in the Eversfield Cell; the daughter of Detachers; dating Luke; senior at Eversfield

Drey (Audrey) Diaz
> Civilian; popular and part of Heidi's clique which includes Sara, Val, Rudi, and Cheri; Lizzard; Sara's roommate in Blackwell; on Eversfield's dance team; sophomore at Eversfield

Duncan
> Vampire; leader of an army set to destroy the vampire hunters of the Clan

Eli Burton
> Civilian; lives in Pasteur; freshman at Eversfield

Elsie (Elspeth) Adams
> Civilian; lives in Blackwell; sophomore at Eversfield; does Val's laundry in exchange for favors

Emilia Rivers
> Senior Warrior and the Eversfield Cell Second; one of Gabe's closest friends; Cosmina's roommate in Tubman

Evie Jones
> Civilian; Tubman's president; senior at Eversfield

Fang
> Vampire; one of Duncan's lieutenants; usually leads groups of vampires to attack Cells; sent to Eversfield along with Kane, Toulouse, Brock, and Ramrod

Fattie Koorey
>Civilian; Lizzard but not part of Sara's clique; Eversfield dance team member; sophomore at Eversfield

Four Eyes
>Vampire; one of Duncan's lieutenants; in charge of the logistics (money, shelter, fake IDs, etc.)

Gabe Lazare
>Senior Warrior and the Eversfield Cell First; Marina's older brother; closest friends are Emilia and Darius; Darius's roommate in Pasteur

Hayden Carter
>Civilian; prospective Lizzard and addition to Val's clique; lives in Blackwell; freshman at Eversfield

Headmaster Flynn
>Civilian; Headmaster of Eversfield Preparatory Academy

Heidi Malik
>Civilian; popular and leader of Val's clique which includes Sara, Drey, Rudi, and Cheri; Cheri's older sister; Blackwell's president; senior at Eversfield

Helle
>Vampire; one of Duncan's lieutenants although she prefers to work only with fellow vampire lieutenant Viper

Izzi Bahn
>Civilian; plays the drums; Lindi's roommate in Blackwell; sophomore at Eversfield

Jade Hernandez
>Civilian; 3rd floor Blackwell house monitor; senior at Eversfield

Jen Crawford
>Civilian; Eversfield dance team captain; lives in Mistral; senior at Eversfield

Juana Martinez
Civilian; Eversfield dance team member; lives in Tubman; junior at Eversfield

Kamila Jackson
Civilian; 4th floor Blackwell house monitor; senior at Eversfield

Kane
Vampire and exceptionally strong Spirit Diviner with skill in all five spirit affinities; one of Duncan's lieutenants; sent to Eversfield along with Fang, Toulouse, Brock, and Ramrod

Kylie Edwards
Civilian; one of Marina's friends, along with Angelo, Yuki, and Mickey; Yuki's roommate in Tubman; on the Eversfield varsity golf team; sophomore at Eversfield

Lex Wilmer
Strong Fire Diviner in the Eversfield Cell; Marina's best friend; Teddi's roommate in Tubman; freshman at Eversfield

Lila (Delilah) Lee
Civilian; Marina's roommate in Blackwell; Val's best friend; sophomore at Eversfield

Lindi Baard
Civilian; plays the drums; Izzi's roommate in Blackwell; sophomore at Eversfield

Lori Lee
Civilian; Lila's mom

Luke King
Wind Diviner in the Eversfield Cell; dating Diana; junior at Eversfield

Marcela Wittermarck
Juniper Troupe leader

Margaret Laufner

Civilian; Val's math tutor; lives in Tubman; Mickey's little sister; freshman at Eversfield

Marina Lazare

Strong Water Diviner in the Eversfield Cell; also a Healer and a Weaver; secret powers with Wind and Earth (Floral and Mineral affinities only); Lila's roommate in Blackwell; Lex's best friend; Gabe's little sister; part of Engaging Eversfield, Eversfield's newspaper; sophomore at Eversfield

Marius Klein

Freshman Warrior in the Eversfield Cell; lives in Douglass

Meg Anderson

Civilian; Lizzard but not part of Sara's clique; Eversfield dance team member; junior at Eversfield

Mickey Laufner

Civilian; one of Marina's friends, along with Angelo, Yuki, and Kylie; Angelo's roommate in Douglass; Margaret's older brother; on the Eversfield junior varsity basketball team; member of Eversfield's math competition team; sophomore at Eversfield

Mr. Clarkson

Retired Diviner and Eversfield history teacher

Ms. Barbaro

Civilian; Chemistry teacher at Eversfield

Ms. Pershing

Civilian; Headmaster Flynn's and Eversfield's primary administrative assistant

Ms. Petoskanov

Civilian; Math teacher at Eversfield

Ms. Taylor

Civilian; Choir teacher at Eversfield

Ms. van Straten
  Civilian; Blackwell's house manager

Ms. Vasile
  Retired Diviner and Harriet Tubman's house manager; also substitute teaches for Eversfield

Ramrod
  Vampire; one of Duncan's best fighters; sent to Eversfield along with Kane, Fang, Toulouse, and Brock

Rudi Fisher
  Civilian; popular and part of Heidi's clique which includes Sara, Val, Drey, and Cheri; lives in Tubman; junior at Eversfield

Russell Lee
  Civilian; Lila's dad

Sam Cohen
  Civilian; 2nd floor Blackwell house monitor; senior at Eversfield

Sandy Sala
  Freshman Warrior in the Eversfield Cell; Victoria's roommate in Blackwell

Sara Howland
  Civilian; popular and the next leader of Heidi's clique which includes Val, Drey, Rudi, and Cheri; Lizzard; Drey's roommate in Blackwell; on Eversfield's dance team; junior at Eversfield

Simon O'Connor
  Senior Warrior in the Eversfield Cell; also marked as having "leadership potential" by the Augurs like Gabe and Emilia but has no official leadership role in the Eversfield Cell; lives in Pasteur

Sofia Kim
  Civilian; Lizzard but not part of Heidi's clique; Blackwell's treasurer; senior at Eversfield

Tasha (Natasha) Masuda
> Civilian; Lizzard and Marina's freshman year roommate; was part of Heidi's clique until she was expelled a week before Lila's sophomore year started; Lila took her vacated spot at Eversfield

Teddi (Theodora) Brown
> Freshman Warrior in the Eversfield Cell; Lex's roommate in Tubman

Tim Montgomery
> Civilian; one of Val's boy toys; on the Eversfield varsity basketball team; Zeke's roommate in Douglass; senior at Eversfield

Toulouse
> Vampire; one of Duncan's best fighters; sent to Eversfield along with Kane, Fang, Ramrod, and Brock

Val (Valerie) Baker
> Civilian; Lila's best friend; popular and part of Heidi's clique which includes Sara, Drey, Rudi, and Cheri; on Eversfield's dance team; sophomore at Eversfield

Victoria Serrano
> Freshman Warrior in the Eversfield Cell; Sandy's roommate in Blackwell

Viper
> Vampire; one of Duncan's lieutenants although she prefers to work only with fellow vampire lieutenant Helle

Yuki Mori
> Civilian; one of Marina's friends, along with Angelo, Mickey, and Kylie; Kylie's roommate in Tubman; on the Eversfield junior varsity volleyball team; member of Engaging Eversfield, Eversfield's newspaper, and of Eversfield's yearbook; sophomore at Eversfield

GLOSSARY

A-Club

    Shortened name for Eversfield's Astronomy Club; club that all Eversfield Cell members belong to that allows them to stay out past curfew regularly; membership by invitation only

Affinity

    Type of Divining; includes Fire, Water, Wind, Earth, Floral, Mineral, Animal, Healing, Weaving, Cyphering, Portency, and Empathy

Animal affinity

    Type of Earth Divining involving animals and magic

Animal Diviner

    One who can work with animals using magic; commonly called a Beastie

Astronomy Club

    Extracurricular group within Eversfield Preparatory Academy theoretically focused on astronomy but actually the group all Eversfield Cell members belong to that gives them an easy excuse for being out past curfew regularly; membership by invitation only

The Augurs

    Group of Diviners with the required skill with both Cyphering and Portency; advises the General and his or her Second and helps with the placement of all Warriors using their combined Cyphering and Portency

Beastie

    One who can work with animals using magic; less commonly called an Animal Diviner

Beechy

    What Val and her clique call Elizabeth Blackwell's Harriet Beecher Stowe common room

Blackwell

Shortened name for Elizabeth Blackwell house

Blackwellians

Generally: members of Elizabeth Blackwell house, but Val and her clique also use it to refer to the unpopular members of Elizabeth Blackwell house

Blessed weapons (blade, sword, wooden stake, etc.)

Weapons enhanced by spells cast by Diviners; the spells make blessed weapons more effective at injuring and killing vampires

The Bloodlust

Gives Warriors a violent urge to kill something and a direction hinting of where the vampire hides; strength and accuracy depend on the vampire's proximity and the crowd surrounding it; triggered by vampires

Border spell

Complicated spell guarding the campus of each of the boarding schools hiding training Cells; immobilizes any vampire that crosses it and activates the Cull and Bloodlust of the training Cell's Warriors; does nothing to humans

The Bureau

Group of up to eight Diviners that represent their respective affinities; advises the General and his or her Second and oversees the training and placement of all Diviners; sometimes refers to the General, the Second, and the group of Diviners (excluding the Augurs) as a whole

Cell First

In command of a Cell or training Cell; also known as the First

Cell Second

The second-in-command of a Cell or training Cell; also known as the Second

Cells

    Groups of about twenty Warriors, a handful of Diviners, a Cell First, and a Cell Second set about the nightly activity of killing vampires; several within each region covering their own geographic territories; named after the nearest city or landmark; report to their respective Guides and Seconds

The ceremony

    When the Augurs decide the future of the Warriors; occurs at least twice during a Warrior's life: when they move up from the group of younger Warriors to the group of older Warriors within a training Cell and when they graduate from a training Cell to a regular Cell; also occurs whenever the Augurs need to fill a vacancy in the Firsts, the Guides, the Seconds, or the General.

Civilians

    Those who aren't vampires, Warriors, or Diviners; can also refer to those Warriors and Diviners who live outside Troupes and Cells

The Clan

    Loose organization of those born to fight vampires, whether that's through supernatural abilities (Warriors) or magic (Diviners); very extended family of vampire hunters living on every continent and consisting of members of every nationality, race, religion, and background; all possess a supernatural drive to kill vampires though it's stronger for some than others

Command

    Supernatural ability of Firsts, Guides, Seconds, and the General to force Warriors and Diviners to follow their orders

The Cull

    Gives Warriors supernatural senses and enhances Warriors' physical superpowers; comes with a nervous energy; triggered by vampires

Cypher
    One who can use the Cyphering affinity

Cyphering affinity (Cyphering)
    Type of Spirit Divining the reveals what's hidden beneath the surface; typically used to assess strength of a newly manifested Diviner affinity and to find Latents

Dampour
    Spell Kane devised to block the Warriors' Cull and Bloodlust from identifying the vampires it covers

Detachers
    Those Warriors and Diviners who decide to live as a civilian without the approval of the General or the Bureau

Diviners
    Vampire hunters with magical abilities to assist in the fight against vampires; types include Elemental Diviners (Fire, Water, Wind, and Earth) and Spirit Diviners (Healing, Weaving, Cyphering, Portency, and Empathy); have a supernatural drive to kill vampires

Divining
    The act of doing magic

Douglass
    Shortened name for Frederick Douglass house

Earth Diviner
    One who can work with the Earth affinities of Floral, Mineral, or Animal using magic

Earth Divining
    Type of Elemental Divining using the Earth affinities of Floral, Mineral, or Animal

Elemental Diviners (Elementals)
    Those who work with Elemental Divining affinities; types include Fire Diviners, Water Diviners, Wind Diviners, and Earth Diviners including the Earth subcategories of Floral Diviners, Mineral Diviners, and Beasties

Elemental Divining

Divining involving the elements; affinities include Fire, Water, Wind, and Earth including the Earth affinities of Floral, Mineral, and Animal

Elizabeth Blackwell house

Girls dormitory within Eversfield Preparatory Academy; houses Lila, Marina, Val, and others; also called Blackwell and Lizzie

Empath

One who can sense and/or control another person's (or people's) emotions through magic

Empathy affinity (Empathy)

Type of Spirit Divining involving sensing and/or changing another person's (or people's) emotions

Eversfield

Shortened name for Eversfield Preparatory Academy

Eversfield Cell

Training Cell hidden within boarding school Eversfield Preparatory Academy

Eversfield Preparatory Academy

Boarding school consisting of grades nine through twelve located near the state reserve south of Juniper; also hides the Eversfield training Cell

Fire Diviner

One who can create, maintain, and control fires using magic

Fire Divining

Type of Elemental Divining using and controlling fire

The First

In command of a Cell or training Cell; also known as the Cell First

Floral affinity

Type of Earth Divining involving the magical use of plant life

Floral Diviner
>One who can work with plant life through the use of magic

Florence
>Closest city to Eversfield and Juniper; almost an hour away without traffic; Florence Cell lives nearby

Florence Cell
>Cell based near the city of Florence

Freddie
>Shortened name for Frederick Douglass house; used primarily by Val and her clique

Frederick Douglass house
>Boys dormitory within Eversfield Preparatory Academy; houses Mickey, Angelo, and others; also called Douglass and Freddie

Future Fashion Designers
>Extracurricular group within Eversfield Preparatory Academy focused on fashion

Gabby
>Shortened name for Gabriela Mistral house; used primarily by Val and her clique

Gabriela Mistral house
>Girls dormitory within Eversfield Preparatory Academy; also called Mistral and Gabby

The General
>Leader of the Clan for a particular continent; unilateral control of the continent's activities; advised by the Second, the Bureau, and sometimes by the Augurs or the lead Augur

The Guide
>In command of a geographic region with the help of a Second and a few Diviners; reports to the General and the Bureau

Harriet Beecher Stowe common room
> Larger common room on the first floor of Elizabeth Blackwell; has a TV, couches, and movies; Val and her clique call it Beechy

Harriet Tubman house
> Girls dormitory within Eversfield Preparatory Academy; houses Lex, Teddi, Emilia, Cosmina, Yuki, and others; also called Tubman and Tubby

Healer
> One who can use magic to accelerate healing

Healing affinity (Healing)
> Type of Spirit Divining accelerating healing using magic

HQ
> Headquarters of the North American Clan where the General, his or her Second, the Bureau, and the Augurs live; it's also where everyone assigned administrative duty lives, where post-graduation Warriors train before joining a Cell, and where the SourceBooks are stored

The Indestructible
> Vampires; undead creatures that must drink blood to survive

JCC
> Acronym for Juniper City College

Juniper
> Town near Eversfield Preparatory Academy; houses Juniper City College; Juniper Troupe lives nearby

Juniper City College
> College located in Juniper; known for its art school

Juniper Troupe
> Troupe residing near the town of Juniper

Latents
> Regular humans born with magical abilities to fight vampires; once their abilities manifest, they're no longer considered Latents

Lead Augur
> Leader of the Augurs; often sits in on meetings with the General, the Second, and the Bureau; in charge of the ceremony placing Warriors in training Cells and Cells

Lizzards
> Popular members of Elizabeth Blackwell house; used primarily by Val and her clique

Lizzie
> Shortened name for Elizabeth Blackwell house; used primarily by Val and her clique

LnL
> What Val and her clique call Eversfield's literature and language building

Louie
> Depending on context, refers to either: (a) what Val and her clique call Elizabeth Blackwell's Louisa May Alcott common room or (b) what Val and her clique call the Louis Pasteur house

Louis Pasteur house
> Boys dormitory within Eversfield Preparatory Academy; houses Gabe, Darius, Simon, and others; also called Pasteur and Louie

Louisa May Alcott common room
> Smaller common room on the first floor of Elizabeth Blackwell; has a TV and exercise equipment; Val and her clique call it Louie

Marts
> What Val and her clique call Eversfield's arts and music building

Mineral affinity
> Type of Earth Divining involving the magical use of minerals and metals

Mineral Diviner
> One who can control minerals and metals through the use of magic

Mistral
> Shortened name for Gabriela Mistral house

Pasteur
> Shortened name for Louis Pasteur house

Portency affinity (Portency)
> Type of Spirit Divining that reveals potential futures typically in the form of visions

Portent
> One who receives Portency visions revealing potential futures

Regions
> The divisions of a continent into geographic areas with one Guide presiding over each region

The Second
> The second-in-command, whether that's of the entire continent as the General's Second, of a region as the Guide's Second, or of a Cell or training Cell as the Cell Second; in certain instances, can overrule his or her leader

Segments
> The divisions of the global Clan into independent continents with one General presiding over each segment

Smience
> What Val and her clique call Eversfield's math and science building

Spirit Diviners
> Those who work with spirit affinities; types include Healers, Weavers, Cyphers, Portents, and Empaths

Spirit Divining

> All Divining that doesn't include the elements; affinities
> include Healing, Weaving, Cyphering, Portency, and Empathy

Tec

> Shortened name for Tecumseh house; used primarily by Val
> and her clique

Tecumseh house

> Boys dormitory within Eversfield Preparatory Academy; also
> called Tec

Training Cells

> Cells in training hidden in boarding schools; consist of one
> group of five or six older Warriors (juniors or seniors), one
> group of five or six younger Warriors (freshmen or
> sophomores), and four Diviners spread throughout the four
> years of high school covering most of the Divining affinities;
> by day normal high school students; by night vampire hunters;
> report to their respective Guides and Seconds

Troupes

> Communities of retired Diviners, retired Warriors, and their
> children who are too young for high school; train future
> Warriors and Diviners and support nearby Cells and training
> Cells

Tubby

> Shortened name for Harriet Tubman house; used primarily by
> Val and her clique

Tubman

> Shortened name for Harriet Tubman house

The turn

> When a human dies and turns into a vampire

Vampires

> Undead creatures that must drink blood to survive

Warriors

> Vampire hunters with supernatural abilities to physically fight vampires (super-speed, super-endurance, super-agility, super-reflexes, super-strength, super-healing, etc.); have a strong supernatural drive to kill vampires

Water Diviner

> One who can control water using magic

Water Divining

> Type of Elemental Divining using and controlling water

Weaver

> One who can combine the elemental and spirit affinities into a spell

Weaving affinity (Weaving)

> Type of Spirit Divining that combines the elemental and spirit affinities into more complicated spells

Wind Diviner

> One who can control the wind using magic

Wind Divining

> Type of Elemental Divining using and controlling the wind

The Wipe

> Erases all of a civilian's memories of a vampire encounter; typically applied by Healers while they heal a civilian of his or her vampire-induced injuries

DEDICATION

This book is dedicated to those who helped it become a reality. You know who you are, but here goes a list of first names and initials: Karen C, Emily D, Cindi F, Laura F, Pat F, Dafne G, Athena H, Cathi K, Trinity M, Jamie M, Jared R, Karoly R, and Tanya W. Without you, this book would not have gotten to where it is today. Thank you so much!

About the Author

As a child, author Betsy Flak spent her free time lost in a book, whether upside down in a cozy armchair, in the bow of her family's fishing boat in Michigan, or on a bleacher during her brother's basketball games. This love led her to declare her intentions of becoming an author at the ripe age of ten.

After a few years of writing fantastical short stories, she took a brief fifteen-year hiatus to become an engineer. But she never stopped creating her own unique adventures filled with supernatural abilities, heart-stopping action, the battle between good and evil, and romantic interests galore. Now — when she's not reading, writing, or editing — you can find her playing roller derby or chilling on the couch with her favorite purple blanket, her two dogs, and her husband.

Want to get to know Betsy? Join her readers group! Go to betsyflak.com/join.

You'll be added to her readers group and be the first to know about book launches, sneak peeks, exclusive original content and updates, giveaways, and other bonuses.

You'll also receive a "Welcome to the Troupe" goodie bag, including a free digital copy of *The Impossible Adventure (The Clan-Vampire Clash: Meet Your Misadventure #1)*, the first installment in a series of interactive stories where you choose what happens, set in the same world as The Clan-Vampire Clash book series.

Made in the USA
Columbia, SC
05 November 2018